# The

# *K*INGS AND *Q*UEENS

# OF *R*OAM

# DANIEL WALLACE

A TOUCHSTONE BOOK
*Published by Simon & Schuster*

*New York   London   Toronto   Sydney   New Delhi*

Touchstone
A Division of Simon & Schuster, Inc.
1230 Avenue of the Americas
New York, NY 10020

Copyright © 2013 by Daniel Wallace

All rights reserved, including the right to reproduce this book or portions
thereof in any form whatsoever. For information, address
Touchstone Subsidiary Rights Department,
1230 Avenue of the Americas, New York, NY 10020.

First Touchstone hardcover edition May 2013

TOUCHSTONE and colophon are registered
trademarks of Simon & Schuster, Inc.

For information about special discounts for bulk purchases,
please contact Simon & Schuster Special Sales at
1-866-506-1949 or business@simonandschuster.com.

The Simon & Schuster Speakers Bureau can bring authors to your
live event. For more information or to book an event, contact the
Simon & Schuster Speakers Bureau at 1-866-248-3049
or visit our website at www.simonspeakers.com.

Designed by Ruth Lee-Mui

Manufactured in the United States of America

3   5   7   9   10   8   6   4   2

Library of Congress Cataloging-in-Publication Data
Wallace, Daniel, 1959-
The kings and queens of roam / Daniel Wallace.
p. cm.
"A Touchstone book."
1. Sisters—Fiction. 2. Magic—Fiction. I. Title.
PS3573.A4256348K56 2013
813'.54—dc23
                                    2012027400

ISBN 978-1-4767-0397-8
ISBN 978-1-4767-0399-2 (ebook)

*In memory of Ellen Navin Lefcourt,*
*Yvonne Velma Henderson, Holland Lucille Wallace,*
*and Joan Pedigo Wallace*

PART I

# THE GIRLS

*R*achel McCallister and her sister, Helen, lived together in the home they grew up in, and as far as anyone could tell (Rachel and Helen included), this is where they would die as well. Though they were both quite young—Helen was twenty-five years old, and Rachel was only eighteen—their paths seemed clear and predictable, each girl so closely bound to the other that to imagine even a day apart was a pointless foray into fantasy. You might as well imagine building a cabin on a cloud.

They lived in a town called Roam, a town founded a hundred years ago by their great-grandfather Elijah McCallister and his Chinese friend and hostage, Ming Kai, where they hoped to make the finest silk the world had ever known. Bordered by a great mountain on one side and a bottomless ravine on the other, and shadowed by dark green forests full of bears and wild dogs, the town—even after a century's existence—felt like the abandoned capital of an ancient civilization: still a wonder to behold, out here in the middle of nowhere, but worn down, broken, nearly empty. One day the vegetable world would reclaim it and all the evidence of every man and woman who had called it home, and those who still lived there (227 people at last count, though the number grew smaller by the day) could only serve as witnesses. The dead outnumbered the living tenfold now. There were so many dead their spirits could no longer be contained in the darkness, and, like deer, their population had spilled over into parts of the town reserved for the living. Sometimes they formed a cool shaft of stray light that leaked into dark rooms, beneath closet doors, into alleyways. There was nowhere you could go in Roam without feeling them, but only rarely would they actually allow themselves to be seen.

Then there was Rachel and Helen.

Rachel and Helen were known simply as *the girls*. That's what people called them. *Have you seen the girls?* they might say. Or, *There go the girls.* For the last seven years, ever since their parents had died, they had never been not together: never. Helen had been taking care of her sister all this time—but it was more than that. It was as if their common losses had brought them so close that a biological metamorphosis had occurred, fusing them forever at the metaphorical hip. The wonder of it was that they were thought of as girls at all, and not simply *girl,* so close were they, so much had one come to depend upon the other.

As inseparable as they were, though, they were more different than alike. One was blind, the other could see; one had the face of an angel, and the other—the other did not.

Rachel was the sweet, the beautiful, the blind one. Her eyes were the color of honeybees, dark eyes with an amber light glowing softly behind them. She wasn't *completely* blind. She saw shapes and sudden colors, a flashing shadow-world. Her eyes showed her the dark mystery-forest where we get lost in our dreams. If she brought something very close—so close she appeared to be kissing it with her eyes—then she could view that very, very small part of it. In a book she could make out a letter or two at a time. *O n c e u p o n a t i m e.* This is how she learned to read. She read part of an entire book this way—a small book with pictures called *Mark the Magical Dog*—but it took her weeks and completely exhausted her. She never read a book again. Still, she liked letters. She traced them in the bare dirt at the end of their driveway the way other children etched houses or trees.

She'd been blind since she was three, when one night she was overcome with a strange fever so intense the town doctor, Dr. Carraway, refused even to use a thermometer. He had seen a fever like this years ago: the thermometer had burst in a boy's oven-hot mouth, and the tiny shards of glass sliced his throat open, the mercury flowing into the wounds. The boy died. Old Dr. Carraway—who still wore a bowler hat and was never without a bloodred rose pinned to his lapel—had seen it all. Combustible hair, earworms, the sudden and inexplicable loss of a man's entire face. He was there the day Roam was besieged by a flock of poisonous butterflies, the night the vines snatched a baby from its crib. He knew Rachel would most likely die from this fever. She was too hot to touch; the edge of her sheets dripped with sweat. The only sound she made was a soft, melodious moan—a death song. But after three days the fever broke; miraculously, she recovered. And, as if it had never happened, as if she had not been halfway to the hereafter, she was soon back to her sweet, happy self. It wasn't until she wandered off into the woods and fell into a gulley that anyone even knew she was blind. Dr. Carraway returned, examined her, and determined that her optic nerves had been singed by the fever, or frayed perhaps; the truth was he had no idea. But if he was right (which he wasn't), it was possible, though unlikely, the nerves might, with time and prayer, grow back together again.

"I was hoping for something having more to do with medicine or science," Rachel's father said.

Dr. Carraway smiled. "Science is a good thing. But prayer is a great thing. After all," he said, "what harm can it do?"

So Mr. and Mrs. McCallister began praying every day for Rachel's eyesight to return. They made Rachel pray as well, though she had even less an idea of what she was doing than her parents did. This was the first of their two fruitless attempts at restoring their child's eyesight. They would literally die trying.

As the years passed, however, it was clear that Rachel was going to be an extraordinary beauty, as if, unable to see herself, she would make the most of *being* seen. Her mother trained her eyes to remain relatively steady, and used tape to keep her eyelids open, in an effort to avoid what she called "that unfortunate blind girl look." She even taught Rachel to blink, and Rachel blinked quite well, and at all the right times. At seventeen Rachel had lava red hair flowing in curls to her shoulders, and smooth almond skin, light brown freckles, and lips—full and fresh, deep orange—that were almost too big, like her mouth, into which it appeared you could fit a tangerine when she smiled. She smiled not because she didn't miss what she'd lost from life, but because of what she still had: her parents, a home, and, most of all, her sister, Helen.

Helen. Her story was even sadder than Rachel's. She was ugly from the day she was born. Dr. Carraway, who by his own account had seen everything, had never seen anything like this. Even one-day-old Helen must have known, as she felt the effect her little face had on those who viewed it. Only her mother smiled when she saw Helen; only a mother could. Her parents did their best to love her, but Helen was the one who went to sleep every night with that face and woke up every morning the same, and no one would know what that did to her.

In town, people turned away when they saw her coming, or walked past her without a word: it was easier for them to pretend she was invisible than it was to pretend she was pretty. Shopkeepers—forced to speak with her—asked after her parents, after her little sister Rachel, but they never looked directly at Helen, not unless she tricked them. "Watch out!" she'd say, and sometimes they'd look her way. Smiling she'd say, "Now that wasn't so hard, was it?"

Helen was eighteen years old when her parents died, and her first act after burying them was to cover every mirror in the house with old grocery sacks. They were covered to this day, the tape yellowed and peeling at the edges. Without a mirror to reflect herself back at herself, there were moments Helen forgot she was the *way* she was. But the moments were brief. She only had to look at Rachel to remember: *I have this face, and she has that one*—the faces they were born with. Helen wasn't evil, but there was a part of her that certainly was. She discovered this part almost accidentally, with her sister on a rainy summer's day.

*H*elen remembered, would always remember, how it all began. They were alone together in the room they shared—not because the house wasn't big enough for them to have their own room; they could have had two rooms each if they wanted—but because, back then, they loved each other. They'd planned to go outside and play that morning, but all of a sudden a storm blew in, and they were stuck inside. The rain made a gray noise as it fell. Helen brushed Rachel's hair. Rachel's little hands were folded in her lap, and she was thinking, worrying a thought like a river washes over a stone until it becomes smooth and round: Helen knew these things about her sister, knew sometimes exactly what was going on inside her sister's head. But not today. Usually, after these long quiet moments, Rachel would ask Helen something everybody else knew—what rain looked like (she'd forgotten), or what color dirt was, or why people wore hats, and Helen would patiently describe and explain these things, because she thought that was her job.

But that's not what Rachel wanted to know today.

"Helen?" she said.

Helen sighed. "Yes, Rachel?"

"What do I . . . look like?"

Helen stopped brushing midstroke. The idea that Rachel didn't know what she looked like—well, of course she wouldn't know. But it had never occurred to Helen. Rachel knew faces—she could feel them—but she didn't know what they *meant*. She was only six years old.

"What you look like," Helen said. "Well . . . that's a big question, isn't it? Have you tried the mirror?"

"It doesn't work for me," she said.

"I know. I was only having fun."

Rachel let this thoughtless admission drift away.

"I ask Mother," she said. "A lot."

"And what does Mother say?"

"She says, 'You shouldn't concern yourself with it,'" Rachel said. "She says it doesn't matter what the outside parts look like."

Helen absentmindedly finished the stroke, and smiled. Smiles were so rare to her face she'd almost forgotten how to make them. "You really want to know, Rachel?" Helen said. "That's what you want?"

Rachel nodded, and in her smallest voice asked, "What am I? Pretty, or—something else?"

"Keep still," Helen said. "I can't brush your hair when you're fidgeting."

Rachel sat up straight.

"I just," Helen started, "I don't know what to say." But she did know; she knew exactly what she wanted to say. This was how it began, all of it, as just a bit of fun—a made-up story.

"I'm not pretty," Rachel said. "If I were pretty, that's what you would say."

"No." And Helen made herself sound so sad that Rachel took her hand. "No. I'm afraid you're not."

"That's okay," Rachel said quickly, though there was water welling in her eyes.

"Good then," Helen said. She gave her sister's lovely hair one more stroke. "Then you're not sad?"

She sighed. "Some. A little." A tear fell.

"It's okay to be sad," Helen said. "It *is* sad."

"But you're pretty?"

"Yes," Helen said. "I am. I'm blessed. Blessed as much as you are cursed." Oh, this felt good! She almost believed it herself—even though the truth was that they were both cursed, each in their own way. "I'm as pretty as the first day of spring, people say. I wouldn't say that about myself, of course. But people say that. I've heard them."

Rachel gently touched her sister's face. "So this is what pretty is," she said, and Helen nodded. Then Rachel touched her own face. "And this is not."

"Oh, my sweet dear Rachel," Helen said, taking her sister's little hand in her own. "Why would you even want to know this? Can't you think of your blindness as a good thing?"

"How?"

"I mean because you don't have to *look* at yourself, sweetheart."

Rachel was waiting. "So . . . "

"All right," Helen said. "But know that when I tell you this I'm *not* being mean. I'm only—"

"I know," Rachel said.

Helen took a deep breath and picked up the silver-stemmed hand mirror on the bed beside them. She looked—not at Rachel—but at herself. "Well, it's kind of hard to describe." She brought the mirror closer. "But I would say that your face is just a bit . . . *not right*. It looks like a face made of little pieces, a face stitched together from the discarded odds and ends of other people's faces."

"Oh. That's not good."

"No, it's not. At the place where they make faces? The face factory? These are the pieces they didn't use, and they gave them all to you."

"The face factory is God, isn't it?" Rachel said. "God made my face."

"That's right. God did this to you. No one else."

"Maybe that's why He took my eyes away. So I wouldn't have to look, like you said. It's a gift."

"You're such a strong little girl."

Rachel, though she was still crying a little, said, "Keep going."

*Stop*, Helen heard a voice telling her. But she didn't. "Does your face feel pretty? When you touch it?"

"I knew you would ask me that," Rachel said. "I don't want to say it but—yes. A little. I thought—"

"That's because you don't really know what *pretty* is. Because you went blind before you figured that out. Your face is soft but—honestly, Rachel—people turn away when they see you."

"Turn away?"

"Because they're afraid of you. They're afraid of your—"

"That's enough!" Rachel said. She grasped her sister's hand, because she was shivering like a struck bell. "I don't think I like you very much now."

"You asked," Helen said.

"I know. I know I asked. I still don't feel like I like you."

But Helen wasn't through. "People will tell you that you're pretty, Rachel," whispering now. "I'm sure you'll hear that all the time. *Oh, you're so pretty, Rachel. Aren't you the pretty one? I've never seen a face more lovely in my entire life!* But they're just saying it to make you feel better about yourself. People do that: they lie to make other people feel better."

"That's nice," Rachel said. "If you're going to tell a lie, I mean, better a good lie than a bad lie, right?" She smiled.

"And when they do say that, just say *Thank you very much.* It's not polite to tell them they're wrong. They *know* they're wrong."

Rachel and Helen sat together for a long time, quietly, their legs hanging off the side of the bed. A moth banged against the window screen; another flew in and out of the lampshade, unable to rest. Helen could have told her then that it was all just a story, that really it was Rachel who was the beautiful one, and Helen who was not. But she didn't. She liked this story, and she liked that there was someone who believed it was true. She wanted the world to be like this, just for a little while longer.

"Don't tell anybody," Rachel said, almost too softly to hear. "But if I had to choose between getting my eyes back and being pretty, I'd choose pretty."

Helen kissed her sister on the forehead. "Wouldn't we all," she said.

This is how Helen changed everything, sowing the seeds of the rest of their lives together, and, eventually, their lives apart.


The next day passed, and the next, and Helen still didn't tell Rachel the truth. She knew she should, but what was the harm in it, really? Rachel didn't know any better and she never had to. Helen *never* had to tell her the truth. It was a ruse that never had to die, so long as she kept Rachel close. And as one day passed, and then another, she wondered: how much further could she take it? What other stories could she tell, just for fun? That's how older sisters can be sometimes. It was almost in the job description.

Three days later, their mother asked them to go to town for some flour. Helen didn't want to: she never liked going to town. And she resented having to cart her sister around with her everywhere she went.

But not today. She had an idea today.

Helen and her family lived in the biggest house there was in Roam. At one time it had belonged to Elijah McCallister, the man who built the house and the town around it. But that was almost a hundred years ago, and since then a lot had changed; everybody said so. Helen didn't know or care anything about that; she only knew what she saw with her own eyes, which was a town that was not much of anything now. A few shops, a grocer, a bar, the shadow of the old mill blocking out the sun. A car came by now and again, but really, the town wasn't big enough to drive in: there was no reason to. Helen figured she could throw a rock from one end of it to the other, if you didn't count the old mill houses littering the outskirts; there were a hundred of those at least, most of them abandoned, empty, and dark. Helen would have been surprised if there were a drearier place than Roam on Earth.

"I hate people," Helen said as they turned a corner and walked into the main square. In the middle of it was a stone statue of Elijah Mc-Callister, who looked like he was about to fall off his pedestal, leaning dangerously to the left. Three of the fingers on his right hand were gone, broken when a tree fell on it years before. "I hate the way they look at you, like your face is the worst thing they've ever seen! That's why you need me, Rachel. To protect you, to tell you the truth."

"Protect me from what?"

"From this town," Helen said. "This town and the things in it." Old Mrs. Branscombe passed them without so much as a nod, as if they were beggars. *Look at my face,* Helen thought. *Could it be that bad?* But it was. She knew it was.

"What things?" she asked again. "Tell me."

"Are you sure you want to know?"

Rachel nodded. Helen was buying time, trying to think something up. Rachel was thinking, too. When Rachel was lost in thought her eyes shivered and pinged in their sockets. Normally they didn't move much at all, and when her pupils were steady they could be piercing, and it made Helen wonder whether Rachel could see a great deal more than she let on. Just to be sure Helen would test her sometimes: she'd put the salt in the pepper shaker, or move a chair into her walking path. How many times must she see her sister trip over a chair leg before she could be assured Rachel was totally blind? There was no certain number.

A dog wandered past them, rubbing against Rachel's leg: dogs loved Rachel. Helen shooed it away.

"Okay then," she said. "I'll tell you."

They came to the old Yott House first, and the stories began to flow. Ghost stories. Helen didn't know where they came from. It was as if the stories were already out there somewhere and she was capturing them, like a butterfly in a net, so real that as she told them they felt true even to her. The Yott House, Helen told Rachel, they called . . . the Yott House of Death. Everyone knows what happened there, she said, though no one likes to speak of it. Helen could only say in a whisper: *Caleb Yott built a lovely sandstone home on the corner. It used to be a grand house (which, in truth, it still is)—grand enough, he thought, to get him a wife. He needed something more than what he brought to the table himself, what with a drinking problem, a bad temper, and a clubfoot. He found a wife, a Chinese woman named Bao, and they were married and had children—a boy and a girl, Franklin and Anita.*

*But it wasn't a happy marriage. Caleb had that temper, and as the years passed, he drank more and more. The story goes that one night Caleb came home drunk and began to argue with Bao, and one thing led to another and he hit her in the head with a brass candlestick. He cracked her head wide open; worse, the children were watching the whole thing transpire from the top of the stairwell, and when Bao was hit Anita screamed and fell down the flight of stairs, and by the time she got to the bottom her neck had broken and she was dead, too.*

*But it turned out Bao wasn't dead—yet. She had enough life left in her to run her husband through with the fireplace poker. But then she died, and the little boy Franklin was alone, his family's bodies scattered across the living room floor like firewood.*

"What happened to Franklin?" Rachel asked, spellbound.

"Franklin ran out into the street for help—and was run over by a horse and buggy. Crushed beneath the hooves."

"That's terrible," Rachel said.

"It is. But it gets worse. After their bodies were cleared away and the blood was cleaned up and the brains shoveled off the living room floor, another family moved in. Husband, wife, son, daughter. And *they* all died as well, in a fashion too grisly to even describe." Helen held her sister's arm tight and pulled her closer, so her lips were touching the side of Rachel's ear. *"And ever since then, every family who has moved into the Yott House has died—by their own hands or by somebody else's, or by the hand of God Himself."*

"But why would people do that? Move to a place where they know something like that's going to happen?"

"Because people always think it could never happen to them," Helen said. "Then it always does."

They kept walking.

Beyond the Yott House was the Hanging Tree. "Ah! Here we are," Helen said. "The Hanging Tree. From this tree—from this beautiful chestnut—over a hundred people had been hanged, and they'd been left hanging there until the meat fell off their bones. A hundred people: one every year for a hundred years!"

Rachel stiffened, but her curiosity always got the better of her. "Hanged?" she asked. "Why?"

"Who really knows anymore?" Helen said. "At first, they were actual criminals. People who did terrible things. In the early years, before Elijah McCallister civilized them, someone would always do something bad enough to be hanged for. But over time people became better. They followed the rules. But hanging had become something of a tradition, and so every year the town voted, and someone was hanged. Usually it was someone people didn't like, or . . . "

"What? Or what?"

Helen paused. "People with some sort of . . . problem. Some sort of physical problem."

"Physical problem?"

"Something wrong with them. Something that made them . . . different."

"Oh."

They stood there for a long time.

"But they've stopped doing that?" Rachel said, hopefully. "I mean, *we've* stopped doing that. Right?"

"Of course," Helen said, laughing. "Of course we have. I can't remember the last time someone was hanged from this tree."

They kept walking.

They walked past the Poison Fields, where nothing had ever grown, not even dirt, and then to the Boneyard where—and again, this was *a long time ago,* Helen told her—the dead weren't even buried. Their bodies were simply discarded there and left to rot. The people of the town were so busy making silk they didn't have time to bury the dead! The poor, the unknown, the evil, and then those unlikeable people they hanged from the tree—they all were left here. The bones are still there.

And after the Boneyard, Helen took Rachel to the most dangerous and deadly place in Roam there was.

The Forest of the Flesh-Eating Birds.

"Where these birds came from, nobody knew. Maybe they weren't even birds at all; maybe they were the last of the flying dinosaurs, with long sharp beaks and teeth like ice picks. They had a magic that allowed them to blend in with the trees. And they were so quiet, so quiet that even if you had eyes you wouldn't be able to see them. *But they can see you.* They can see everything. They're part of the darkness all around them, and if you come too close or linger too long—even here, where we're standing right now!—they'll fly out in a great flock and before you have a chance to turn away they'll be upon you, and all that will be left of you is *nothing*, not even a bone to clatter against the sidewalk. Very few people have walked through the Forest and lived."

"I might," Rachel said. "Birds like me. Remember that time—"

"Not these birds, Rachel," Helen said. "These birds don't like you at all."

"Oh." This set her back, Helen could tell. "Is the whole world like this?"

"The whole world? No," Helen said. "There are better places than Roam. There's a place I've heard of not far from here. It's a land of light and honey. The sun comes up in the morning and paints the town all daffodil yellow, warming the porches and the windowsills. The dew clings to the grass until the sun melts it, and the air smells of pine needles—fresh like that. The sky is a milky blue and at night every star comes out to shine on the perfect little houses and the happy people inside them.

"Everyone goes about their day with joy in their hearts; they do honest work. Laughter: sometimes that's all you hear. People laughing. Everyone's happy. It's a clean place. In the morning the streets themselves look like they've been swept, but it's just the natural wind, taking away with it what it needs to, but leaving all the beauty behind."

"Oh," Rachel said.

"I could go on, but I won't. Just know that *everything* about it is wonderful, more wonderful than you could ever imagine."

"How do you know about this place?" Rachel said.

"Why wouldn't I know?"

"You never said anything about it before."

"Because you weren't *old* enough before," Helen said. "I don't know that you would have been able to understand."

"Have you been there?"

"Of course I haven't been there! There's only one way to get there from here. And it's dangerous. Very dangerous. "

"There's more than one way to get anywhere," Rachel said.

Helen flicked Rachel's arm sharply with her index finger: it's how she gave her blind sister a stern look. "How is it you know so much all of a sudden?"

"I don't," Rachel said and rubbed her arm. "Why is it so dangerous to get there?"

"Because to *get* there," Helen said, "you have to go through the Forest of the Flesh-Eating Birds. And if somehow you were lucky enough to get past the birds, which you wouldn't be, there's a ravine, a ravine so deep you can't see the bottom of it. You'd fall in and no one would ever find you." This was actually true—there *was* a ravine—but if there weren't she would have invented one. "They built a bridge across it a long time ago, our ancestors, but it was almost impossible to build and it didn't last much longer than it took for them to get over it the first time."

"Why?"

"Because it was made of twigs and pine straw and spit is why," she said. "And hope. Which the world is sorely in need of these days." Helen took a deep breath and sighed: telling stories was hard. "But if you got past *that*, and then walked for days and days, you would come to the river." Helen had heard her parents talk about a river, after they came back from seeing the doctor in Arcadia where they went to get medicinal water for Rachel's eyes. "Oh, the river is a wondrous thing, unlike any other river in the world. It's magic. Everyone who bathes in it changes. Whatever ails them is cured. It's what people say, anyway: no one from Roam has ever been to it. Not for lack of trying, of course. The bones at the bottom of the ravine are proof enough of that."

"Whatever ails them," Rachel said.

It made Helen sad to look at her. Not just because she was so pretty and all that prettiness was wasted on her, but because Rachel wanted so much to be something that she wasn't, and could never be. Her world was a small dark box, and the only thing outside of the box was the world Helen created for her. The sad part was watching her struggle against the sides of the box. Helen tried to love her, but there were just too many things that got in the way.

"That sounds like such a wonderful place," Rachel said.

The sighs of the dying brushed past them, and Helen turned away from her sister.

"I just thought you'd want to know," Helen said. She brought her sister close in a tight hug: the lies she told—and that's what they were, she knew that—made her feel empty, lost, and alone. At least for a moment or two. And that's when she needed her sister most of all. "I'm sorry if it hurts. I'm sorry that I told you. Sometimes I tell you things I shouldn't. Just don't think about it."

"I just don't understand," Rachel said. "Why hasn't anybody built another bridge?"

"I said don't *think* about it, okay?"

"Okay," Rachel said. "I won't."

But Rachel *would* think about it. She would never stop thinking about it. Helen had spoken to some deep need inside of her sister, and this picture Rachel had conjured—of this faraway town and the river, the beautiful river—would live inside her mind and grow, and over time—especially after their parents died, not too many years from now—it would become as real as anything else in her world. It was a failure of Helen's own dark imagination, however, that she never for a moment thought that Rachel—her blind little sister—would actually try to go there on her own.

# ROAM:
# A SHORT HISTORY,
# PART I

*I*t's impossible to say exactly where Roam is. A small settlement lost somewhere in a blanket fold of American terrain, between a range of mountains, a light in the forest, a sudden something in the middle of an infinite nothing—it doesn't matter anymore. But for a few golden years, long before Helen and Rachel were born, it was a sight to behold. It was once the home of a great silk factory, and its owner, Elijah McCallister, had built the town to go along with it, inspired by the grainy black-and-white pictures of castles he'd seen in a book once as a child. His ambition had been to create a new world, something he could embellish or destroy to his heart's content. With Roam he did both.

Elijah himself was a small man, five feet tall in thick-soled shoes, with the face of a sullen angel, and made up of equal parts brilliance and cruelty. He'd had a tough life. His parents abandoned him on a park bench within a gated children's playground when he was only seven; he swung all day and into the evening before he realized they weren't coming back. He spent the next nine years in the St. Alphonso Home for Wayward Boys, and if he was not wayward before going in, he surely was on coming out.

For a year after that he lived on the streets, creating a life out of the refuse of the fortunate: shirt, pants, belt, jacket, a watch, a hat, a knife, food and drink—he found what he needed in the gutter and the alley-ways, and what he didn't find he stole. Finally he got himself a place—the back room of a subbasement apartment near the harbor, next door to a cobbler's shop, a room he shared with a twelve-year-old mute girl, her syphilitic grandfather, and a tall, thin man they knew only as "Jim-Jim." A lot of people in that gray and crumbling city would have said he had it pretty good, but it wasn't good enough for Elijah. He eventually left the city and took a train to San Francisco, where he signed on as a cook on a private frigate, and sailed around the world.

And there he was but two years later in a Chinese saloon in Hainan, when he spotted a young man named Ming Kai selling something pretty from a small wooden cart. A cloth of some kind. Ming Kai looked—well, to Elijah he looked exactly like every other Chinese man. He motioned Ming Kai over. Ming Kai bowed and showed Elijah his wares. Later Ming Kai would realize: this is how a life is changed. Not gradually, over time, but in a moment, a moment as simple as this one. As the tips of Elijah's fingers rested on the shiny, colorful surface of this strange and delicate object, he felt fireworks go off in his heart: it was merely silk (though Elijah didn't know what it was called yet), and Elijah had never felt silk before; there weren't many who had. Never in his hardscrabble life had he even imagined a thing as soft and cool as this, as shimmering and beautiful. Red, blue, orange, green. Every color so bright and delicious. Ming Kai smiled at him beneath his Chinese hat as Elijah ran his fingers across the fabric's surface.

"Is this made . . . by *people*?" Elijah said. "By actual human beings?

Or did it fall off an angel's back and float down from heaven itself?"

Ming Kai spoke no English, but men don't have to know the same words to speak the same language. He understood exactly what Elijah meant. Ming Kai shook his head: no, it wasn't made by people—but then yes, he nodded that it was. He placed his index finger over his mouth—a secret!—and beckoned Elijah to look beneath his cart. There was a small box full of what appeared to be worms, or caterpillars, and small cocoons the size of a tooth: white, covered in thread. Ming Kai pointed to the worms, then he pointed to the cocoons, then he pointed at himself. And Elijah understood.

"Nature and man together," Elijah said, nodding. His eyes glowed with possibility. "The man and the worm." Ming Kai nodded, happy, not yet knowing how much he would regret this encounter. "It's a secret, isn't it?" Elijah went on. "No one knows how to do it in my country, not like this. But you do, don't you? You know the secret." Now Elijah had completely lost him. Ming Kai cocked his head to one side.

"Do you realize what this could mean for us?" Elijah said. "It's like it says in the book. *A well-guarded secret coupled with avarice and ambition is the birth of all good things*." (Elijah had read a book on how to be a successful person.) "We'll be rich, you and me!"

Ming Kai still had no idea what Elijah was saying but hoped it was something along the lines of, "I have a lot of money and I want to buy this silk from you, and your life will become better, and your family healthy and happy." In a sense, Elijah was saying that. But in reality it was the preface to a plan that unfolded like so: Elijah invited Ming Kai aboard the ship and took him down to its bowels, and there he lopped him on the head with a piece of wood pulled from the side of an orange crate. He tied Ming Kai's hands and feet with twine and stuffed a bandanna in his mouth and stowed him behind a stack of salted pork. He took great pains to hide him, but it wasn't really necessary; sailors brought Chinese men and women back home with them all the time.

But it wasn't Ming Kai he was hiding so much as it was the box of worms—and the secret inside Ming Kai's head.

It would be three long months before they made it back to America. That worked in Elijah's favor, as he used the voyage to teach Ming Kai English. By the time they arrived in San Francisco Bay, Ming Kai could confidently approach a street vendor and say, "A dozen of your freshest oysters, please." Turned out he loved oysters.

But this isn't why Elijah taught Ming Kai English. He taught him English in order to learn the secret of silk. Elijah was young enough to remember the one-room schoolhouse where he learned to read and the teacher, Mrs. Hauptman, who taught him. She was first-generation German, and spoke with an accent, and liked to whack her students on the back of the head with a ruler when they made mistakes. But he learned how to read and write goddamn it and so did Ming Kai. Ming Kai's first complete sentence was, "Please never untie me, for if you do I will kill you, and I don't want to become a man who takes another man's life."

"That's a long sentence," Elijah said. "Too long to follow." And he whacked him across the back of his head with a piece of wood.

From San Francisco they took a train to Chicago, and in Chicago Elijah bought two horses, a donkey, and a wooden cart, which he loaded with guns, food, hammers, and nails, and the strange pair made their way into American wilderness. For the first three hundred miles or so, going roughly south, Elijah kept them on the main roads, the muddy thoroughfares of grassless dirt and wheel ruts any idiot could follow. Then he remembered the book. *Blaze a trail into oblivion and create your own paradise.*

"Tell me how it's done," Elijah said as they slowly navigated among trees, across rivers, up mountains so steep they almost fell off of them, backward, as though they were falling from the sky. "I'm serious: I need to know."

But Ming Kai stayed quiet. At night, every night, he cried himself to sleep. Elijah had never heard a Chinese man cry; their tears seemed sadder, purer, and more beautiful than the tears of a white man, and after a thousand tears like this Elijah's heart opened for him, and as they watered their horses in a stream one day Elijah put his arm around Ming Kai's shoulder.

"You," he said, "are my friend. I know it doesn't look that way. We started off badly. I hit you too much. I feel bad about that. But I want to make amends. Tell me what it is you want—anything—and I will see what I can do to get it for you. And perhaps in return for that you will tell me the secret of silk."

"Set me free," Ming Kai said. "Let me return to my home and my family. Wash out my skull and every memory I have in it of you and this great tragedy that has become my life."

Elijah brought Ming Kai closer, and hugged him harder.

"I can't do that," Elijah said. "I would like to. I mean, if I were different, if the world were different, if this story of ours weren't already written down somewhere, I would like to do this. That's the thing, Ming Kai. This story—our story—is fated. We're in this together. I'm nothing without you, and without me you'd be pulling that rickety cart around a crowded square that smelled of piss and rotten vegetables. You and I are part of something big. Do you think it was chance that brought us together? That I just happened to be sitting there, at a table at one of the smaller towns in China, when you walked by?

"This is no accident, Ming Kai. You will tell me how to make silk. We will make silk together and become great men. You will thank me. You will love me. This will happen regardless. But now, what I'm doing now is offering you something more. What can I do for you, Ming Kai, that will make your life that much better?" And he held up his fingers just the smallest width apart.

Ming Kai was silent. Then he said, "I want my family. My wife

Sing Loo and my two little boys. I want you to bring them here, to America. Then I will tell you the secret of silk."

"Done!" Elijah said. "At the next town I'll telegraph a man I know. He's in the British Navy. He will do this for me. We'll have them all brought over and you will be happy and together we will make silk! You and me!"

"Yes," Ming Kai said, hugging his old captor, his new friend. "Yes."

And then, looking into his eyes, he said the word that would change Elijah's life.

*Mulberry.*

"Mulberry?" Elijah said.

"This is what we need. Mulberry trees. To make the silk. Let us find this tree, and I will tell you more when my family arrives."

"Yes!" Elijah said. "You drive a hard bargain, but yes!"

"But I will also tell you this," Ming Kai said, narrowing his eyes so they might burn into Elijah's soul. "No good will come from what we do. No flower grows in a poisoned field. We may not see it now, but our children will, and our children's children. They will be the ones who finally suffer. They always are."

Elijah laughed. "What, is that some kind of Chinese curse?"

"No," Ming Kai said, flicking the reins. "It is the truth of the world."

And off they went into the heart of America, in search of the wild mulberry. The curse preceded them, blown on the wind through space and time. One hundred years would come and go before it found Helen and Rachel McCallister, Elijah's great-grandchildren, and Markus, the last of Ming Kai's line. Generations would pass before they could be born into the world, but the curse would find them, nonetheless.

# GHOSTS,
# PART I

Ghosts were everywhere in Roam, but only two people could see them: Helen McCallister and Digby Chang. Digby Chang was the smallest man in Roam. He had a ruddy, pockmarked complexion and was completely hairless, head to toe. He looked like a sausage with legs. Some people thought he was a midget, but, as he would be the first to tell you, he wasn't. Not that there was anything wrong with being a midget, but if you weren't a midget, as he wasn't, he felt it incumbent upon himself to clarify and elucidate the fact of the matter, which is that he was not a midget, but rather as close as a man could come to being a midget without actually being one. He was simply a very small man, and he never thought a thing about it.

Digby ran the town bar, a bar he inherited from his father (a somewhat taller man of the same name), who had inherited it from his father and his father before him. In the beginning it wasn't even a bar at all, but just his great-grandfather Wei selling drinks from a bottle of potato vodka he had found on the side of the road as he was coming into town, a bottle of barely potable alcohol that had been accidentally dropped there or, more likely, thrown in anger: it tasted like piss. Wei dragged a half-dead log into what would become the main square, set the bottle on top of it, and in five minutes he had made the first real dollar in this town. In a sense, Digby's family was one of the founding families of Roam—a kind of royalty, if such a thing were possible, or even desirable, out here in the middle of nowhere.

People called it Digby's, or Digby's Bar, even though it had never had a proper name. Digby didn't even call it a bar: he called it a *tavern*, because a tavern sounded like something magnificent and historical, whereas a bar was just a place where people went to drink. Beer, whiskey, even potato vodka—he had it all, though business had gotten so bad over the last few years that if someone came in for a glass of water that was okay, too. He even served ice cream to the kids, when there were any. He had a big tub of vanilla in the icebox, but it had been there so long it was starting to look like chocolate.

Digby liked to say he had more ghosts in his tavern than he had customers, which used to be funny—until it started being true. Ghosts *were* his customers. He didn't call them ghosts, though, because that word summoned up images of ghoulish night-visitors who stole the faces of children while they slept (that's what his father used to tell him ghosts did), and Digby didn't believe in that sort of thing. But there was no disputing it: most of his customers had passed away. Age, accident, disease, all those things life tended to throw at a person you either survived or you didn't and when you didn't you died and were buried and then—then? Apparently, this: revenants with no clear lines, gray, fading in and out of focus as you looked at them. They didn't appear to be representatives of the afterlife so much as they were vestiges of this one, so Digby took to calling them either *leftovers* or *old-timers*—*leftovers* when they irritated him and *old-timers* when he was feeling warmly, the same way his dad called the Chinese *Orientals* when he liked them and *chinks* when he didn't, and those of mixed race *combos*.

At any rate, there was nothing to be done; Digby had adapted to their constant presence. They were there when he opened up in the morning and there when he closed his doors at night, sometimes exactly as he'd left them, murky images of the people they once were and yet completely recognizable. They talked, fought, spit, laughed, and cried like anybody else who'd ever come into the tavern, but they didn't drink. If they drank, it would have been different; they'd have spent some money. Instead, they just took up space. Why here? He imagined it was no different now than it was when they were alive: they had nowhere else to go. Digby knew that feeling: as he had neither wife nor family himself, the tavern was his home, too.

He opened up today, as usual, at two. Regardless of what it was like outside, inside the tavern it was all shades of gray and weary light, dust and smoke hanging in the air, perpetual cloud cover.

"Digby?"

One of them always called out his name when he walked in the door. *Digby?* As if his presence here was a surprise. As if he didn't own the place. Today it was Fang Martin. Fang was one of his father's good friends, round and wrinkled and happy, with a thin white sheet of hair on his head.

"Fang," Digby said.

"We were talking," Fang said, nodding toward He-Ping, his best friend, "and Ping said, 'I wonder if Digby will be coming in today, and, if so, what time.'"

Digby sighed and closed the door behind him. He turned on the neon beer sign, YANJING, indicating the tavern was now open for the living customers, too. "I come every day, at the same time every day," he said. "I am a human timepiece."

"And that's what I told him!" Fang said, laughing. "That's what I told him."

Halfway to the box of rags on the other side of the room, Digby stopped, looked back over his shoulder. "Where's Chen?"

"Chen got himself a place," He-Ping said. He-Ping didn't sound one way or the other about it, but Digby knew He-Ping had been waiting on a place for a while now. "On Orchard. Where Martin used to live, before he took off."

"Ah," Digby said. Even his spiritual clientele was diminishing. Soon even they'd be gone and then . . . he didn't want to think about it.

"Chen!" Fang said. "Glad to see him go myself, if you ask me. He smelled like cabbage."

Fang had not been such an obstreperous spirit when he was alive. Digby remembered him as a sweet, quiet, serious man, second shift in the silk mill. He would be the guy who held the door for one person and would end up holding it for the next ten. A cobbler in his spare time, he could turn an old piece of ham into a shoe if someone needed him to. And he would do it without complaint. Digby, in fact, couldn't remember Fang saying more than six or seven words his entire life.

Dying (he broke his neck one morning when he fell out of bed) changed all that. Fang was *loud* now. He cackled at nothing all day and night. He made terrible jokes. He never shut up, and there was nothing Digby could say or do to make him; his pointless joy was everything to him. At first Digby wondered if Fang was not Fang at all, but some otherworldly vision usurping his father's friend's body and face. But Digby learned soon enough that this is the way it was with all of the old-timers: the roles they took on in the hereafter were different from the roles they played in life. It was as if through dying they were given a chance to become someone else. He-Ping Rogers, the grocer, had been a great practical joker; he'd give you back change for a five when you and he both knew you had just given him a ten, and just before you got angry and irritated with his insistence that you *did* in fact give him a five he would laugh and say, "I kid you, Digby Chang. Here is your five dollar." Impish. Frivolous. (He had been trampled by a wild horse; it was just terrible, the horse tracking He-Ping's insides all over town, a hoof-marked trail of blood you could still see.) Now He-Ping sat in a chair along the far wall in silence, watching the goings-on without so much as a smile. Those who'd lived the big lives, the expansive lives, they were the quiet ones: Digby had seen Elijah McCallister himself now and again, and sometimes you barely even knew he was in the room. If you tried to talk to him he'd wander away. Elijah was one of the old-timers whom Digby wished *would* talk; oh, the stories that man could tell.

Digby thought Fang should take a hint and shut the hell up, especially first thing in the afternoon. But it wasn't just Fang. The bar was full of leftovers, a dozen or so, many of them laughing, yelling at one another, spitting, swapping tall tales about this thing or that. He-Ping looked like he was thinking about something, and the women (there were a couple of them) seemed to be waiting to be noticed, beams shining out of their eyes as if there were tiny lighthouses behind them. One of them smiled at Digby as he pulled a bulb cord, and he tipped an imaginary hat her way. The truth is, as much as he might like to complain, he liked their company, and they didn't hurt what little business there was—nobody else could see them. But Digby was a bartender: he saw everything.

"This town," Digby said to himself and shook his head. "It's not what it once was, but then, nothing is, is it?" He waited for someone to say something, and then answered the question himself. "No," he said. "Nothing is."

"You don't look so good, Digby," Fang said. "You look like you just rolled out of bed." Fang winked. Same joke over and over and over. "Get it?"

"I get it," Digby said.

"Like you rolled out of bed and broke your neck. The way I did."

"I get it," Digby said again.

Fang laughed and laughed and then sighed and sat down at a table and sighed again. "So who's up for a game of cards?"

No one was.

There was a commotion outside, and Fang and some of the others stood to look out the window and see what it was. A car door slammed.

"It's the Morgans, all packed up and everything," Kelly Neighbors said, looking out. Kelly only had one hand; she lost the other in the factory. Digby thought it would have been nice to get your hand back when you died, but that wasn't the deal, apparently. "And here comes Sam Morgan,"

"I guess they're leaving town," Fang said. "They lived over on Abby Lane, right? The nice two-bedroom."

"Mattress roped to the top of their car," Kelly said. "Wonder how long that will last."

The old-timers laughed. There was a mattress graveyard half a mile up Silk Road.

Then Sam Morgan pushed through the barroom door and didn't stop walking until he made it to the bar and the old-timers quieted down. Sam was a regular. There weren't many regulars left: the lumberjack came in time and again, and Jonas, the mechanic, who had a thing going on with the McCallister girl—the homely one, Helen—he came in twice a week at least. Sam Morgan was among the last.

"Sam Morgan!" Digby said. He always greeted his customers with a sense of the exclamatory, as if they were the one person out of all the people in the world he had been waiting for. "You look tired but hopeful; a thoughtful man of action. A god among men. *That's* Sam Morgan."

Sam Morgan took a seat. His head was too big for his tiny shoulders; it looked like it belonged on another man. He had the face of a mustachioed bulldog. "Looks like I'm the first one here today," he said.

"And you may be the last," Digby said. "All I know is that I'm happy to see you. What can I do you for, Sam Morgan?"

"Something that's wet, cold, and packs a punch," he said. "Maybe a mug full of that Arcadian brew."

"The perfect elixir to imbibe before a long drive," Digby said.

"With two kids and a sad wife," he said, "I'll need more than one."

Digby served his customer and gave it to him straight. "Starting over isn't easy," he said. "But you can do it. Believe it and it will happen."

Sam Morgan threw back the drink. "That's bullshit," he said. "It's going to be a slog from here on out. Two kids, a wife, and empty pockets. I can't even sell my house."

"It's not a seller's market," Digby said. "Sadly."

Digby looked over Sam Morgan's shoulder: the old-timers were grinning. Sam Morgan followed Digby's eyes, saw nothing, turned back. Digby smiled reassuringly, and Sam Morgan nodded toward his glass. Digby refilled it.

"The damn thing is," Sam Morgan said, less to Digby than to himself or to no one at all, "you don't think—you never imagine—that a whole town can die. *An entire town.* It's even started to smell like it's dead. You notice that?"

Digby said, "There's an unpleasant olfactory presence in town, I will give you that." It was hard to recall the way things used to be. Were things *ever* the way they used to be? Digby seemed to remember from his childhood a brightness, a sense of possibility, the belief that Roam's best days were ahead of them—but did he remember that, or was it just a story that his father kept telling him? The silk factory had been closed for a generation, and from that day forward Roam had commenced its ending. The miracle was that Roam was here at all and not just a scar on the landscape. Or maybe that's how long it took to put a town out of its misery.

Still working things out in his head, Sam Morgan said, "Nothing lives forever, I guess. I guess the whole world will die one day and it'll be a cinder of nothing, and no one around to know or care."

"Ash," Digby said. "Nothing but ash. Not even a memory left to say what it was."

"That'd be better, in a way. Instead of this having to go on with it all."

Digby took Sam Morgan's hands in his own and held them tight. He looked right into Sam's eyes: the stool Digby kept behind the bar allowed him to do that. "My friend," he said, "a man is sometimes required to do things he'd rather not, in part because he is a man and has no real choice in the matter."

These words seemed to strike Sam Morgan in the way Digby wanted them to. His eyes cleared, his jaw tightened, and he straightened those shoulders of his. "You're right, little man," he said. "Damn if you're not right."

"I have never been more right in my life," Digby said. "My last gift to you—free of charge."

Sam Morgan wiped the foam from his lips. "The kids want some goddamn ice cream," he said.

"Wonderful!" said Digby. "Chocolate or vanilla?"

*T*he old-timers watched Sam Morgan drive away until no one could see or hear his car anymore.

"Well," Kelly said, breaking the silence. "I guess that's me. My turn, right?"

"That's right," Fang said. But his face was still, his eyes empty. "Your turn. And good for you. Sam Morgan had a real nice place." Fang looked over at He-Ping, leaning against the far wall, and He-Ping looked back at Fang until he couldn't anymore.

"Don't worry, Fang," Kelly said. "People are clearing out of town faster than ever. Your turn's coming."

Digby wiped down Sam Morgan's spot at the bar. He kept his tavern clean, same as his father had. "I still don't get it," he said. "Why do you need a place to live? Being dead and all."

"You won't get it," Kelly said, "until you *are* dead."

"It's a second chance," Fang said. "A do-over. Things not having gone so well the first time around."

"Then I better make the days I have left really count," Digby said, and gave him his best bartender's wink. "Then maybe I can skip the trip back."

Kelly smiled at Digby and got up to leave. She walked through the door as if she were a regular customer, and her old friends sat down and closed their eyes and let the moment wash over them like a breeze.

What an odd bunch, these dead people. But maybe it was a mistake to think of them that way. Maybe being dead wasn't an ending at all, but more of an evolution, a new chapter. They had qualities that surprised him, that's for certain. Their ability to laugh, for example, and to want things, to desire. Digby had always thought of death, if anything, as the end of desire, and he'd thought about it that way with some relief. He was also disappointed to learn that housing continued to be an issue into the afterlife. In fact, there appeared to be but three things the old-timers *didn't* do anymore: eat, drink, and make love— which, Digby said, were the only three things he wanted to do. The old-timers made him, more than ever, want to live.

·  ·  ·

$\mathcal{W}$hile Digby had been surrounded by ghosts all of his life, the first ghosts Helen saw were those of her mother and father, the night after the car accident that killed them both.

Helen had decided to go; it was her last chance. Along with whatever grief the loss of her parents inspired—and there was grief—came the knowledge that her life would not go well from here, an awareness of the sisterly caretaker she would become. She saw her story looming before her as if in a magic crystal ball. She was eighteen; Rachel was eleven; there was no one else to take care of them, so they would have to take care of themselves. Helen would lose everything when she left—the world she'd made for herself and Rachel, and the only person who believed her beautiful—but she had sustained that story long enough, too long, and she knew that if she didn't leave she wouldn't stop. While the neighbors sat with Rachel downstairs, Helen found the small wooden suitcase in her mother's walk-in closet and packed a few essential items: a pale blue blouse, a skirt, her red dress, two pairs of underwear, three pairs of socks, and some of her mother's jewelry. She slipped quietly down the stairs and out a backroom window. She threw the suitcase out ahead of her and then followed it into the herb garden, brushing herself off as she stood. And there she came face-to-face with the ghosts of her parents. They were not much different as ghosts than they had been as real people, because there had always been something dead about them to her. If anything they looked more alive, brighter, well polished. They had loved her, she knew this, and they may have been the only two people who ever really did, but she felt as if they'd raised her the way they would a plant: they made sure she had everything she needed to thrive—food, water, sunlight—but kept her rooted to this pathetic patch of soil called Roam.

Helen had never seen a ghost before. She waited to be scared, but Mr. and Mrs. McCallister weren't frightening, despite the fact that they had only just died. There was something natural about them, something real: she had never before believed in ghosts, but now that she saw them she believed. It was as simple as that.

"*Helen,*" Mrs. McCallister said. A mother's voice: no one else was able to pack that much meaning into just that word, her name. "How could you?"

Her father didn't have anything to say. He just stood there and glowered.

Helen looked beyond them for a moment. The fog was rolling in like a cloud of cotton. Her mother and father were ghosts; she could have walked right through them to another life. But she didn't. All it took was for her mother to remind her: her sister was all she had.

Then her parents were gone, and Helen crawled back inside the house. *How could you?* For a long time Helen thought her mother meant how could she do this, leave at a time when her sister would need her the most? But it wasn't that; her mother knew Helen would never—could never—leave. Her mother meant, *How could you do what you've been doing to your sister for the last five years? Telling her these stories? Making up this dark and terrible world, and taking your sister's face for your own?*

The dead know all our secrets.

Later that same night, long after Helen thought Rachel had gone to bed, she heard Rachel's little feet padding down the hallway to her room. The door edged open, and Rachel slipped in. Moonbeams glowed through the window in narrow beams, spotlighting her sister's face as she entered. Helen had never seen her sister's eyes so sunken, her cheeks raw from wiping away the tears. Still, even through all of this, so beautiful. But she had stopped crying now. Rachel stood by her bed and held out her hands and waited until Helen took them. Then Rachel held them tight.

"It's just us now," Rachel whispered.

"Yes," Helen said. "Just us."

Helen brushed a strand of her sister's hair back behind her ear, and when she did could feel how hot Rachel was: the back of her neck was dripping wet.

"You'll protect me?" Rachel asked her.

The moonlight disappeared behind a cloud, and then the cloud passed and Rachel's face was bright with the moon again. "We'll protect each other," Helen said.

*S*o Helen stayed. She liked to imagine sometimes, just before she fell asleep, the life she might have had *if* . . . if her parents hadn't died, if she'd been beautiful, or been even plain. She closed her eyes and dreamed. *After years of taking care of her blind little sister, Helen Mc-Callister left Roam and traveled the world. The great minds and swarthy lotharios of her generation sought her out. After one night with her, many men simply killed themselves, realizing they had achieved a happiness impossible to replicate. Why go on? She gave herself freely, for such was her way. She had given herself to her sister for all those years, and now it was time to share herself with the rest.*

The dreams came, impossible dreams in any world, but she dreamed them just the same, and when she woke up, nothing, of course, had changed; nothing.

The ghosts of Mr. and Mrs. McCallister appeared to Helen on just that one night, and thereafter spent most of their time with Rachel, who couldn't see them anyway, or no better than she could when they were alive. (It was an irony that at least *some* of the ghostly shapes the world presented to Rachel were in fact the shapes of real ghosts, watching over the only person they believed could not watch back.) Years passed before Helen saw another ghost, and it wasn't her mother or her father. It was a man, standing beneath the chestnut tree in the front yard. She thought he was staring at her—she'd come out on the front porch for some air—but he was staring at the house, at one window and the next, then the side door, the path leading to the entryway. He was a small man with a white beard and gray eyes. He glowed like a dim bulb. She knew who he was in an instant, because there was a portrait of him in her living room, a portrait she looked at every single day. Elijah McCallister. He didn't want anything to do with her, though; he just wanted what everybody else did: a house, a place to live.

# ROAM:
# A SHORT HISTORY,
# PART II

ing Kai and Elijah traveled into the wilderness for days and days, but at the next town Elijah did as he said he would. He telegraphed his naval friend, a man whose life Elijah had saved from a sea monster—some great shark or whale, he couldn't remember—and asked him to get Ming Kai's family and bring them to America. Ming Kai told Elijah the name of the street where his family lived, and a positive response arrived from Elijah's friend early the next day: it would be done, and gladly, he wrote; anything for the man who saved his life. Of course, it would take some time—six months, perhaps a year, because Ming Kai's village was far from the coastal provinces and only reachable by horse—but it would be done. Elijah told Ming Kai, and Ming Kai shed tears of the greatest joy.

Happy now, Ming Kai and Elijah searched for the elusive mulberry. They traveled deep into the wooded hills and mountains of the virgin country that spread out before them like a soft green dream. Civilization, such as it was, was left far behind. They trod on earth that had never known the step of a human foot. Occasionally they'd encounter Indians, who would give them meat and water and then disappear into the forest like ghosts. (Even then Elijah knew that one day he would have to kill his share of Indians. It wasn't something he wanted to do, but it was something he would have to do to become the man he planned on becoming.)

The journey was hard. In the beginning Elijah and Ming Kai were full of hope and a wild bravado, they felt like two reckless gods making their own path in a new world. They became like brothers. But after many weeks of making paths they began to feel desperate. Tired, hungry, sick, dirty, and scared—for there were *lots* of bears in this part of the world—at the end of each day they felt they could go no farther . . . and yet they arose the next day and did. Elijah saved Ming Kai's life twice: once from a snake and once from rock slide. Ming Kai saved Elijah's life three times: once from a giant cat, once from a poisonous berry, and the third time from an Indian woman (though Elijah didn't feel this time should count because he really wasn't in danger, so they were even, as far as he was concerned).

And then one day, Elijah gave up. He simply stopped and sat down on the forest floor.

"I can't go on," he said. "I am done. This is where it has been written that I will die."

"I see no such writing," Ming Kai said, looking about.

"I will die here and be remembered by nobody. All my friends will forget me. At least you have a family, Ming Kai. They will miss you. Your sons will tell the story of how a white man came and took you away and you were never seen again. At least you have that."

"Yes," Ming Kai said. "At least I have that."

"Let's pick where our graves shall be," Elijah said.

Elijah stood. He found a flatness not far from where it was written that he would die. "This seems like a nice enough spot," he said.
"What do you think?"

Ming Kai sniffed the air. "I don't know."

Elijah looked more closely at the ground and sniffed himself. "I
think you're right," he said. "This is where the bears come to shit."

But Ming Kai shook his head. "I think—I think it is too soon to
die."

For Ming Kai's nose—which, like so many Chinese organs, was
advanced beyond the reckoning of his Caucasian brother—smelled
what was surely the mulberry tree. Mulberry trees smelled like red
wine and wet grass, and his grandmother. He walked to the edge of
the rise, the flattened expanse on which just moments before they had
planned to bury themselves, and his Chinese eyes saw it, growing wild
in the valley below them. Not one, not two, but a hundred of them.
Elijah followed his stare.

"Is that . . . ?"

Ming Kai nodded. "Yes," he said in a whisper. "Yes."

But there was a problem: between the two men and the bushes they
had been seeking for who knows how long was a ravine, a ravine as
deep and dark as the mouth of hell itself. A bridge would have to be
built. Ming Kai knew how: they cut down two dozen saplings, each
half again as long as the ravine itself, and tied them together with rope
until they formed a solid frame, and let the thin and fragile platform
fall from one side to the other, where it rested. Elijah looped a tree
stump with a lariat and swung across the ravine on it—agile as a mon-
key—where he secured the posts and waited.

"Come," he told Ming Kai.

"But—"

"It will hold," Elijah said.

"The horses—"

"Even the horses."

It didn't really even matter to Ming Kai anymore. It would have been just the same to him if he had fallen to his death into the ravine. But the bridge held, and the rest of their lives began.

Ming Kai ran down the hill; Elijah followed. From the first tree he found he clipped a leaf and ate it, just to make sure, and by his smile Elijah knew: he was sure.

They were home. They embraced like friends who could not have known each other longer, and fell to the ground and rolled around in the leaves and bear scat like a couple of little boys. They hugged and rolled; they rolled as one. They came to their senses soon enough, however, and stood and breathed deep and surveyed the world around them, a world that over the course of the next quarter of a century would be changed beyond recognition. Ming Kai saw the trees, and smiled; Elijah saw what the trees would do for him. His smile was briefer than Ming Kai's, but bigger.

"I've been thinking what we'd name it," Elijah said. "Once we made it here, once we found it, the place where our fortune would be made. What would we call it? I bet you've been thinking the same thing."

Ming Kai shook his head. He had but one thought, and that was of his family.

"If I were an Indian," Elijah said, "I'd call it Happy Man Valley. But I'm not a goddamn Indian. So I came up with a lot of names as we were riding. I came up with a new one every day. There's a peculiar and intoxicating power in that. Naming things is probably the second best thing in the world, next to actually inventing, creating the thing you get to name. Anyway, as one day became the next and the next and the next day after that and we rode all over every godforsaken mountain and valley and plain, I came upon the only name that would do. *Roam*. Because we have been roaming, my friend. And there will be others behind us, roaming as well. More and more will come. We will make our silk and our homes and our families and they will come here, to Roam."

Ming Kai nodded. "Yes," he said. "And when my family arrives, then we shall begin."

"Yes." Elijah sighed, not entirely sure they would ever arrive. They were a long way away from everywhere. Even Elijah wasn't sure where the two of them were now. But why borrow trouble? It might happen.

Meanwhile they needed shelter, and so over the next month they built two cabins: a small one for Elijah and a bigger one for Ming Kai and his family. The cabins were made entirely of cedar trees, trees that were tough to cut and hew but would last forever. Then the rains came and the valley flooded and they were surrounded by an ocean of water for days. Summer became fall and fall became winter, and Ming Kai kept his word about waiting and said nothing about the silk, and so when the snow melted Elijah mounted his horse to ride back to the last town he remembered passing through. How long ago was that? Weeks, months, years? It was all a blur now. But he had no choice but to return for supplies and—they hoped—Ming Kai's family.

"I'll be back as soon as I can," Elijah said. "And while I'm gone feel free to start the whole silk-making process—"

"When my family is here," Ming Kai said. "Only then we shall begin. But come quickly. The worms are dying."

Elijah cursed him and left.

*A*nd Ming Kai waited. Days became weeks, weeks a month, one month, two. He wondered if he had been abandoned. He wondered if Elijah had been eaten by a bear, since Ming Kai was not there to save his life. If so, he would die here as well, alone in the heart of America, in a place no Chinese had ever been before and perhaps should not have ever been. At night the sounds from the forest were nightmarish—piercing cries and malicious hoots. Ming Kai would grab his gun and shoot into the darkness, and in this way he killed many shadows, and scared some bears and maybe a wild dog or two. During what quiet there was he missed his home, the lean-to his family lived in, the small thatched hut he'd built down by the sea they sometimes visited if he'd sold a bit of silk that week. He would never see the sea again, that much he knew for certain. But none of that really mattered if he could have his family. All he wanted was to be loved by those he loved. This is the kind of man he was.

*H*e could hear the wagon coming long before he could see it, and at these first sounds his heart began to beat like a hammer on a nail. He tried to bridle his hopes, for he could not have lived through the disappointment if he thoroughly imagined them, his wife and sons, only to see Elijah arrive with a wagon full of wheat and rice.

At the top of the ridge, far, far away, the wagon came into view. Elijah was at the reins, and he paused briefly to raise a hand and wave it Ming Kai's way. This had to mean he had been successful, for what man would raise his hand and wave if he had not?

So Ming Kai looked closer, and there, right beside Elijah, was Sing Loo, his wife. Sing Loo! Oh, how beautiful she was! She was even more beautiful than he remembered—and he had remembered her many times as the dark nights passed. And there, the two little black dots bobbing in the wagon behind her, Chang and Tan! They had grown. He had missed a part of their lives because of Elijah McCallister, and he hated his friend for that. But now look what he had done for Ming Kai: he had atoned. Ming Kai waved at them until his arm turned to rubber. Oh, happiness! He felt as though he were being born all over again. It was the ecstasy of his life, of being alive, to have one's ultimate dream realized, and this had been his dream from the day Elijah knocked him out and kidnapped him. He couldn't wait. He ran up the hill to meet them.

The wagon and Ming Kai met but a minute later. Ming Kai's chest was heaving as he tried to catch his breath. Elijah had a smile on his face so large it looked as if his entire head could fit in his own mouth. *This is the beginning*, Ming Kai was thinking. *My life has been returned to me.*

Ming Kai stood, frozen, a smiling statue of himself, but then, slowly, his smile waned, and finally disappeared altogether. He looked at Sing Loo, and then at the two young boys. A tear came to his eyes. Then, he spoke.

"That is not my wife," he said. The two smiling children in the back peeked at him and laughed, then hid behind a bag of corn. There was a little black dog with them, a puppy, and it barked once. "Those are not my sons."

Stunned—or so he appeared—Elijah looked at the woman beside him, the woman who had not said a word through the course of their travels because she knew none he would understand. He looked at the darling black-haired children behind him, who had not cried once on the long journey, who seemed forever bright-eyed and happy, and at the cute little puppy he had purchased for them at the last outpost, because Elijah wanted to be thought of as the kind of man who would buy a puppy for a couple of Chinese kids, even if he was not.

"Not your wife?" Elijah said. "Not your sons?"

Ming Kai shook his head.

All joy had drained from Ming Kai's face: it had become hard, petrified. He said something in Chinese, and the woman said something back to him.

She had a sweet voice.

"Her name is Wu Li," Ming Kai said. "She is from Shanghai. She is not my wife."

"But . . . " Now it was Elijah's turn to fall mute. At that moment it was hard to say whose heart was more broken, Elijah's or Ming Kai's. Both had dreams that were shattered: Ming Kai's dream of love, and Elijah's dream of riches. Ming Kai wanted to die; he knew he would never see his real family again. But Elijah was the sort of man who, in the absence of authentic hope, created his own. He was the sort of man who could build a town in the middle of nowhere in order to conform to a dream, the sort of man who saw a wall not as a thing to go around but as something to be driven through.

He snapped the reins, and the horses began their descent to the place that would one day be Roam. Ming Kai had to move out of the way lest he be trampled—it was as though Elijah were no longer able to see him. But as the wagon passed, Elijah spoke.

"You'll get used to them," he said.

Ming Kai did get used to them. It took some time, but he did. They were not his family, but they were still *a* family, and they were much better than no family at all. He gave up the secret of his silk to Elijah, and Roam was born. And like everything that had ever been built in the history of the world, it was built by those who had nothing and, almost certainly, never would have anything more than that, people who sacrificed themselves for a future they would never see, almost all of them Chinese.

In America, Ming Kai learned, it is easier to be happy than sad. It's better to forget what was and to remember what is, or better yet, what might be. The old self is wiped away like chalk on a blackboard, overwritten with new words in a foreign vocabulary. There is no history here. In America you can fly, because there's no past to weigh you down. Only here could this place, which had been nowhere forever, become a town. And it grew so very fast, fast beyond imagining, and soon, sooner than anyone could have believed—especially Ming Kai—there was a road, and buildings, and homes, and stores. It was all so fresh, so new. It *smelled* new, and for a full year after construction began you couldn't breathe outside without swallowing a handful of sawdust. Chinese poured into Roam. What had taken Elijah and Ming Kai months to discover took the rest of the world a matter of days. Words travel on the wind, across the sea, into the ears of anyone willing to listen. Steel and braided wire and coal were brought in by the wagonful from as far away as Arcadia, and a mechanic named Shapiro was kidnapped and forced to design and build the factory. He died before it was done—worked beyond exhaustion—but Elijah was able to finish it himself, because he had the kind of mind that could subsume another man's thoughts. He just made it bigger—twice as big as the design called for. It grew into a great steel giant. Ming Kai had never seen such quantities of silk emerge from its warehouse doors. Moths were everywhere, too: in every window, in every lamp, their carcasses littering the muddy streets like dead baby angels. But even before all of this happened—on the day he saw his new family, in fact—Ming Kai knew he would have to become a new man. China was thousands of miles away, and he would never return; best to let go of the memory as well. *Good-bye, family and the old tarnished world. Hello, sweet and glossy future!*

As Elijah had predicted, Ming Kai got used to his replacement family, and like fish growing legs and learning to crawl on dry land, everyone changed. Sing Loo became Sarah, and the boys were named Thomas and Norton, and together with Elijah, Ming Kai and his worms created a new world; the future would see them produce enough skeins in a month to drape the entire town of Roam in a billowing sheet of silk. There was so much beauty: is there anything more beautiful than silk? Every bed in Roam was covered in it. Women wore the loveliest silk dresses, and some men wore their silken pajamas out early in the morning, taking their dogs for a walk. And there was no man, no matter how poor, who couldn't boast a drawer full of handkerchiefs. It was a soft town with a sweet sheen, and Ming Kai had helped create it. That was something. That filled a spot inside his large heart.

*O*nce they were settled, Ming Kai had Elijah over for a feast. The boys played in the dirt beneath the table, and Elijah smoked a fat cigar.

"Thomas and Norton seem like good boys," Elijah said. "And Sarah, she's a good cook."

"Yes," Ming Kai said. "What you say is true."

Elijah stood, and it seemed as if in that moment all the blood drained out of his face. He turned a chalky white, and his cold eyes flared. The old Elijah died then, and a new one was born.

"Before we go any further in our enterprise, you should know: they are yours," Elijah said. "But everything else is mine."

# GHOSTS,
# PART II

*T*here was a fire burning down the street, and from what Digby could see of it—which wasn't much, since all he did was poke his head out the tavern door—it looked like it might have been the fire station itself. He wasn't particularly worried about it, though, because fires in Roam had about the same ambition the rest of the population did: soon it would die out on its own. There were a lot of fires these days. Sometimes it was just a great big pile of old furniture, or books, or clothes, or whatever got collected during the course of an entire lifetime spent in one place (always too much to take with you to the new life), but some of the other fires were a good deal bigger. Entire homes, shops, businesses—turned to ash. Digby understood the rage, he understood the bitterness. But to burn down your own home? The place you raised your children? It seemed unnecessary. Were Digby himself to leave Roam—and at this point in time he had no plans to, but who knew what tomorrow might bring—he would make sure the tavern was clean, the lights were off, and the keys were on the counter along with a note wishing the very best to whomever wanted to have it.

He took another step out into the day and craned his neck to see around the door. Yes, it *was* the fire station. He wondered if Sam Morgan had started it before he left; he used to volunteer down there. Sam Morgan, driving away in that beater with the mattress strapped to the top. Is there any sadder sight? A man, a wife, two kids. A family with nothing to call their own except all the time in the world. And that car, same as the rest of them around here, cobbled together from the parts of half a dozen other cars, not cars at all really but rumors of what cars were supposed to be. Digby knew there had to be a place where cars were actually *made,* that there was a time when they were new and shiny, but by the time the cars got to Roam they were seven different colors, cannibalized, chopped up, three doored, loud as all creation. He'd seen people using the trunks as bathtubs. He witnessed one poor soul warming up a sandwich on the engine block. The steering wheels were sometimes completely missing and in their place were two blocks of wood wired to a metal rod, and inside the car no place to sit at all: you just had to squat. This was the trade-off of living in what Digby thought of as a frontier community: it took a while for the future to get here, and by the time it did it was the past.

The old-timers liked a fire, though. Most of them left the tavern to get a closer look at it, gathering at its edge, as if to warm themselves. Digby watched them file out the door, hundreds of them, all dressed up in their pants and dresses and hats, strolling down Main Street as if they actually lived here, as if this were still their town.

Digby shook a cigarette out of its pack and struck a match on the wooden post supporting the portico. Again he was beset by that sadness, a family trait; his father had it so bad that there were days he wouldn't get out of bed at all. He would just lie there, staring at the ceiling. All Dr. Carraway had to do was look at him to know what it was: *nostalgic melancholy*, which he described as a deep sadness brought on by thoughts of the past, and since sometimes all a man *had* was the past, this nostalgic melancholy could be quite dangerous, in some cases even fatal. The only cure was to paint a picture of the future so bright and powerful and real that it overwhelmed the patient's obsession with times-gone-by.

The past that Digby's father was thinking about had everything to do with Allie Wei, his first girl; he was thinking of her jet-black pigtails and her eyes—one brown, one blue—and of the day they made love in the mulberry trees behind the factory, and fell asleep, and woke up the next morning naked, overlaid in a layer of silk, the dusty fibers sent airborne during the manufacturing process. She died a year later, her lungs ravaged by the silk dust. He thought he had stopped thinking about her when he met and married Digby's mother, but it had been but a temporary reprieve, and when he turned fifty he was overwhelmed by almost palpable images of her. They possessed him. So Dr. Carraway wrote out a prescription for Digby's father: *Stories. Three times a day. Morning, noon, and just before bed.* They were to be stories not of what was, or what is, but of what could be. That was the only thing that could cure him.

Mrs. Chang had never been much of a storyteller, so little Digby took on the job. But he only had one story to tell, and he had his mother leave the room to tell it. *When you die*, he told his father, *you will find Allie in the field behind the factory. It will be exactly as it was. She will be naked and covered in silk dust. So will you. But she will never die again, and neither will you, and you'll be together forever.*

*Then let me die*, his father said.

*You* will *die*, he said. *But you have to finish this life first. Keep this story in a little box beside your bed, and look at it every morning when you wake and every night before you sleep. It will make you happy.*

•    •    •

*H*is father was happy for the rest of his life.

Digby had no one to tell him stories, and who knew if they would even work with him, because his melancholia came from the past *and* the present. It was this town; it was Roam itself. It was in the very air he breathed. To live with what had happened to his home . . . It was as if he had to watch a good friend die, and then had to view the corpse every single day for the rest of his life. It was almost impossible to remember the Roam that once was, now that it had been abandoned, burned, broken, and worn down by time itself, all because of the curse born with it (or such was the old story people told). He grew up just as it was beginning the long, slow descent into decay, but he could remember all too well the town it used to be, its Main Street lined with shops and bustling with people, all of them dressed in the silk produced in McCallister's factory just half a mile away, hidden behind a line of poplars as if it were the secret engine that powered the town. And it was. The day the factory died was the day the town began to die. It was the rich who left first, taking with them all the money, secure in their ability to find a life elsewhere. Left behind were the workers, mostly Chinese and combos, who had nothing at all. Now almost every storefront was dark and empty. A few old-timers had moved into them: Digby could see them in the windows, as if on display. The quiet was eerie, too, another absence that had all the qualities of sound: he could hear the silence, even feel it.

Digby stood by the door of his tavern and had these thoughts. Then, in the silence, he heard the dogs. They belonged to the lumberjack who lived in the woods at the edge of town. Lumberjack Smith, the sole human being who had actually come to Roam in the last few years and stayed here to live. When he heard the dogs barking Digby knew this meant the lumberjack was coming into town for a drink, as he did every day. The dogs followed Smith everywhere, about a dozen of them, each one as black as the next. The closer they came to town the more they barked, and when they reached Main Street they began to howl, howl as if they'd gone completely mad. Digby thought it was because they could see the old-timers, too.

# YARD SALE

*T*he saddest part of the day—of everyone's day, really, of every day everyone in the entire town had to live through—was when Rachel and Helen set up their little shop on the northwest corner of the intersection at Twelfth and McCallister. They were there every Monday by ten (unless it rained), and today was no different. *Here come the girls*, said old Mrs. Branscombe, half to herself, half to her old dog Comer, a basset hound she'd named after her dead husband because she could not imagine living out the rest of her life *not* saying his name. There they were: Helen and Rachel pushing an old metal cart down the sidewalk, the one they borrowed from the big grocery store that had closed its doors years ago. Rachel insisted on pushing it, as heavy and unwieldy as it was, while Helen walked ahead with long, aggressive strides, as if she were challenging you to try and stop her. Townsfolk at their windows gawking, shaking their heads, sighing, *the* *girls, again.* Helen didn't care what they thought. She knew how they felt, but it fed her determination to do it, every Monday, at ten, until what she and Rachel were selling was all gone.

Tied to one side of the cart with rubber ropes was a card table with a fake alligator-skin top, which they unfolded and placed just before the stop sign. Rachel and Helen sat in two old wooden chairs behind the table, and Helen had a cigar box—PUNCH CIGARS, HANDMADE IN SPANISH HONDURAS, the box said—that served as her cash register.

What were the girls selling? Everything. They were selling everything they had, one thing at a time. Helen had it all worked out, what they were selling and when—the order, as it were, in which they would be dismantling their lives.

They'd started with their parents' things. Their parents had the most, so they were still selling them, ten years after their deaths. All their clothes, every coat and every dress, every pair of trousers. They had almost sold every sweater (there were many sweaters, since Mother and Father both wore sweaters of various weights and warmth deployment all year long, cold-blooded creatures that they were). Every sock, hat, tie, and belt—everything but their underwear, which Helen had thrown away in the days just after they were buried, unable to stand the idea of her dead parents' underwear in the house. All of their things: books, pens, cuff links, hairbrushes, and boxes and photos of old friends, all of it available for purchase on the corner of Twelfth and McCallister.

After this, they would begin to eat away at the rest of it, all those things belonging to the house itself, and then what was Rachel's, and then—Helen would probably stop there. And with all the money she'd earned she'd buy some new things for herself.

They had a ways to go. There weren't a lot of people in town left to buy things, and those who remained couldn't bring themselves to approach the girls. But sometimes Jonas came by to flirt, and that was nice. He never bought anything unless Helen made him, though, promising with her smile the recompense he never stopped wanting.

There was a sturdy magnolia growing there. It had a nice strong branch jutting out over the sidewalk, and it was here Rachel hung the clothes. A dress of her mother's, a pair of slacks belonging to her dad. Then a coat—his jacket—the herringbone he wore almost every day, still saturated in pipe smoke, a bit threadbare. It was a wonder he wasn't wearing it when he died. Rachel pressed her face against it and took a deep breath. She pressed the palms of her hands against the tattered and—she smiled—ticklish wool blend. She stuck her hand in the pocket.

"Look," she said, holding up her fingers. They were speckled with tobacco flecks. "Everything is here except for him."

Helen took Rachel by the wrist and brought Rachel's hand close to her face and smelled it and, as though she were testing some food that may have been too hot, or poisonous, tentatively stuck out her tongue and captured a small brown remnant of Mr. McCallister. This dust, proof he'd once had a place among the living, transported her back into the old world, one of youth and love and possibility, the big world, before it had become so small and dead.

"Let's keep this jacket," Rachel said.

But Helen shook the jacket out, watching the brown flakes scatter and fall.

"Everything must go," she said. She hung the jacket on the tree. "It's for the best."

"But, Helen," Rachel said. "These things are all we have left of them. Once they're gone—"

"Exactly," Helen said. "That's the idea."

"I want to stop," Rachel said. "I want to stop doing this."

Tears welled in her sister's eyes, and Helen wondered, as she always did when her sister cried, if there was something different about them, if the tears of a blind girl had a quality the tears of the seeing did not.

She held her sister close. "You smell good," Helen said. "Like a flower. And listen to the birds. They always come out for you."

These small kindnesses were usually enough for Rachel. But not today.

"It's not *right*," she said. "And it must look . . . wrong. A blind girl and her sister setting up shop on a corner."

"Oh, Rachel," Helen said softly, still holding her sister tight against her, tighter now, too tight. "This is what people have always done. Ever since long ago. For generations it's been the same. When people die, you take their things and send them out into the world, and in that way—"

"I don't believe you," Rachel said, pushing her sister away. "I've never seen anyone do that before. Who else does that?"

Helen almost laughed. "No," she said. "You're right. You wouldn't *see* anyone doing that anymore. But people used to set up shop on the corner all the time."

Helen knew that if she said the same thing over and over again, and said it with conviction, eventually Rachel would believe it. Even Helen found herself believing some of the stories she told. Sometimes she felt like she was living in more of a dream world than the one she'd created for Rachel.

"A long time ago," Helen said, "but not *that* long ago, you would see people on every corner of this town, selling their things. It was called . . . cornering. And some corners were the good ones, and some were the bad ones . . . " But Helen stopped midstory: somebody was coming.

"I think we have customers," Rachel said, cocking her head to one side, like a dog.

"No," Helen said, sighing. "It's just those boys."

Those boys: Gus Dyer and his quiet tagalong Johnny Clare. They always came around on sale days and never bought anything, just picked up things with their sticky hands and stared at Rachel, especially Gus, who was clearly smitten by her. He stammered and blushed as if Rachel could see him. It was—almost—adorable. Helen tried to keep Rachel behind her when they came by, but today she was too late. They were there before she had a chance to protect her.

"Hey," Gus said. He was chewing on something—a twig. It made his lips green. Little bits of bark were in his teeth. Helen wished Rachel could see this. "Hey, Rachel. Hey, Helen."

Neither of the girls said anything. Rachel had been instructed in how to be with boys. She had been told how they were.

"Can we help you?" Helen said.

"No," Gus said. Johnny Clare just shook his head.

"Y'all can scoot then," Helen said.

"We're not hurting anything." Gus had never been scared of Helen, for some reason. It might have been because he wasn't smart enough to be. "Do you mind if I speak to Rachel?"

Helen laughed. "She has nothing to say to you."

"That's right, Gus Dyer," Rachel said, but without much conviction. "I have nothing to say to you." She was smiling. Helen realized she was actually trying to flirt with him.

"See?" Helen said. "Get on out of here."

Gus didn't move. He looked back at his friend Johnny Clare. Johnny didn't say anything, either. Everyone was quiet until Gus spoke. "Well," he said. "That's what I wanted to say to Rachel. We're going. My folks and me. Leaving Roam."

Rachel actually gasped. "No," she said.

"What do you care?" Helen knocked against her sister's shoulder with her own.

Rachel appeared to gather herself. "I don't," she said. "It's just . . . you can't give up on Roam. Our great-grandfather founded this town."

Gus nodded. "I know," he said. "But we're not giving up. There's just not much left to hold on to."

Suddenly Johnny spoke up. "Gus and I are about the only boys still here," he said.

"Men," Gus said, correcting him. "We're men."

A black dog wandered in the yard behind them, stopping to look at the gathering as if it might be something the dog wanted to be a part of. Then it disappeared behind the Treadways' house.

"Anything else?" Helen asked. "You're scaring away our customers."

Gus looked behind him, to his left and his right. No one was there.

"Just one more thing," Gus said. "Rachel."

*Rachel.* She'd never heard her name spoken like that before. Helen wasn't sure she had heard anyone say her name like that, either.

"Yes?" Rachel said.

"We," Gus started, then rethought it. "Johnny and me and a couple of others—not just us—Laura Anne's going to be there, too. But we're going down by the bridge and just, you know, have a farewell party. Say good-bye with smiles on our faces instead of frowns."

"The bridge?" Rachel said. "What bridge?"

Helen would have liked to kill Gus Dyer now.

"The old bridge down by the ravine," he said.

"That bridge is gone," Helen said. "Long gone."

"It's old," Gus said. "And I wouldn't trust it. But—"

"There's a bridge?" Rachel asked again.

"There's no bridge," Helen said.

Gus and Johnny looked at each other, and then at Rachel, and then at Helen. There was a story in Helen's eyes, and somehow they could read it. It wasn't a short story, either; it was a long one, and it was all about Helen and Rachel and who they were to each other, and even about the things Helen had told her. It couldn't have been clearer if it had been written in a book.

"There's no bridge," Rachel said.

Gus and John kept looking at Helen, and Helen kept looking at them. "Okay," Gus said. "Jeez. There's no bridge. Can you come anyway?"

"Can Helen come, too?"

So much happened in the world beyond what Rachel knew. That Gus and Helen were having their own silent conversation at the same time Rachel and Gus were talking to each other was nothing she could have even imagined. That people were able to speak with their eyes— of this, too, she had no idea. But she would learn.

"I don't think it's that kind of party," Helen said. "Is it, Gus?"

"No," Gus said, defeated. "It's not." Gus took one last long look at the most beautiful girl he would ever see in his life. "Bye, Rachel."

"Bye, Gus. And bye, Johnny Clare."

So the boys left. Helen watched them walk away while Rachel appeared to be putting some of the table's trinkets in a kind of order. Even Helen could feel how sad her sister was, though, sad in a way Rachel could never express, sad for missing out on something she had never, and would never, know. When the boys turned the corner Helen looked at the house standing there—empty now for a week—and saw Tammy Chan looking at her through the living room window. Tammy died ten years ago, in the flood. Helen remembered how her body had been found at the top of a pine tree, but she didn't look that worse for wear now. Tammy Chan smiled, and lifted a hand to wave, and Helen almost did, too—force of habit. She stopped herself, because it didn't feel right to be waving at a ghost, even if one waved at you first. Distracted, then, she didn't hear the *click-click* of a real person approaching. Dorothy Samuels. Rachel liked Mrs. Samuels. It hadn't been easy for Helen, keeping the two of them apart, but, for the most part, she had.

"Girls," said Mrs. Samuels. "Good morning."

"Morning," Helen said. She watched as Dorothy glanced at her and then quickly to Rachel, where she let her gaze linger. *She can't even look at me,* Helen thought.

"Good morning, Mrs. Samuels," Rachel said. "How are you today?"

Mrs. Samuels had been a good friend of their mother's. She was close to fifty years old, the age their mother would have been. Mrs. Samuels did things like put a kettle on the stove to boil water for her coffee each morning, and work in her garden, and make pies for charity auctions and the like (back when they had charity auctions in Roam), while her husband carved walking sticks from tree branches. It seemed so strange to Helen that they were still able to do all this while her own parents had melted away into the soil.

"I'm very well, thank you, Rachel," she said. "Older than I've been." She held out her hand and Rachel took it in both of hers, and Rachel ran her fingers across them as though she were reading the topography of a map. Rachel sighed, her face tilting toward her sister. Mrs. Samuels was nice.

"What can we do for you, Mrs. Samuels?" Helen said. "We have a number of new items today."

"So I see." Mrs. Samuels's voice was tinged with sadness and— Helen heard it—the sharp edge of disapproval. "So I see."

She let her eyes wander across the card table—past the deck of cards, the set of three blue pens from different stays at the Concorde Hotel, the chipped, stained coffee mug—until they stopped on something, transfixed.

"Your mother's brooch."

"Yes," Helen said.

Now Mrs. Samuels was able to look at Helen, and Helen back at her, each woman filling her own space in the world and each of them unwilling, or unable, to move from it. At moments like this you could see Rachel suspecting something but unsure enough even to say what it was she thought.

"Helen?" Rachel said. "What's happening?"

"Nothing, Rachel." Helen was still looking at Mrs. Samuels. "Mrs. Samuels is interested in Mother's brooch."

"May I see it?" Mrs. Samuels asked.

Rachel's hands, eager to be a part of whatever was going on, clumsily moved among all the objects until she came to it. She clasped it in both hands, to make sure, and then held it out for Mrs. Samuels to take.

"Thank you, Rachel," she said.

She took it, looked at it: it was a beautiful Chinese flower. Or at least it had the feeling of something foreign, of something faraway, of something magical. The way the jewels and stones glowed, even in darkness. Someone said they were just garnets and orange jasper—but there was definitely something about them. Rachel swore the flower had an aroma. To her it smelled like a camellia.

"It's beautiful," Rachel said, "isn't it?"

"It is," Mrs. Samuels said.

"You must have seen her wear it many times."

"More than that," Dorothy said. "I gave it to her."

"Oh."

Dorothy looked at Helen. "Your sister knew that, I'm sure," she said. "Didn't you?"

Slowly, Helen nodded. "I think I did know that."

Dorothy held the brooch with both of her hands, just as Rachel had. "How much?"

Rachel was flustered. "We couldn't sell it," she said. "Not to you, Mrs. Samuels. Just take it. Please."

"Don't be silly," Dorothy said. "I insist. How much for this lovely brooch? Helen?"

Again their eyes locked in wordless battle. "Five dollars," Helen said.

"That's much less than it cost me, even all those years ago. Are you sure?"

"Fine. Ten."

"*Helen*," Rachel said.

"Ten it is," Dorothy said, opening the tarnished golden clasp of her small black purse and gingerly removing a weathered bill. Helen quickly snatched it from her and dropped it into the cigar box.

Dorothy held the brooch for only a moment more. Then she said, "Here you are, Rachel. A little present."

She crossed to the other side of the card table and carefully pinned the brooch on Rachel's dress. Then she hugged her. "It looks beautiful. You look like a queen."

"Like a queen? Really?" Rachel said, unable to stop herself.

Dorothy was crying now, softly. "Remember her," she said. "Remember your mother. If she were here she would tell you to stay hopeful. Things could change: they always do." And she squeezed Rachel's shoulder before she turned and walked away.

"Hopeful for what?" Helen called after her. "Hopeful for *what*?"

But Mrs. Samuels was already gone around the corner.

Rachel and Helen stood there, both of them appearing to look at Mrs. Samuels as she left them, but neither seeing her. Helen's eyes were clouded, too.

"That was nice," Rachel said, fingering the brooch on her chest.

"Yes," Helen said, as she felt her strength returning. "Now we have money for the cake."

There were other customers that day, but only a few, and none of them spent any of their precious money. When Rachel said she smelled rain—she was good at that—they packed everything up and covered their things with a tarp and almost made it home before the first drops started falling. It was a warm rain, the kind you could steep a tea bag in. So although they were just a few feet away from the awning that would bring shelter, they stopped and let the rain fall all over them. *The girls, would you just look at the girls.* It's what you would say had you seen them, standing in the warm summer shower.

They both closed their eyes and raised their heads toward the heavens. Rachel's hand reached out, her fingers gently waving like the fronds of a sea flower, until they found Helen's wrist. Then she clasped their wet hands together.

"What they said about leaving," Rachel said then. "The boys."

"Idiots," Helen said. "What makes them think anywhere else is going to be better than Roam?"

"It just made me think," Rachel said. "Maybe we should go, too."

"Really?" Helen said. "And do what, where?"

Rachel had no answer for that, of course. "Or maybe—maybe I should leave. Just me. I'm a grown woman now."

"Really?" Helen laughed. "A grown woman? A grown woman can take care of herself, Rachel. I don't see you doing that anytime soon. Or ever."

"Because you never let me try."

Helen bit her bottom lip to keep from screaming and let go of her sister's hand. "Go ahead," she said. "Try. See how far it gets you. You couldn't find your *shoes* without me! Actually, Rachel, sometimes I feel more like your servant than your sister. 'Get this, get that. Clean this up.' It's never ending. Literally."

"I don't want to be a burden to you," Rachel said. "I want to show you—"

"I think it's too late for that, Rachel. It's a lifetime too late for that. Have you ever considered what I've given up for you? I could have gone anywhere, done anything. But then Mother and Father died, and I had to babysit my little sister instead."

"I'm sorry," Rachel said. She was crying now, though she couldn't tell the tears from the rain. "I'm so sorry. But is it too late? Mrs. Samuels just said—"

Helen looked at her sister. Her dress was translucent against her body. Not too long ago little blind girls were put away with other little blind girls in an asylum, because no one even wanted to know such people existed, blind people with their twisted faces and bad posture and eerie stares. Could have happened to Rachel, too, after their parents died. No one would have blamed Helen had she done that. But she didn't, and now it was too late. Over the years it had happened: now Helen needed Rachel more than Rachel needed her.

"Don't leave me," Helen said. And then, almost too softly to hear, "Please."

"Never," Rachel said, but with less conviction than Helen would have liked. "Where would I even go?"

The rain came down harder. Against the metal porch covering it sounded like thunder.

"Never," Helen said. And she took her sister by the shoulders and shook her, pressing her lips to Rachel's ear. "*Never! Never! Never!*" she said.

And Rachel, through tears, said, "Let go of me, Helen. Please. "

But Helen wouldn't let go, and they stood like that until the rain stopped and some of the wet dripped out of their clothes. Then they set the cart on the porch and walked into the house Elijah McCallister had built, so many years ago, and tried to pretend that nothing had changed, when everything had.

# ROAM:
# A SHORT HISTORY,
# PART III

Silk made Elijah a very rich man, and as rich men have always done, he built a house far too big for a man to live in. It was elegant, magnificent, absurd. It would have been absurd anywhere, but in Roam, an invented place in the middle of nowhere, it was gloriously, mythically, absurd. In addition to being huge—you had to look at it twice just to see it once—it was also recklessly beautiful, the largely uninhabitable manifestation of the mind of a madman lucky enough to find a thing through which he could channel his ambition. In his dreams his house swallowed everything and everybody; America lived inside of it instead of the other way around. The imported Chinese kept coming, half of them working in the silk factory and the stores and clearing the land to build a bigger factory and more stores; the other half working on his house, building wing after wing after wing, soon to no purpose at all but his own deranged desire to hear the incessant sounds of progress hammering in his ears. Elijah liked to be able to see new rooms, new porches, new staircases; it wasn't necessary that they lead somewhere.

At least there was a town in which the house could exist. For quite some time Main Street was the only street, and only was called Main Street after there was a second street, and then a third. It was laid out much like any other town—thoughtlessly, and in haste. Here is where the rich people lived, and here the workers. This is where the white people shopped, and here was the special store for the Chinese, which had everything they could ever want, as long as they didn't want that much. There was a barn and a bar and a general store. There was a place to eat. One young man opened a haberdashery, and that was welcomed by men and women alike. People lived and died. They loved and laughed and cried. It was the same here as it was anywhere else in the world; people were no more or less sad, no more or less happy, no more or less anything. Roam was new, but at the same time it wasn't anything new at all. The only difference was, it was Elijah's. He made the laws and invented the money. His house was like a second town—even he never saw it all—and rumor had it that within its labyrinthine bowels he sired many families with the most excellent of the Chinese women and had children—one of them a son, to keep his blood and name alive—who never saw one another, though sometimes separated only by a wall and a door. They say he had more children than a dozen men, and though he never married a single one of their Chinese mothers, he professed an abiding fondness for each—and in fact treated them all with the gentleness one usually reserved for stray dogs and babies not your own. Outside of his own home he forbade the comingling of white men and yellow woman; he called their offspring combos and created a slum just for them. He created everything, the worst of it and the best of it as well, and for a little while—a week, perhaps, give or take a day—Elijah was content.

Ming Kai was not.

All these years, as Ming Kai had watched Roam grow from a patch of mulberry trees into a real town, he was kept separate from its success. Even though it would never have existed without him, he was of value only for as long as Elijah wanted to know his secret. Once Elijah knew the secret of making silk, Ming Kai became just another person in Roam, another person to perform a small part in the drama of Elijah McCallister's life.

But not entirely. When Elijah needed to talk to someone, it was always Ming Kai he sought out. When the pressures of running the town became overwhelming—and they did, occasionally, though Elijah would have no one else in the world know it—he turned to Ming Kai. They would talk from night into the morning about the bears, about the combos, about the past. Ming Kai mostly listened; he could go for some hours without saying a word. Still, in the morning Elijah would clap him on the back and say *Thank you, my friend. You have been a great help.* And to Elijah he did feel like a friend—his only friend.

It had been years since they talked like this. Now Ming Kai felt like just another man; no one knew who he was, what he'd done in his time. After giving up his life to come here, this was too much to bear.

Ming Kai had never even been to Elijah's office. He had seen him in it, since his office was at the very top of the factory, and Elijah always seemed to be at one of the windows, looking down at his workers with his hard, cold stare. But today Ming Kai went up, and he knocked on the door until he heard Elijah's voice: "Enter!" he bellowed, as though he were a king.

Ming Kai shuffled in and waited for Elijah to look at him. It took a minute or two. Elijah had a stack of papers on the desk in front of him—invoices, order forms, payroll—and he was going through each and every piece of it. He did not become who he was by trusting someone else to do even the menial task of bookkeeping. But no one could ever have done it as well, because it was more than just a job for him. It was his life.

"Yes?" he said. He still didn't look up. "What is it?"

"It is this," Ming Kai said.

Finally Elijah looked. Ming Kai had something in his hand, but Elijah couldn't see what it was: it was so small it hid behind Ming Kai's skinny old fingers.

Elijah sighed. "Well? What the hell is it?"

Ming Kai showed him. It was an old, gray worm. It looked starved, even dead. It only moved when Ming Kai gently touched it with the tip of his finger.

"The worm is sick," Ming Kai said.

Elijah almost laughed. "You see all this work I have to do, Ming Kai, and you interrupt it to bring me one sick worm?"

Ming Kai shook his head. "All the worms are sick. The trees, too: they are dying."

"All of them?"

Ming Kai nodded.

Elijah looked away from the worm, from Ming Kai, as if his eyes were tracking down a thought, an idea—a solution. Beneath the two men, the sound of the factory and its whirring machines seemed to diminish a bit. But maybe that was their imaginations. "Well," Elijah said, finally. "Cure them."

"I cannot cure them," Ming Kai said.

Elijah looked into Ming Kai's eyes. He knew what was in a man's heart just by looking. This is how he had become who he was: by seeing what was in a man's heart, and taking it from him. "Can't—or won't?"

"Maybe I can cure them," Ming Kai said. "But I want—I need—something in return."

"Oh? And what would that be?"

Ming Kai stood very tall then, and his face turned very serious. "An apology."

"From me?" Elijah said. "For what?"

"For ruining my life," Ming Kai said.

Elijah straightened a stack of invoices that looked about to fall off his desk. "What's *done* is *done*," he said. He had moved on; this conversation was over. "Nothing I say can change anything now. I can't help you, Ming Kai."

But Ming Kai persisted. "All I want from you is this," he said. "Not money. Not land. You can have everything. Nothing has to change. Just to say to me you know what you did, so I am not alone in knowing this. Tell me you are sorry and I will fix the worms."

Elijah sat down in his huge desk chair. There was no bigger chair in Roam. It was made of birch and oak and the weathered skins of animals he had killed—bears, deer, a couple of rabbits—and stuffed with down. In it he looked miniature, like a little boy, but no one told him this. No one ever told him the truth: he thought he looked powerful. Elijah put on a pair of glasses and picked up a red ink pen and began going through his invoices, initialing the bottom of each page as he read through it. He had initialed thirteen pages before he looked up again and saw Ming Kai still standing there, waiting. Then he looked back down and initialed the next page, and the next.

"Then it is over," Ming Kai said, setting the old worm gently on top of the stack of papers. "The worms will die, Elijah McCallister," he said. "And without the worms, so will everything else."

"Don't you dare threaten me!" Elijah said. "I know you—you wouldn't dare!"

He walked around his desk and grabbed Ming Kai by the shoulders. "You!" he said. "You! I should, should—"

But before he could finish the sentence, he gasped, choked, and fell to the floor. Ming Kai calmly watched him fall. Then he sighed, took a deep breath, and knelt beside him. He paused, bent closer, as if listening for something. "What?" Ming Kai said into the silence. "What did you say?" He nodded. "Yes," he said. "Nothing. Just as I thought."

Then, with a few hard thumps to his chest, he saved Elijah's life. But now it was only a matter of time.

As Elijah died, so did Roam, and not over the course of months or even weeks—but days. It was as though the town were not merely his invention, his creation, but actually *him*, that they were connected somehow by an invisible artery, the art and the artist one. He developed a malaise so consuming and heavy he felt it inside of him, like a tumor, and he attempted to have it pressed from his body by something even heavier. He lay on his back and had a large plank placed on top of him and then rocks placed on top of that until he couldn't breathe. Finally, he prayed. Nothing came of that, either.

For years Roam had been usurping the world around it like a hungry machine. Even after the town became a town, with its stores and bars and whorehouses—along with the homes, some of the nicest with golden commodes—the construction continued. Pointless structures were built, huge empty warehouses, beautiful roads to nowhere. But after the worms died all of that stopped. The Chinese—and they were still coming by the boatload—suddenly found themselves with nothing to do. Most disappeared into the forest. Many of the whites stayed, however, as did the combos. They didn't know who or what they would be outside of Roam.

The factories produced not a skein of silk ever again. This is how they learned: Roam was and always had been at the mercy of an insect.

*O*ne month to the day after saving his life, Ming Kai made the trek from town up the hill to Elijah's mansion. He entered without knocking and walked slowly up the winding staircase to the bedroom. The desiccated body of Elijah lay barely breathing in the huge bed, tiny, hardly a smear of life left in it.

Ming Kai stood beside the bed and looked down at him. Elijah was only fifty years old, but he looked twice that.

"There is nothing left, Elijah," Ming Kai said. "Nothing for me, nothing for my family. We are going. We leave today."

"Have you ever thought," Elijah said, and then he stopped to breathe. He couldn't speak above a whisper. Each word he spoke took a day off his life. But his eyes still glittered with bitter amusement. "Have you ever thought how, if I hadn't been in China on that day, or you had stayed at home to play with your real children, none of this would have ever happened?"

"I have thought of nothing else."

But even so, Ming Kai had grown to love his replacement family in a way that surprised even him. He dreamed of his true wife and sons, and wondered what became of them. He imagined beautiful lives for them, even though he knew that no such thing was possible without a husband, a father. He longed for them in the way any man with a heart would have longed for them.

Ming Kai took Elijah's hand in his own.

"My replacement wife tells me, 'Forgive him.' She says it is the only way to take back my life. But everything bad that happened to me happened because of you. Everything. Yes, I should forgive you. It is what a stronger man would do. But I can't. I won't. Not if I live to be a hundred years old."

"We made something beautiful, Ming Kai," Elijah said.

"This town was cursed from the beginning."

"It was you who cursed it!"

"No," Ming Kai said. "You cursed it when you brought me here, when you took me away from my home, my family. When you made me hate you." He shook his head. "And yet I love you, too, which is strange to me."

But why waste his breath? Ming Kai thought. This man would never change. He moved to leave, but Elijah wouldn't let go of his hand. He held it more tightly than a dying man should have the power to do.

"*Die with me,*" he said. His voice hissed. "It's only right. We made this town together. Every nail in every board. Even the combos: we created a new kind of human being. Together. We should die together, too. It's you and me, Ming Kai. You and me. It always has been."

Ming Kai shook his head. "This is not how I want my life to end," he said. He still had much to live for. He saw a world beyond this one. Elijah didn't want Ming Kai to have a life at all.

Slowly, Elijah's other hand rose, shaking from the sheets, and as it did Ming Kai saw in it a gun, a pearl-handled gun with a long black barrel. Elijah pointed it at Ming Kai's chest. Ming Kai only smiled.

"A worm is born a worm," he said. "Then it becomes a moth. It is born twice. It has two lives. We should all be so lucky."

Elijah fired, but his hand was swaying back and forth so, like a weather vane in a high wind, that the bullet missed Ming Kai and lodged itself into the far wall. Ming Kai stood, staring at the man he loved and hated more than any other man in the world. Elijah fired again, and the shot broke a window. Ming Kai bowed, turned, and walked away, slowly, bullet after bullet flying past him. Elijah fired until there were no more bullets left, pulling the trigger long after Ming Kai was gone, the click of the hammer against the empty chamber matching his own heart's last beats. When his last concubine discovered him the following day, she took his withered body to the town square where his body was burned in a fire so glorious it's said its flickering fiery tongue warmed the moon.

Ming Kai didn't see his old friend burn: he was long gone by then and vowed that he would never return. He made a new home for himself in a valley, a valley that turned out to be not that far away from Roam, though it may as well have been on the moon. But as the years passed—and many years passed—Ming Kai thought more and more about Roam and the life he led there, and he visited it in his dreams, and he talked about it, talked until he could talk about nothing else. The stories he would tell! The golden world his memory created! What a paradise it was. His great-grandson Markus listened to the old man tell these stories, and *he* believed them; this vision of a better life, far away from the sad, secluded valley where he had always lived, possessed him. He would go there one day, he told himself. And he would take these stories with him.

# JONAS,
# PART I

*D*ripping wet, the girls left the cart on the porch beside the broken swing and walked into their home. The house was decrepit: every year another piece of it fell apart, or was blown off in a wind—shutters, drainpipes, window trim; much of it hung from the sides of the house as if by invisible screws and nails. The lawn had become as wild as any forest; still, the entry hall had a ceiling as high as some of the buildings downtown and a magnificent winding staircase: a penniless drifter would feel like royalty walking down that staircase. The house had a sitting room, a living room, two dining rooms—one meant to be used and one *not* to be—one and a half kitchens, ten bedrooms, four full baths, and a run for the dogs (if they'd had any); the backyard was half the size of McCallister Park, where the swing set and seesaw and gazebo were. Everything was in a state of such disrepair that men from organizations who concerned themselves with such things had visited the girls and made ominous warnings about the town's ultimate responsibility for their safety—it had come to that— and would, if improvements were not made, be forced to take such action as was necessary.

The dead, though—the ghosts who had taken up residence in the abandoned residences around town—saw things differently. The house to them was less a real house than a symbol representing the McCallisters' (and, by extension, Roam's) gradual deterioration, a deterioration that was inevitable. The rose gardens grew wild, the kudzu swallowed the dying oaks, and the lawn itself took on water when it rained until the water never went away and a small pond formed, a place where the neighborhood children came to fish with their home-made poles, kids Helen chased away.

Rachel had taken only a few steps inside before she stopped. "Someone's here," she said.

Helen nodded. "Jonas, probably."

"Smells like a car engine," Rachel said. "And drink."

"*Definitely* Jonas."

Jonas was the man Helen let come around, and he'd been coming around for years. Rachel didn't like him much, and Helen didn't like him much, either. But liking the man you had around and liking having a man around were two different things. He was sprawled out on the green love seat, his ropey arms resting across the top and his legs spread so far apart it was like he was daring you to throw something at him. He used to work on cars, and still could, but now there were so few cars left to fix he just took the broken ones apart and sold their insides to the occasional lumberjack who came through. He wasn't much, but he could take Helen's mind off of things. That was enough.

"I ate that ham sandwich in the crisper," he said. Helen could see a little mustard yellowing the corners of his mouth. "It was just a half, and kind of stale. Hope that's okay."

"That was Rachel's lunch," Helen said.

"I'm not that hungry," Rachel said. Her voice was even softer now than it usually was, and she turned her blushing face away, as if to avoid his gaze, as if she could feel the eyes of Jonas burning into her.

"I've been wrestling with a radiator all morning," he said. He was chewing a piece of gum. Jonas could make one piece of gum last all day—probably had it tucked in his upper lip while he ate Rachel's sandwich. "Man works up an appetite wrestling a radiator. Then I spent some time with Digby over at the tavern."

"She said it was fine, Jonas," Helen said. "Everyone knows what an appetite you have." Here is where she would have winked at him, normally. One of the nice things about having a blind sister is that it was a little like having a child: you could say things that went right over her head because she couldn't see to make the connection. But Helen didn't wink; she was still upset by what had happened outside. How could Rachel believe, even for a moment, that she could live without Helen? Jonas winked, though, and licked the mustard off his lips. Then he let his left hand nestle snugly into his crotch, staring hard at Helen, zeroing into her eyes until all he could see were her pupils. "You two are wetter than a fish."

"You surprised us," Helen said.

"Good surprise, I hope," he said.

"I asked you to call first."

"Same difference," he said. "You know you'd just say to come on over. Or not. Then I would anyway. I thought we could work on your car." Winking again.

"Uh-huh."

"And?"

"Well. It does need work," she said.

"Okay then."

But that was enough of that. Helen didn't want to talk to him any more than he wanted to look at her, because he was as stupid as she was homely. She sometimes imagined what a baby of theirs might be like, and when she did she almost cried.

"I guess I'm going to my room," Rachel said. She reached out with her right hand and found the butterfly-backed chair. Her north star. Rachel was able to negotiate around the holes in the floorboards, knew which doors were frozen at angles, skipped over the slats in the stairs that couldn't bear the weight of even her slight frame. The winding staircase did not make her feel like royalty; she felt like a mountain climber descending a precipitous slope.

"Sounds like fun," Jonas said, running his fingers along the sofa's knotted weave, looking at Rachel up and down.

Helen saw him. "Stop it, Jonas," she said.

"Stop what?" said Rachel.

"Nothing," Helen said. "Nothing."

Helen shook her head, trying to clear it. That Rachel could even think of leaving her stirred up the darkest place inside of her, that place she'd discovered the rainy day she'd been brushing her sister's hair, the day they switched faces.

"I have an idea," Helen said to her. Her voice was unbelievably bright and buoyant and cold. "Actually, Rachel had one."

"I did?" Rachel said.

"You said you want to see what it's like to be on your own," Helen said. "Remember?"

"No, Helen. I—"

"That's what you said, Rachel. You said, 'I'm a grown woman.' So be a grown woman. See what it's like. It'll make me happy if you are, that's for certain: my life would be a great deal easier if I didn't think I was going to be babysitting you for the rest of it. Jonas and I are going to go out for a while. We're going for a ride. You stay here. See how you like it without me."

"Don't be mad at me, Helen," she said.

"Who said I was mad?"

"I only want you to be happy."

"If I were you I wouldn't worry about me," Helen said. She kicked Jonas, who immediately stood. "I'd worry about you."

As Helen walked past, Rachel reached out for her, but Helen was just out of reach.

"I love you," Rachel said.

Helen stopped. When was the last time she'd heard Rachel say this? It didn't matter: today she was as hard as stone. "Of course you do," Helen said.

Jonas followed Helen out the back door like an old dog, trailing a few steps behind. She gave him the keys. Helen could drive, but she liked it better when Jonas did, so she could roll down the window and let the wind blow against her face: on some days, when the air had that cool layer beneath it, there was nothing better than that feeling. Rachel always sat in the backseat, as quiet as a mouse.

He started the car up and backed it out of the drive and into the road.

"What was that about, with you and Rachel?" Jonas said. "Is she going to be okay?" He paused, carefully putting together the words of his next thought so as not to enrage her. "It's just—it wasn't nice, the way you said what you said."

"I'm messing with her," she said, "the way I do. It's a joke, okay? She'll be fine. We won't be gone that long. Just long enough for her to see what it might be like for her without me."

And off they drove in her parents' car, turning into the street so fast they almost hit a dog. Helen looked back and saw Rachel at the living room window, following them with her eyes by the sound the car made as it got farther and farther away. It was the first time the sisters had been this far apart in nearly a dozen years. Nothing in the world would be the same for them after this, from now until forever.

# THE QUIET

*T*he lumberjack left his dogs outside the tavern and took a seat at the bar, the caked dirt falling off his arms like bark. Digby was a small man, but in the lumberjack's presence he appeared miniature, like a doll. Each existed at opposite ends of the spectrum of what a man could be, freaks of dimension. Smith was the lumberjack's name, and what a frightening man to apprehend he was. His face was stained by time and etched by weather, like the side of a stone mountain. His cheeks were so deeply furrowed Digby thought that if he could pry apart the folds of skin he might find some burrowing creature, or a growing plant. His eyes were so sunken he appeared to be looking at you from twin caves in his head. His beard was like a forest. Digby could get lost in it—that's how big it was, and how big he was. To be in the same room with a man who could eat you—that was something. Even the old-timers seemed frightened of the lumberjack, as if there were something he could do to them that hadn't been done already.

Smith never said anything, but this didn't stop Digby from speaking to him.

"The usual, Mr. Smith?" he said as Smith rumbled in. Digby got no response, positive or negative, so the usual it was: one part vodka, one part rum, two parts beer, all poured into the largest receptacle Digby had: a terra-cotta flowerpot. He'd covered the drain hole in the bottom with four pieces of chewed gum that, when dried, provided the perfect stopper.

Smith threw it back, and then pushed it again toward Digby. Digby mixed another.

"I hope you've got everything you need out there, in the woods," Digby said. "But what's a man need, really, other than a roof, a woman, and a meal?"

Digby smiled the way a man smiles for another man when something manly has been said.

Smith said nothing. He was struggling with some thought, or some memory: Digby could see that clearly. He'd seen the look before: Smith was sad.

"It must be a nice respite, though, regardless, to be off the mountain. Done with the felling of trees, et cetera. No more *Timber!* All that. You must have a tale or two to tell from those days, Mr. Smith, those days on the mountain, a tale of lumberjacking and . . . "

Even Digby found it hard to continue talking when met with a veritable wall of silence and disinterest. And yet he continued.

"I once had a romantic liaison with a woman who lived in a tree. She built a tree house in a sprawling oak not far from here. I climbed that tree like a little squirrel the days of our assignations. There was something especially romantic about that, looking out a window hewn from used plywood, to see the leaves changing, turning red and gold, a cloud floating by above."

Nothing!

"I hear it's brutal, being a lumberjack, an environment only the strongest of men can endure. It's almost a calling, isn't it? Like the priesthood. Which simply makes me wonder why you came here, to Roam. You must have a story. Everyone has a story. I should create a bit of silence and within it let you tell yours. I shall shut my piehole, as they say. The floor is yours!"

Sometimes Digby talked too much. A good bartender knew when to shut up; it was his father's greatest skill. So now he would be quiet, and the lumberjack would feel the need to fill the quiet with the sound of his own voice. Digby fiddled with the bar keys in his pocket, and then stopped even that. What followed was the most profound emptiness, the living and the dead together in this small place and not a one of them saying a word.

As Smith finished off the last of his concoction he met Digby's eyes with his own, briefly, but long enough for Digby to see into them and ferret out some understanding of the man's predicament.

Smith's heart was broken. More than broken: it was crushed and shattered. That's why he was the way he was.

Outside, the dogs started howling like mad. One was scratching at the door; another was on its hind legs, trying to see in the window, others howling like mad. It was a crazy canine symphony. *Maybe that's why he's so quiet,* Digby thought. Maybe this was the only time he could get even this far away from them. Smith dropped a few dollars on the bar, almost seeming to nod at Digby. Then he left, and the dogs left with him, their howls receding, becoming no less constant but somewhat less urgent the more distant they became.

"Sad," Digby said. "He tries to hide it, but he can't. I can see it plain as day. The sadness follows him around like one of his dogs."

Digby said it more to himself than to anybody else, but Fang heard him. From a dark corner the chalky light that was Fang appeared and walked toward the bartender, and once to him placed his hand on Digby's chest, and it went straight through to his heart: Digby felt the odd warmth of it in his blood.

"You're a good man," Fang said. "You're the last good man in this whole town. All the good that could be squeezed out of this forsaken place was used to make you. That's why you're so small, my friend: there just wasn't that much left." Fang laughed. "And that's why you can see us, you know, and nobody else can. You see everybody, even that lumberjack."

Then He-Ping and Fang joined in what sounded to Digby like a coordinated not unhappy sigh. He-Ping said something and laughed, and then Fang made a comment about the weather, and soon everything was back to normal.

# THE LUMBERJACK
# AND HIS DOG,
# PART I

r. and Mrs. McCallister made the trip to Arcadia once a week. Arcadia, though only thirty miles away from Roam, felt like an entirely different world. It was built on the ruins of an old Indian trading post, and when the Germans and the Dutch settled there (and killed the Indians) they were inspired by the Greeks to call it Arcadia—an unspoiled, harmonious wilderness. There was no way to get there from Roam until a small road was finally built by Elijah McCallister. It was known as the Silk Road, because it was the main artery via which silk left his town, but also because it was as thin and slippery as a silk thread. Deaths on the road occurred so often that it was almost more newsworthy when someone survived it.

The McCallisters survived it once a week. Braving the journey was a courageous act, and not something one took lightly: Mr. McCallister slept poorly on Thursday nights, and usually left the bed long before sunrise to wander the house, in an attempt to steel himself by drawing upon the history of all that had happened in it over the years. Mr. McCallister—Edward—was the son of Charles McCallister, who was the son of Elijah McCallister, who was, they said, one of the bravest explorers (and certainly the most courageous entrepreneur) the world has ever known. Edward's father, Charles, had been quite bookish and dark, and Edward had become much more like him than he had become like his grandfather. Whatever strange and heroic virus there was lurking in the blood of Elijah McCallister, it had diminished and finally disappeared in future generations.

And so off they went, Mr. McCallister in his brown suit, white shirt, and bow tie, his father's pocket watch tucked snugly in a vest pocket, his thin forty-two-year-old face unmarred by time because he so seldom used the muscles in it; and Mrs. McCallister in her cream-colored dress with the roses, in her slip and stockings, her sensible black shoes with the copper clasps, her only jewelry a wedding band and a small golden locket on display between her collarbones, her face round and serene, like that of an angelic cow. She was a tall woman with dark eyes that could hold you where you stood with the power of a strong man's hands. That's how she met and married Edward McCallister: she saw him one day, this reedy eighteen-year-old boy, mowing the lawn of the big house on the hill. She was on her way to a knitting class. When she saw him, she stopped and stared and somehow knew. He saw her staring and stared back, and as the world kept moving all around them they were still, alone in each other's eyes.

Mr. and Mrs. McCallister continued living their life together in slow motion. They were old even when they were young. They felt that doing anything too quickly—whether it be moving, speaking, even thinking—usually resulted in a mistake of some kind. Both of their children were the result of a methodical plan, based on cycles tracked by temperature, the moon, and sperm motility, which was said to be greater during the summer months. This was how Mr. and Mrs. McCallister, in a black car as big as a boat, navigated the treacherous cutbacks and blind curves of the Silk Road once a week: slowly.

And why? For Rachel, of course. In Arcadia there lived a Dr. Oscar Beadles. Beadles was a small, withered, balding man whose hands, due to a circulation problem, were blue. He was from the old country and had come for the water: he'd heard tales of its medicinal powers. By the time the tales had reached him, they were a bit garbled and it wasn't entirely clear what the water really did: make old people young, or young people old? Did it promote hair growth or restrict it? He wasn't sure. All he knew is that for a story about water to come all the way from the new world to the old there must be something to it, and if there was an opportunity to sow the seeds of his genius somewhere, he had to take it. When he got to America he made his way to Arcadia and discovered that there was indeed a magic water, a river rich with a unique mixture of subterranean minerals science had yet to fully understand but that Dr. Beadles was certain could aid him in creating a perfect elixir, a medicine with powers so vast and subtle it would cure not just one thing, but *all things*.

Every morning he captured the water from a spring just as it left the underground cavern. He placed the vials as deep into the hole as he could, because it was his feeling that prolonged exposure to sunlight degraded its magical, medicinal properties. But after eighteen years of the most rigorous scientific experimentation, he had succeeded in curing only one thing: blindness. Like many breakthroughs, it had happened quite by accident: one of the hundreds of mice he was working with had been born blind (or it certainly *looked* blind, it *acted* blind), and one day, after many treatments in which its entire little body was submerged in the mineral-rich Arcadian water, it miraculously regained the ability to see. Each treatment saw a marked improvement in its vision. Soon it was able to find its way through a simple maze, and then one day—Beadles would swear to this—it made eye contact. With him. They actually *looked* at each other. The mouse would have achieved perfect twenty-twenty eyesight if what was to have been its final treatment hadn't gone on just a moment too long and it drowned.

Clearly further experimentation was required.

Unfortunately, Beadles had no other blind mice—but a blind human being, he decided, would be even better. Eyes are eyes, after all. He made inquiries and discovered, to his amazement, that there was not a *single blind person* in all of Arcadia, a town with a population verging on the thousands. And why? *It must be the water!* Beadles thought. He was definitely on the right track.

But, while there were no truly blind people in Arcadia, there were a number of people who couldn't see that well, people who needed glasses to read, to drive, to walk without stumbling. This meant their eyes were far from perfect, and some improvement could be made. If he could cure blindness, he could certainly cure those on the darkening road toward it.

So he placed an advertisement in the *Arcadian Daily News*:

SEEING IS BELIEVING!
IF YOU DON'T THROW AWAY YOUR GLASSES
AFTER ONLY 3 TREATMENTS
THE ENTIRE PROCEDURE IS FREE!

It was a huge success. Eyeglass-wearing Arcadians lined up for the treatments. Freshwater from the underground river was bottled into dark brown eyedroppers, and everyone from the president of the Arcadian Bank to little Joey Cooper the paperboy, whose glasses were as thick as pop-bottle bottoms, took their turn in the dentist's chair Beadles had found in a salvage yard. "I now will remove from the room all the light," he said as he flicked the switch, leaving him and his patient in complete darkness. "This, to confiscate all stimulation from the nerves of the eye." The people of Arcadia delighted in his way of talking. It was his accent, his tortured syntax—and, of course, his moderately hunched back—which made them never question the *Dr.* he had placed before his name. They believed him; they believed *in* him. "Now I will emit a shower of photons. Do not be alarmed: they will not harm you. They will merely determine the presence of phosphors in your eyes. Once that has been determined to my satisfaction, we may proceed."

Phosphors, Beadles went on to explain, are responsible for many problems of the eye, in that they *emit their own light,* and can destroy the *visual receptors.* He would then push a small red button on the end of a long white tube and people would be astonished and amazed to see a ghostly, glowing image of Beadles grinning before them, his teeth brighter than anything else in the room.

"Let me see," he would say, and the patient would nervously watch as the teeth approached—it was indeed very frightening for some—until Beadles had seen what he needed to see.

"*I detect the presence of phosphors,*" he would invariably announce and, producing a bottle of his water, would drop one large drop of it into each open eye. "Very good. Yes. And we are . . . done."

He turned the light back on and glared at his patient. "Better, yes?"

"Better," the patient said. How could one say otherwise to Dr. Beadles? He so wanted you to be better. "Yes, I do think I can see better now."

"Then you won't be needing these."

And he would take his patient's glasses and deposit them into a disposal bin. By the end of the day his trash can was full of them, and his reputation as a miracle worker spread far and wide, all the way to Roam.

He was the McCallisters' only hope.

•   •   •

$\mathcal{M}$r. and Mrs. McCallister did not speak to each other during the long drive. The fear that many a young person has when contemplating spending their entire life with another person—*Will we run out of things to say?*—had in fact been realized by the McCallisters: they had run out of things to say. Each had shared with the other all the information they cared to. Mr. McCallister had told her about his mother, Constance, who drank, and his father, Charles, who spent most of his time alone in the basement reading and building balsa wood models of old British frigates; Mrs. McCallister told him about her best friend, Katie, who had been born with only one leg. He had told her about his first kiss, with a Chinese girl in the weeds behind the old silk factory, and she in turn told him about a secret correspondence she had with a boy she never met: they would leave notes for each other in the hollow trunk of a dying elm, until one day the notes stopped coming, and she never knew why. She assumed he died. And though Rachel and Helen were always doing something that might provide conversational material, the McCallisters each knew how the other would respond to any gambit, so there was no good reason to get into anything. For the last six years they had simply not spoken, a decision they reached without having to discuss it at all. Their lives as a couple had been simplified to a single united desire: all they wanted was for their daughter to see again.

Unfortunately, there had been no improvement whatsoever. They had done everything Beadles told them to: after the sun went down they applied the drops—three of them, at three-second intervals—into their daughter's eyes. Each week they would report the lack of progress, and each week Dr. Beadles asked them if they were administering the drops correctly. *Are you turning off the lights? For how long? Is she leaning back at the correct angle? If not, the drops won't seep into the nerve endings, where they need to go.* At one point he even suggested bringing Rachel to Arcadia and throwing her into the underground river, something that had never been done but in her case (which was clearly extreme) might be necessary.

"We are not throwing our blind daughter into an underground river, Dr. Beadles," Mr. McCallister said.

His wife concurred. "Though we appreciate your zeal to see Rachel cured," she said, "that course of action seems unwise."

"So she cannot swim?" he said. Then he tapped his huge forehead with his index finger. "Of course she can't! What was I thinking? Little blind girls don't swim."

"That's actually not true, doctor," Mrs. McCallister said, and—not for the first time—exchanged a worried glance with her husband. *Why do we risk our lives every week to see this man?* "She *can* swim. Even so . . ."

Coming here for Rachel only made them feel that much more love and pity for Helen. But what could they really do for her? Yes, Mr. and Mrs. McCallister were hard to get to know—and when you did get to know them, you knew them to be quite tedious—and aggravatingly slow drivers. But they loved their children. Both inhabited the same amount of space in their hearts.

Helen, though, didn't see it that way. Clearly, to her, there was no contest: they loved Rachel more, and it was during her parents' trips to Arcadia that Helen nursed her rancor. Not simply because Rachel was a burden, but also because her parents did nothing of equal value for Helen, nothing to make *her* life better. Helen yearned; there were things she wanted. Mostly what she wanted was another life. She wanted another world. She wanted a planet of her own. High school had been a nightmare. The vast, brick building with its long, dim hallways and cold, metal lockers. Once a thriving place, it had begun to resemble the abandoned Indian temples they read about in Mrs.

Crittendon's tenth-grade World History class. The gray, linoleum floor squares—and there must have been ten thousand of them—were broken, peeling, betraying the dark and tarry surface beneath. Helen's class would be the very last to graduate; after hers, there weren't enough students left to justify the school's existence, though the building was still there and always would be, a hulking relic of hope. That's why Rachel was homeschooled, and why for so much of the time her teacher was Helen.

Helen wanted a man, or better yet *men*, men who were capable of penetrating her permanent mask to find the young and hungry woman within, a woman who would let them do things to her they could only imagine. The truth was she felt she had nothing else to offer. All week long, from Monday to Thursday, she trolled the streets of Roam, pretending to be on some errand for her parents. At the grocery she would lean her sturdy body against a boy and lock her smoldering eyes with his and take a slow and sultry bite from a crisp red apple—a maneuver she picked up from some romance novel she'd read. At the hardware store she would run her fingers up and down a wrench handle and breathe in short, hot inhalations, leaving her scent everywhere she went. She transformed herself into something pungent, rudimentary, and available.

They would come as soon as Mr. and Mrs. McCallister left for Arcadia. When the doorbell rang she locked Rachel in her room and opened the front door for whomever it happened to be. Grease monkeys, house painters, street sweepers, the police, a lonely clerk, and those twins Larry and Jerry, who, when it came time for their turn, would fight for her affections until one of them dropped unconscious to the ground and the other dragged himself into the house—cut, bruised, and bleeding.

Everyone did their best to ignore the little blind girl upstairs who was slamming her shoulder against the door and wailing to be set free.

And even though she wished she'd never had a sister, especially the blind one she ended up with, after her parents would return with the Arcadian water (*We're back!* her father would announce each and every time) and placed the vials in the refrigerator for after the sun went down, Helen would take each vial and pour each of them out into the sink, filling them up with water from the tap.

*V*ery soon it became clear to the McCallisters that these trips to Arcadia were a waste of their time, yet they kept going. Even though in their hearts they knew Dr. Beadles had no science to offer them, he did at least persist in believing in the impossible; this was better than nothing. "I wish I could find another blind mouse," Dr. Beadles said when he saw them. "It would lead me in the right direction. Still, it may take some years to . . . it *is* science, but not an exact one."

He never did find another mouse. He bred them like mad, until he had an entire room full of them, ten in some of the cages, twenty in others, the cages stacked one on top of the other nearly to the ceiling. Some mice had only two legs, others no hair whatsoever, but all of them (as far as he could tell) had perfect vision.

Then one day a miracle happened. Beadles was eating breakfast in the Arcadian Diner when he heard two men talking in the booth behind him. They were lumberjacks, these two men, big and thick as trees themselves. Lumberjacks in Arcadia—there were about a dozen of them—had a reputation for being wild, terrible, violent men for whom human life was no more precious than a garden weed. Most of the year they lived together on a mountaintop miles from town, cutting down trees from dawn to dusk and eating whatever wandered too close to the burrows in which they lived. They came back to Arcadia for a month every year to sell their trees and see their wives, who in turn would need eleven months to recover from the poundings they endured from their otherwise abstinent mates. Beadles heard a name. *Carla*. At first the doctor naturally assumed it was a wife these two were discussing. But it wasn't.

"So how's Carla doing, Smith?" one of the men said as he chewed on a mouthful of egg and sausage and toast.

"Well. Not so good," Smith said. "She's getting old. She still has three good legs, though. That's something."

"One more than my dog."

"Not much hair on her hindquarters."

"My dog has none at all."

"And blind."

"Blind?"

"Can't see a goddamn thing."

"That's terrible."

"Well, it happens."

"Yes, I reckon that it does."

"Even so," Smith said, and this he said with resolute passion, "I'll love that dog until all that's left of her is a mangy old tail and a couple of rotten teeth. We've been through it all together, her and me. I see myself in that dog. It's almost—I don't know—I wish my wife were more like Carla."

The lumberjacks laughed. Beadles kept quite still; he needed to let the words settle in his head like snow in a little globe. *Blind*. A blind dog! Clearly this was fate taking a moment to intervene in his life and in the life of the poor little blind girl Rachel McCallister. It was not a mouse he needed at all: *a three-legged dog* would lead him from the dark Arcadian wilderness into the glaring light of the bulb that is Science.

Beadles slid across the warm red vinyl booth and stood before the two behemoths like a bent blade of grass. Neither man looked up. Neither stopped eating until every last vestige of food was gone from their plates, and from around their plates, and from their shirtfronts and mustaches and beards. But once done they glanced over at the thin, somewhat hunchbacked old man with the rivers of purple veins running through his shaking hands. Though the lumberjacks were sitting and Beadles was standing, they were looking directly into each other's eyes.

"Hello," Beadles said.

The lumberjacks said nothing. One raised a hand for the waitress to bring them more plates piled high with bacon and eggs and toast.

Beadles continued. "I don't want to suggest that I was listening to or even overhearing the conversation the two of you were having. I am not the sort of man to eavesdrop. I would say, however, your words did seem almost to float on the air from your table across to my own, which in any case is a short distance, and, having arrived, they were, I would say, impossible *not* to hear, just as one would have no choice whether to hear a car backfire, or a bird sing. Very difficult not to hear, if one can hear, if one has ears; it's involuntary, you see. We hear things whether we want to or not, and in this way the words you were speaking to one another entered my ears and thus here I am to speak to you, for what I heard—involuntarily, as I said—piqued my interest in a profound way."

This is what the lumberjacks, who weren't listening, heard:

*I dooooonebeneben hehehehehe having sayword flairiedalirad rrrrrrrrrrrr bleblebleee my own treeeeees hasod oidufois my ears gada gada goooo mmmmmm mmmmmmm bird sing hfuey bladdie gggggggggggggrrrrrrraaaaaaaaaaaah.*

"What?" Smith said, the one to whom Beadles wanted to speak.

"Your dog?" Beadles said. "I'm given to understand it is blind?"

Smith looked at the other lumberjack as if to confirm the presence of this strange, tiny man who was speaking to them.

"Blind as a dead man," he said.

"Sad," Beadles said. "Heartbreaking, even to a man of your great size. But what if I told you . . . what if I told you I had it within my powers to restore her eyesight?"

"If you told me that," Smith said, clearing his throat, "the first thing is, I would be unconvinced, then I would wonder if you were insane, and then I would ignore you entirely and return to my breakfast. Then later, as the day went on, I'd wonder why a stranger would approach me and say something like that, because even though I would know that such a thing is impossible it would make me hopeful in the way people get. In the end, I would be angry. I would be *very* angry. I'd want to kill you, and then feed your bloodied limbs to the same blind dog you said you could cure."

He returned to his breakfast.

"Beadles," Beadles said, extending a limp, shaking hand. He was afraid Lumberjack Smith would take it into his own hand and crush it into a fine powder.

The lumberjack stared at the appendage hovering before him. "Smith," he said.

"Then Mr. Smith," Beadles said. "May I call you Mr. Smith? Mr. Smith. I must tell you that I am a scientist, sir, on the cusp of a breakthrough which will astound the world. Your dog may be the key to that breakthrough. Imagine: not only would your precious dog see again, but her name would live on through time as the dog whose eyes led to a cure for blindness—and not just for her, and not just for other canines, but for us all."

Smith deposited a chunk of half-chewed food to a back corner of his mouth. You could see the muscles in his face twitching, jaw muscles nearly as big as Beadles's arms.

"I am skipping all those other parts I mentioned before and am going straight to the very angry stage," Smith said evenly, "to the wanting to kill you part. As my father used to say, I was born at night but not last night, and I can tell by looking that you are a kook and a quack, having seen many in my day. Believe me, I am prepared to do awful things."

"Awful things," the first lumberjack said. "Because after he kills you, I'll kill you, too."

Beadles was about to say it would only take a *bit* of testing, that it would not harm Carla in the *least*, that it was really no more than the administering of *water, three times a day*. But he didn't. His scientific mind knew it was impossible, but something in the way they said what they said made Beadles believe they *could* kill him twice. So he smiled, and nearly bowed, and did his best to drift away.

*T*wo weeks later, Beadles watched the lumberjacks (including Lumberjack Smith) pack up their things and head back to the mountains. They took everything with them they could: hardware, guns, ammo, food, warm clothes. One long flatbed truck was stacked two-men-tall with boxes. If the truck died—as it sometimes did on the long, uphill journey—the lumberjacks could easily push and pull it to their destination. That's how big and strong they were.

It was a rainy day. The exhausted wives and girlfriends of the lumberjacks stood beneath awnings and umbrellas, waving at the large men as they disappeared into the gray sheets of falling rain.

From his office window, Beadles waved, too.

As night fell, it was still raining. Water rushed down from the mountains, flowing like a thousand tributaries through the streets. Wearing a child's yellow parka (the only one he could find at the department store, all of the adult raingear having been taken by the departing lumberjacks), Beadles crept through the dripping darkness, a metal leash in one hand and a piece of flatiron steak in the other.

He followed the blind dog's plaintive howls—mournful,

heart-piercing howls—until he found her. Whether the howls were for Lumberjack Smith, or because she was tethered to a rope in his back-yard in the drenching rain, it was impossible to say. Beadles crouched and watched her. There was no doghouse, no hope of respite from the rain. She paced as far as she could in one direction, then the same in the other. She had worn a small rut in the yard, and now the rut was a little stream. Beadles felt a great sadness for her—he saw something of himself in the dog—but this reassured him of the rightness of what he was doing. Great men were rarely good men, but what he was doing *was* good. He wasn't happy about all the mice he had made to be born and then drowned when it became clear they would be of no use to him. He wasn't comfortable playing God. But he wasn't God tonight; in this instance, he was merely borrowing an absent lumberjack's blind dog, and nothing bad could possibly come from it. Nothing! When Lumberjack Smith returned from the mountains, his dog would have her sight back. Rather than kill Beadles, he would thank him, and perhaps over time they would become friends. The doctor and the lumberjack.

Poor Carla. She was hardly the animal Beadles had imagined she'd be. He'd thought a lumberjack's dog would be as big as a bear, or feral as a wolf, its yellow eyes glowing in the night. But as he crept toward her she began to whimper. She cowered low, her tail between her legs, her belly covered in mud. "Carla," he whispered. "Not to worry, old dog. It's okay." But she was worried. Her lumberjack was gone and she had been left outside in the rain—by the lumberjack's wife, no doubt. She was shivering, shaking in fear; so was Beadles. He held out the steak he'd brought for her, but he didn't need it: she would have gone any-where, with anyone, to escape the life she was forced to live. He untied the rope and hooked her to the leash. He pulled, and she followed him.

Beadles looked back at the house as they were leaving. A woman stood at the window. She was sad and dark, the way most of the lum-berjack wives were, but she didn't see him or—or, if she did, she didn't care that he was doing what he was doing. They walked back to his office unmolested, the old man and the three-legged dog matching each other's pace as they fought their way through the rain.

*C*arla was a sweet dog. After a day or two she seemed happy in Beadles's care, slept most of the day curled up on an old blanket, wagging her tail every time Beadles entered the room for her treatment. He thought she was a brown dog, but when he gave her a bath discovered that she was yellow and white, with soft warm fur Beadles liked to bury his fingers in. She was very much blind: her eyes were gray smoky orbs. And yet she seemed always to be *trying* to see, her head moving one way and another to capture the source of a sound. He desperately wanted to cure her. Though he had always wanted to meet Rachel McCallister, he was glad now he hadn't: the sense of responsibility he felt toward Carla was so overwhelming he knew he couldn't bear the actuality of a person, a real human being, counting on him for everything.

The treatments, however, were unsuccessful. Three times a day for five weeks he brought his dropper into the room, squeezed the rubber end, and let the magic water fall gently into her smoky gray eyes. If nothing else, the drops were soothing, because she always raised her head when she heard the door open, waiting (he imagined) to feel their efficacious cool. But her eyesight did not return, not even a little.

Beadles chose not to tell the McCallisters about Carla. Each week came and went much as the one before: they would be waiting on the street outside his office every Friday at one (their visits coincided with his lunch), and he would ask if there had been any improvement, and they would say no, and he would give them a fresh batch of water he had that morning drawn from the stream just as it left its underground home, and they would return to Roam, hopeful in the way only the hopeless can be.

As was he. He believed in himself, believed in his quixotic ambition, letting the failures of the previous day disappear as each new day dawned. Yesterday was not today. The past did not predict the future if he could learn from his mistakes.

And this, he began to believe, was the problem: he *wasn't* learning. He simply maintained his obstinate belief that the water he drew from the rivulet in the meadow was enough to achieve his ends, when clearly it wasn't. It took Carla to make him understand. She slept with him now. In the morning he would wake and find himself holding her close, her warm body spooning his the way he imagined a man and a woman would spoon, and he felt something for her so strong that he could only call it love. He loved her, and she him, and more than anything he wanted her to see that love beaming from his eyes.

He could see smoke rising on the distant mountain now. One day, too soon, Smith would return, and Beadles knew what would happen then.

A change in treatment was called for.

$O$ne spring morning he took Carla with him to the meadow. She walked easily on the leash, hobbling on her three legs without complaint. The day was bright and beautiful. The meadow was like a dream of a meadow, the way the breeze gently bent the stems of the daffodils and the tall trees cast purple shadows across the valley. Many years had passed since he'd first come, searching for rare herbs he thought might grow here. That was when he'd discovered the entrance to a cavern where the river flowed, a small opening beneath an overhang, just big enough for a man to walk through without stooping; he had been too frightened of the dark to enter then. There was no trail. Beadles and Carla had to slide down a precipitous and rocky embankment; he didn't know how they would make it back up, but he was sure they would find a way.

At the entrance to the cavern a cold wind stung his face, and Carla, for the first time, simply refused to follow him, at least not until Beadles rubbed her neck and whispered in her ear *It's okay*, just as he had the night he'd found her. She took a step forward, and together they walked into the darkness.

As soon as they entered the cavern he could hear the river, flowing neither sweet nor gentle but raging. He paused. After a moment his old eyes adjusted to the gloom, and the cavern walls appeared to glow. It was as if he and Carla had entered a secret palace. The river had carved out a giant hallway through the rock, and a kind of path on a gentle slope leading deeper and deeper into the underground world. When Beadles looked down at Carla, he saw that her fur was sparkling, covered in snowy flakes of mineral wonder, so that she looked magical, effervescent. He did, too. Radiant, the two of them made their way down to the river.

And there it was. Beadles had never seen anything like it. It rushed through the cavern with the power of something suddenly unleashed. But it wasn't sudden: it had been running like this forever. Who could say how long this river was, or indeed, if it ever even stopped? "Look," he said to Carla. "There is the remedy for your eyes." This was not science anymore, if it ever was; it was religion. This was his god, the answer to all things, the source of the mystery. Carla barked once, sharply. He had never heard her bark before, not like this; she must have felt it, too.

He looked for a safe place to baptize her. He took her to the shallow edge of the river. Everything was happening as he hoped it would, as he had dreamed it would. He kneaded Carla's neck. *This is where it will happen*, he thought; all his effort would be justified, his life's work fulfilled.

He walked into the water with Carla.

It was cold, so cold. After just a few moments he was no longer able to feel his toes; his calves stung as if the water were full of needles. Carla whined, but he said *It's okay*, and again she trusted the sound of his voice. When the water was up to her neck, and past his knees, he placed a hand on top of her head and pushed it under. He held it there for three seconds, four . . . She was entirely submerged. Then he let her go, and she raised her head and looked at him. She *looked* at him—met his gaze with her own. Between them he saw the colorful flakes falling softly through the air. He took a deep breath and let them coat his lungs.

"My God," he said. "My God—it worked."

It *was* miracle water. He felt it coursing through his very blood, felt it saturate his body. He bent over to look into Carla's eyes to be sure, to be completely sure, and he was. If you can see love, he thought, Carla was seeing it now. And so was he.

Oh, finally to have done something right! He would bring the girl here, the little blind girl Rachel McCallister, and he would take her to the water, to this very pool, and with his hand on the back of her neck he would push her under, and when the water fell away from her eyes she would see, and her parents, who had shown such faith in him, who *believed* in him, would finally get everything they wanted. Their little girl would see again.

Then the current changed, and he felt the stones beneath his feet begin to slide. An undertow. He took a step backward, but Carla, whose little feet didn't have the hold his did, was pulled forward. He held the leash with a solid grip, a strength he didn't know he had, that he had never had: this water had made him stronger. But he was not strong enough; she was being drawn away from him. He held the leash tightly, he would never let go, never, and in the next instant they were both dragged into the river, hostage to the current. *It's you and me, girl,* he said to her, though he knew she couldn't hear him over the roar of the river. *You and me.* And the river took them. From there it became a journey deep into the heart of the earth, but it wasn't dark. The heart only became brighter the closer to it they came, and Beadles gazed at it, he gazed *into* it, until he could see absolutely nothing at all.

# THE LUMBERJACK
# AND HIS DOG,
# PART II

O n Friday, the McCallisters quietly prepared for their weekly trip. Without exchanging a single word they dressed, prepared a lunch for Helen and Rachel, and got into the car. Mr. McCallister backed the car down the driveway, and in his slow, careful way looked left, then right. Then he looked left again. Then he pulled out into the street.

The back windows of the car had been left open the night before, in order to facilitate the passage of air. Mr. McCallister believed that stagnant air was a cause of illness and, in fact, secretly wondered if this was why Rachel became blind in the first place: had she been subjected to stagnant air? The perfectly healthy life would, according to Mr. McCallister, be lived in a place where one enjoyed a constant breeze—not a wind, but a breeze, a gentle and continuous waft of air. Island people, he had read, live long lives free of any illness whatsoever. Therefore he always left the car windows open just a little, and it was through this small opening, on this particular morning, that a bird had accidentally flown, and, not knowing what else to do but fly, continued until it hit the opposing window. It slammed into the glass and fell to the floor, stunned, motionless, and completely unseen by the McCallisters as they began their trip to Arcadia.

It was a goldfinch.

*A*fter bringing Carla back to his office Beadles had stopped seeing patients, so his disappearance had yet to be noticed. It's conceivable, in fact, that it *never* would have been noticed were it not for the return of the lumberjacks, Lumberjack Smith among them, that same Friday. They came down the mountain in their huge flatbed trucks loaded with lumber and went to their wives, who were waiting for them, naked and trembling on their beds, waiting for that familiar weight to press mercilessly upon them, like being crushed beneath a house. Lumberjack Smith sated himself quickly—the first time was always quick—but as he lay beside his wife he suddenly raised himself on his elbows and looked out the bedroom window.

"Where's Carla?"

His wife sighed, knowing this was going to come up eventually. "I don't know where Carla is," she said.

"What do you mean you don't know where Carla is?"

"One night a man came—"

"A man?"

"That little man," she said. "The old one. The one who took everyone's eyeglasses away. He took Carla."

Lumberjack Smith lay in silence. Finally, he asked, almost in a whisper, "And you didn't stop him?"

"It was raining," she said. "I thought—"

"*Thought?*"

"Maybe he was saving her," she said. "Maybe you had told him—I don't know."

He looked at his wife, at a loss for what to say, with so many violent feelings battling inside him. "You don't know anything," he said.

Luckily he had not undressed, had not even taken off his shoes. He was a fast man with long strides and a few moments later he stood before the door of Dr. Beadles's office, his heart pounding with a yearning, a yearning to find his precious Carla, as well as a yearning to do awful things to Beadles. He imagined a number of ways to kill him and tried to settle on a single one before going in. But standing there he realized he was too late: the smell of death was thick as fog, even in the hallway outside the office. The door was unlocked, but he tore it off its hinges anyway. Carla wasn't there, of course, and neither was Beadles. The smell came from the corpses of a thousand dead mice.

*B*ut the McCallisters, who had no idea their savior had died, kept to their schedule; you could set your watch by their departure, block by block. The left on Elijah McCallister Boulevard (9:01), followed by the hard right on Silk Road (9:03), and then they drove past Dark Green Lake and out of town (9:05).

Mr. McCallister looked forward to this long drive; it gave him an opportunity to think. What was it about driving that allowed him to have the strange and mysterious sorts of thoughts he had, thoughts that never would have entered his mind had he been back home sitting in a chair? It was as if the wind itself blew things into his head. He imagined impossible scenarios. What if a giant bear suddenly presented itself to them, leaping from the forest into the middle of the road? (And by giant he meant fifteen feet tall at least, with teeth as long as his arm.) What would Mrs. McCallister do if he pulled into the lot before one of the motels they passed on the way to Arcadia—the

Peach Blossom, say—and he turned to her and suggested, *Let's stay the night here*. He never would—he never did—but he thought about it, and the scene played through his mind as if it were really happening. *She blushed, turned away, smiling, and said,* Let's do.

He thought about the past. He became a sort of amateur anthropologist when he drove to Arcadia. He imagined what the world must have looked like a hundred years ago. He considered the life of his grandfather Elijah McCallister, a man who had single-handedly cleared a forest and built a town, who made a factory, who built a beautiful home where his descendents lived to this day.

At 9:07, the goldfinch regained its bird-sense, looked around, panicked, and took off. Its first and last stop: Mrs. McCallister's hair. Its little feet became caught, and it flapped its wings in terror. In the silence of the car, its appearance could not have been more disturbing—a masked man wielding an ice pick could not have been more terrifying. Mrs. McCallister screamed; Mr. McCallister turned to her. His mind was a hundred years away then, and at first he didn't know what he was seeing; at first he thought his wife's hair had come alive somehow. *But hair is dead*, he thought, *hair is dead*. He then surmised that a bird had flown out of his wife's head. This was his last real thought. *A bird has flown out of my wife's head*. He was in shock, and stayed that way for the rest of his life.

The car broke through the wooden railing and plunged into the lake, and both of them (and the little goldfinch, too) drowned.

Within the hour everyone in Roam knew what had happened. A big crowd gathered to view the accident: the lake was only six feet deep there, and the car could be seen clearly. It appeared to be parked at the bottom of the lake. James Harding, mayor of Roam, who felt as mayor it was his job to do it, jumped in. He peered through the window.

The McCallisters looked like they were still alive. They were sitting in the front seat, belts securely fastened. Harding said later that it looked like they'd simply let the water take them. (No one admitted what they were thinking, that maybe they had done this on purpose, that their home life had finally become too much to bear, what with Rachel blind and Helen, with her epic face.) He said that as he stared through the driver-side window, Mr. McCallister's head suddenly turned and appeared to look at him. Harding said his heart almost burst in his chest. Mr. McCallister looked somewhat surprised, he said, his small eyes wide open to take it all in.

And in Mrs. McCallister's hair there was a bird.

# JONAS,
# PART II

*J*onas drove this same car the day they left Rachel behind. The sun had turned the front seat into a hot plate. They drove around the lake and past the metal barriers the town had installed after the Mc-Callisters' accident. Helen peered over them into the shallow water, feeling not grief, not anger, but emptiness, the absence of feeling. She had been sad once, and angry, but those feelings had been buried beneath the sediment of a life that had been willed to her seven years ago. *If her parents had lived*: was there any bigger "if " in her life? Most things still would have been wretched, of course—nothing could change that—but some things would have been different. She would have been a part of the real world and not this patchy substitute she had created for her own amusement, a world for her and Rachel. In the beginning, when they were children, it was nothing: kids did that sort of thing all the time, especially sisters, they made things up, and they'd see how far they could take it. But it had gone too far; even Helen couldn't remember all the details she had concocted. The complexity of her creation was what made it come alive, she thought—it was so mysterious, and therefore lifelike, in so many ways. It was the ever-changing totality of her grim vision that brought her the greatest joy, and not because it was inherently cruel (and it was, she knew that) but because she had made it all herself. She had taken the world and turned it inside out for both of them, and now the only beautiful thing in it was Helen herself. There were even times she believed in it, believed in the birds and the Boneyard and the story about the husband and wife who killed each other and who continue killing each other to this very day. And how she had given herself a new face, one that, in Rachel's eyes, was as glorious as any face had ever been.

This is what she had instead of love.

After her parents died there was talk about what to do with the car. Roam was not equipped with a crane large enough to raise it (one would have to come from Arcadia), and some felt it was better just to leave it and let time and the water do what it would. But the day after the funeral, Dark Green Lake turned crystal clear. This was attributed by some to the intercession of a higher power, rather than to the great plankton holocaust that had in fact taken place. The car appeared to be on display to anyone driving past, the bottom of the lake like a showroom floor. You couldn't see it without thinking of the McCallisters, Mrs. McCallister with the dead bird in her hair, Mr. McCallister clutching the wheel. Couldn't see it without thinking of those girls, all alone. A man was sent to Arcadia, a crane truck dispatched, and the long black car was raised like an ancient ship from the six-foot-deep water. Jonas, being the expert with cars, was there that day, and for a lark turned the key, which was still in the ignition. The car started immediately, and, the seats still soggy, he drove it to its home. To this day the car smelled of mildew—even with the windows down, as they were now, the wind blowing Helen's hair straight back, as though she were flying.

Jonas kept looking over at her, smiling.

"This is good," he said. "Getting out, you and me."

Helen said nothing. She stared straight ahead with her hands in her lap. They passed by the Bentons' house. They were having a yard sale. Everything was in the yard, even the bed, the meat freezer, the kitchen table, a big box of shoes, and, hanging from a tree, dresses. No one was at the yard sale but the Bentons. She slipped down in the seat and closed her eyes. She wondered if anyone would see her, wondered what they would think if they did. *There goes . . . a girl.* They would have to know what she was doing because everyone knew everything in this town whether they knew they knew it or not. People could smell it, smell change, smell difference, new things. *Where is Rachel?* they would wonder. They would see Helen, and then they would wonder where Rachel was and what the little blind girl was doing. Helen herself wondered. *Where is she? What is she doing now, without me?* She felt as if some part of her had been severed, or scooped out of her like ice cream. She had no idea it would feel this way.

"I said—"

"I heard you, Jonas."

He looked back and forth, from her to the road. Some time went by, and then he cleared his throat.

He said, "Sometimes I wonder what it's going to be like."

"Wonder what *what* is going to be like?"

"Everything," he said. "Roam. Me. You. Me and you."

Helen let a little time go by, her eyes still closed. "No one knows what's going to happen," she said. "That's why they call it the future."

"I know. It's just—you wonder, too. I know you do."

Now she opened her eyes. "Why are you *talking* so much?"

"I don't know," he said.

"Just stop it," she said, and he did.

They turned off the main road and crunched down the gravel drive to the shop. Helen didn't want to be here now. The sun filtered through the kudzu and pine trees and glowed on the dirt. The air singed her lungs. The shop was a sheet of corrugated metal resting on top of two sketchy wooden walls, open on both ends. Scattered over the scrubby half-acre around it were the rusty husks of a dozen dead cars, gutted of all value and waiting to be sold for next to nothing to a man in a flatbed who occasionally came through Roam, and to the lumberjacks, who flattened the metal and used it to fortify the holes they lived in for most of the year. And that one lumberjack who lived in the woods outside of town, Smith his name was, he'd bought some of it, too, even though he lived in Roam now and wasn't a lumberjack. If a car could be fixed, though, Jonas could fix it. He was a genius with cars and an idiot with everything else. This is what everybody said, and everybody was right.

He put the car in neutral, turned it off, and let it coast to a stop beneath the shadow of the metal overhang. Then he put it in park and just sat there, looking out on his kingdom. Now that they were here, it was all about him waiting to have her: Helen knew his mind didn't have room for another thought.

"So," he said. "You want to get out of the car and look around?"

It took her a little while to hear him. "Look around?" she said. "No. No, I don't think so."

Jonas didn't know what to do next—but when did he? He shook his head and took in a deep breath through his nose.

"I think I've finally hit the bottom," she said. She still wasn't looking at Jonas. If he turned into a gnat and flew away she wouldn't have noticed. "I thought I had already, but I hadn't."

"What are you talking about, Helen?"

"I think I've done everything I can do to her now. The way she looked out the window—that face. That was a new look from her, that kind of . . . despair. All that's left from here on out is more of the same. She knows it and so do I. I've taken everything from her, and for the rest of our lives this is how it's going to be: me taking more, even when there's nothing more to take."

Jonas looked at the dirt beneath his nails and tried to pick some of it out. "You and Rachel, y'all are like peas in a pod, aren't you?"

"What's that supposed to mean?"

"I don't know," he said. "I thought that's what you were saying."

Helen rubbed her forehead with her fingers. Jonas reached toward her tentatively and touched the hem of her blue silk dress.

"You want to get on over to the shop?" he said. "I mean, if you want to we could."

"No, I don't."

"Okay," he said, giving patience a try, and failing. "What do you want then, Helen? What is it you'd like to do?"

She sighed. "Not this," she said. Then she said, "I think I'd rather die."

"*What?*" He held the steering wheel in both hands as if he were driving. "Don't say that. That's not funny, Helen."

"Seriously," she said. "I want you to kill me." Even she didn't know where this voice was coming from. A feeling had somehow hijacked her tongue, and it sounded about right, so she stuck with it. "How about you kill me and stick me into one of these cars," she said. "No one will ever know."

"Kill you," he said. He laughed. He gripped the steering wheel until his knuckles turned white. "I'm okay just sitting here, talking. Or I got a better idea. How about we get out of the car and get some fresh air. That'll make you feel better."

The air inside the car was so hot the sweat on her arm burned. Her forehead was glistening. Jonas reached over and placed a gentle hand on her knee.

"How do you even stand to look at me, Jonas?"

"Are you kidding?" he said. "It's the easiest thing I do all day."

He started unfastening his seat belt. The sweat flowed down her face now, burning her eyes, and for a moment she couldn't see. She shouldn't have left Rachel like that—not because it was any worse than anything Helen had ever done to her before, but because Rachel knew Helen for who she was now, and if she didn't know for certain, she would, and soon. It had been easier when Helen thought she would never be caught—as long as Rachel didn't know it was possible for Helen to imagine her own self as the picture of that person she had painted for Rachel. And it was this, more than the darker parts of her own heart, that made her malice so successful, and necessary. Rachel let Helen believe she was better than she was.

Jonas slid quickly across the seat and took her hands in his and brought them to his lips, where he kissed them. He kissed them front and back. "What's wrong with us today?" he said. "We're usually thinking the same thing."

"We're never thinking the same thing, Jonas. *Never.*"

She said this last part so emphatically that he looked at her like she had just run over his dog and was feeling pretty good about it. His eyes were little pools of pain. He'd become that boy again, the boy she met while he was picking up used nails from the gutters in front of the houses. She'd shown him what she wanted him to do to her and he'd done it, and he'd done it again and again over the years as she kept searching for that feeling, any feeling at all.

She took his hand and placed it on her leg. "But we're thinking the same thing now," she said.

"So you're okay?" he said. "Because it's fine with me if we just stay here and talk. I mean, Helen, I've never said this before, but I—I—"

"I'm okay," she said.

He smiled. "All right then. Good. That's all I wanted to hear."

"Show me the shop," she said. "Where you work. I want to see it. Maybe . . . maybe you can work on me there, too."

"Okay," he said. "Sure. But that's not, I mean—we don't have to."

She winked at him. She hated it when he was this happy, that he could let her make him so. She opened her door; he opened his. But only he got out. She waited until he was well on his way to the shop before moving over to the driver's side of the car. He always left the key in the ignition. She turned it, the engine roared, and she gunned it backward, sweeping in circles through the dust and the flying gravel, in this parched lot full of rusting corpses, and she was gone. In the rearview mirror she saw him watching her go, not even moving, probably too rattled to know what to do. "Sorry," she whispered. She took the car back toward Roam as fast as she could drive it, and would have made it in more than enough time had she taken that hill a little bit slower. But she hadn't. The car lifted up as though it were about to take flight and then came crashing down, and when it did something broke, the engine died, and the car rolled to a stop beside a big tree. Now she had to walk. Now she knew she would be too late. Rachel would be on her way to the bridge by now, and there was nothing Helen could do to stop her.

# JONAS,
# PART III

*I*n a town full of sad men, Jonas Whittle was perhaps the saddest of them all. His mother and father had never married—in fact,
they'd only seen each other a couple of times; one of the times is when
Jonas was made. They were seventeen years old. His father's name
was Mason; her name was Britannica. She was pregnant with Jonas for
six months before Mason even found out, and when he did he had a lot
of trouble believing it was his, and maybe he never really did. His folks
made him promise to marry her as soon as the baby was born, though,
and he agreed because his father said he would kill him if he didn't.
But there were complications during the delivery: Britannica bled out
and died. When he heard about what happened to her, Mason had a
good idea how things were going to spin out, so he tried to leave town
that same night—he'd never wanted a child, and he definitely didn't
want one he had to take care of by himself, especially one he didn't

really believe was his. But his escape was foiled by a rainstorm of such strength and duration that the lowlands around the town flooded, became a sea, and turned Roam into a temporary island. When the water subsided a few days later he tried to leave again, but by this time the hospital was on to him, and the old doctor met him on the road with the baby in a box. He set the box on the ground in front of Mason and said, "He is yours." Mason thanked him, watched him go; then he took the box out into the woods, placed it in a clearing near a bear den, and walked away. He turned to cast a final glance, and something about how the box began to tremble moved him, cut him deeper than he was able to endure. He picked the box back up and took it home. It was, he would later say, the worst thing he had ever done in his life. Whatever plans he had, whatever dreams, hopes, ambitions—they were all gone now. The rest of his life was over. He named the baby Jonas, because he thought that was the name of the man in the Bible who was swallowed by the whale, and no one told him different.

Mason and Jonas Whittle lived at the far edge of town where the forest was most ferocious, where if you stood in the same place for too long you were likely to disappear beneath a blanket of vines. A lot of time was spent just killing things that were green. Jonas went to school through the third grade. Sometimes his father forgot to pick him up and he'd spend the night with one of his teachers, who fed him whatever strange food they were eating, put him to bed, and took him back to school the next day. The first time a teacher questioned Mason about this, he took Jonas out of school and put him to work. Most of the day the boy was sent out looking for gutter nails—nails you might find in the gutter, used, discarded, but good enough if they were straightened, nails his father used for various building projects. As Jonas grew older, Mason accidentally taught him about cars; he had Jonas hold the hoods up on cars that didn't have a setter, and as Jonas watched, he learned things. This went on for some time. After his father died—a car hood fell on his head one day—Jonas took over the business. He was good at it, but with business slowing down the way it was, he fell back on his first skill, collecting nails. He had some run-ins with the lumberjacks. They were so big, so full of life, Jonas looked like a scrawny sapling compared to them. They made fun of him, and he let them. But when they started saying things about his mother—how many times they'd had her themselves when she was a young girl, how (who knows?) anybody could be Jonas's father—he scrapped with them. He put up a good fight, too. He'd get a few ribs broken, a bone now and again, but he held his own. They couldn't kill him, hard as they may have tried. *Being left in a box in the woods has its upside*, Jonas thought. *Makes you tough.*

Maybe it also helped to have nothing to live for. If Jonas did have anything to live for through those years he didn't know what it was. He didn't have any friends. He didn't know how to read much beyond a stop sign. He had no family at all.

Everything changed the day he met Helen. He was in the gutter outside her house and she was sitting in the porch swing, watching him. He knew that if he thought about it long enough, if he really looked at her, he'd realize she was the ugliest woman he'd ever seen, and maybe the ugliest there ever was. But he didn't really think about it. Because even he, who knew next to nothing, knew how she was looking at him and what it meant. They didn't have to say a single word.

He didn't know what her name was for a week. The first time they did it was against a tree along the backside of the house, her skirt pushed up around her hips, his pants pooling around his ankles. Like animals, really. And he didn't have a problem with that. The problems only started later, when he actually started to care for her. He couldn't say exactly how this happened: it wasn't his plan. He had no hope or dream of it, nor even the idea it was possible. But just being with her so often over the course of weeks and months and then years . . . well, everything changed for him—though not in a way that he could show or talk about. He had an idea he might have said something today, out at the shop, but he never got the chance. Instead, he watched her drive away, abandoning him in the middle of nowhere, dust from the wheels settling into his eyes as he buckled his belt and kicked at the ground.

# A HUNDRED SILENT
# WINGS

She couldn't find her other shoe. On that list etched inside her head—*The Simple Indignities of Blindness*, it was titled—the inability to find the other shoe was at or near the very top. How one shoe strayed from the other was a mystery to her. She removed them at the same time, in the same place, the same as everybody, because who takes off one shoe and then walks half-shoed someplace else? And a shoe without a foot in it couldn't go anywhere. So where was it? She tried to avoid getting down on her knees, because she didn't like the way that must look, the blind girl crawling around the living room like some sort of animal. And she was still wet, dripping from the rain. (For someone who couldn't see, Rachel was very sensitive to *being* seen.) She envied the instant information a pair of eyes must deliver. She had her own sources of information, of course, other senses, but some of what she thought she knew was, by her own admission, partly imaginary. It was never completely clear to her what was real and what wasn't. This had its advantages, of course: though she had been told time and time again that there was no bay window in their home, she always imagined a bay window, like the bow of an abandoned ship on the hill overlooking the town.

She held one shoe in her hand as she inched across the living room, letting her toes sweep the carpet ahead of her, hoping to bump into a canvas tennis shoe, her favorite, now held together by tape and string. Such grace, even when looking for a shoe. Even when she was in a hurry.

She had to leave before Helen returned.

*Ah!* Here it was, beneath the coffee table, behind the Roam telephone book inserted beneath a leg to keep it level. Her thumb ruffled the book's cornered edge. All the numbers of all the people who lived in Roam were here, the ink barely raised from the surface of the fine rice paper, but enough so she could feel it. It seemed so odd, when you thought about it, that you could just open this book, pick a number, and call up anybody, even if you didn't know them at all. Just call them up and say, *Hello. My name is Rachel. To whom am I speaking?*

With her shoes on she was ready to go. No need for a change of clothes; no need to pack a lunch. She brushed her hair to a soft shine and slipped on a cotton sweater, then left through the front door as if she were going to the store—confident, quick, almost not really blind anymore. The outside world hadn't changed the way the world inside her had. The inside had changed in the blink of an eye, knowing what she knew now, knowing what she had to do—but the outside world changed more slowly. She knew it. Walking through Roam was like walking through a painting of Roam. She knew where she was going and how to get there, and had you seen her and not known who she was you wouldn't have been able to say anything other than that she was a pretty girl on her way somewhere.

In her mind there was a map, a map etched from years of patient practice with Helen. Rachel counted steps as they walked until the town became a series of numbers, a mathematical construction in which the path from the drugstore to the market was not a left on Chestnut and a right on Main, but left 126 steps and right 212. Helen didn't know she was counting. Helen didn't know the half of what was going on in her head.

It was late already. She was about to do something reckless. She very well might die. But no single life was made to live forever; each had its own span of days. Were a fly to live for a week he would be famous among other flies for his longevity. Rachel's own parents lived, all their years combined, for not quite a century, and yet one could say they left the world too soon. Rachel could certainly say that, and so could Helen, for it was upon her the weight of their absence set most heavily. It was Helen who continued living but who each day gave a bit more of her life away without even having lived it herself. Too much. Rachel understood. She knew why Helen had left her alone. She would have done the same. She was saying, *You need to go.*

She was scared but felt free and real.

It was a lovely day. She could feel the dying sun on her cheeks. The trees were crowded with so many cacophonous birds she had to press the palms of her hands against her ears as she walked beneath them. When she did this she could hear her own breathing. She could hear her heart beating. It felt like she could hear the wind blowing through her head.

There was a bridge. She knew there was a bridge. And beyond that?

Wonders.

*R*achel could feel the eyes of Roam on her as she walked, alone, toward the woods. The first person she met was the Widow Harrington.

Rachel heard her old lady footsteps—the heel of her shoe dragging against the sidewalk.

"Rachel McCallister?" the widow said. "What in the world?!"

Rachel knew what that meant: *Where is Helen?* But Rachel didn't have the time to stop and talk to her. She kept walking. "It's a beautiful day, isn't it, Mrs. Harrington?" she said, as she passed.

843 steps to the Forest. 842, 841 . . .

*J*uliana Scopes was the second person she met on the way to the Forest. Juliana was Rachel's very first, and very last, friend. Mr. and Mrs. McCallister had struggled with what to do with Rachel after she went blind—how to present her to the world and how to present the world to her. After much discussion they decided to pretend she *wasn't* blind, or at least to do the same things they would have done had she not been. So they had Juliana over for a playdate. Juliana lived one street over and had been born the same week as Rachel; when they were babies Mrs. McCallister imagined a future in which they grew up to become the best of friends. Then Rachel went blind.

Regardless, Mrs. McCallister insisted that Rachel be treated no differently than any other child, and on the first day of summer she had Juliana over. They spread out a blanket in the backyard beneath the apple tree, and Mrs. McCallister took an apple and cleaned it and cored it and gave half to each girl. Juliana knew there was something wrong with Rachel from the moment she got there, the way her eyes couldn't focus on anything, how her hands were always reaching for something that wasn't quite there. Juliana was scared at first, and held tight to her mother's legs. But as soon as Rachel tripped over the roots of the apple tree and fell, and then fell again as she was trying to get up, Juliana laughed and saw how much fun this could be. "Let's play hide-and-go-seek," she said.

"I don't know that's such a good idea, Juliana," Mrs. Scopes said.

"Let them play," said Mrs. McCallister. "Rachel wants to, I can tell."

Rachel did want to. She counted to ten while Juliana hid. Through force of habit, Rachel even covered her eyes with her hands, and this, to her mother, was the most heartbreaking thing. It was a long ten seconds, long enough for Mrs. McCallister to begin to regret her decision.

"Ready or not, here I come!" Rachel called, and her pointless seeking began. She took one halting step after another, walking in small awkward circles. She did this for a couple of minutes, flattening the grass around her in a strange meandering pattern. Mrs. McCallister watched with a smile frozen on her face, as if perchance were she to maintain her composure, were she able to believe that something good would come from all of this, something actually would. After a few minutes Juliana quietly approached Rachel until she was just behind her. Rachel heard her—turned, lunged—but Juliana just got out of her way. This happened again, but the third time Rachel somehow tagged her.

"You peeked!" Juliana screeched, until she realized that cheating, for Rachel, was impossible.

Mrs. McCallister thought it best to continue the playdate some other time. After that Helen was the only friend Rachel had.

Now here Juliana was again. Even before Rachel heard her she could smell her: a cloud of sugary perfume filled the air, so thick as to be dizzying. She was with someone.

"Oh, my," Juliana whispered, but not nearly so softly that Rachel couldn't hear. "It's Rachel McCallister."

"The blind girl?" a man's voice said.

"Yes, the blind girl!" Juliana whispered quite loudly. "Now lower your voice!" she said even louder.

Rachel tried to keep walking—732, 731, 730—but at the last moment Juliana spoke to her, and Rachel felt she had to stop.

"Rachel," she said. "This is—I am—Juliana Scopes. You probably don't remember me."

"Of course I remember you," Rachel said. She needed to keep going; the longer she was on the streets the greater the chance she'd be discovered by her sister or be taken home by some do-gooder. But she had to act as though everything were fine. "I do hope you're well."

"I am," Juliana said, but Rachel could hear in her voice that she was staring at her the way people felt so free to do, knowing Rachel couldn't see them back. "Father, you know Rachel."

"Of course. Hello, Rachel."

"Mr. Scopes."

"Your sister isn't here," Mr. Scopes said. "She's with you, usually, isn't that so?"

"Usually," Rachel said.

Juliana and her father exchanged a look: Rachel didn't have to see to know that. A bird flew down and—briefly, just long enough to say it had—perched on Rachel's shoulder. Then fluttered away.

"Well, would you look at that," Mr. Scopes said.

"Animals have always liked Rachel," said Juliana. "I guess it's one of those things that comes with it."

"It?" Rachel said.

"They see what we see," Mr. Scopes said, the way a father says it, with that deep voice, as though he knew what he was talking about when he was talking about something he had no concept of at all. "Because blind or not, I have to admit: you're the prettiest girl in Roam, Rachel. Present company excepted, of course," he said to his daughter.

"Thank you, Father," Juliana said, "but I have eyes." An awkward silence. "I didn't mean—I only meant that without a doubt there's no more beautiful girl between here and Arcadia than you, Rachel."

"Please," Rachel said. "Please stop."

"To wake up every morning and see your face on the pillow beside him," Mr. Scopes said. "I don't know a man who could easily say no to that."

Rachel felt as though they were throwing rocks at her. "Helen told me that people could be cruel," she said. "I just never imagined how cruel. You should be ashamed of yourselves. You should, but I know you won't be. Anyone who could say such things doesn't have the capacity for shame."

She heard them reeling, felt the shock, the sudden surprise. "*Rachel*," Juliana said, aghast, breathless. No one expects a blind girl to have the temerity to say what's true.

"*Juliana*," she said, mocking her. "If you are no prettier than I, you must have the face of a dog."

And she walked away, just like that. Again she heard them not making a sound, and Rachel thought: *How the world seems to change after one decides to leave it.*

729.


*T*he third and last person Rachel met before she made it to the Forest was Mrs. Samuels. Mrs. Samuels was in fact the last person she wanted to meet, because other than her sister she seemed to be the only person in the entire world who truly cared for her, or who thought about her enough to care. Rachel wondered why—because Mrs. Samuels had never been particularly kind to Helen. Rachel sensed that cool distance between them when Mrs. Samuels came upon them selling their things on the corner. With Helen and Mrs. Samuels, it was as if much less were being said than thought, known, and felt. So maybe it was simply pity. Pity the poor ugly blind girl who has taken everything from everybody and given nothing in return.

Still, Mrs. Samuels seemed truly happy to see her.

"Rachel," she said. And again: "Rachel. Look at you. You're—"

"I know," she said. "I'm wearing the brooch."

Mrs. Samuels placed her hand on Rachel's arm and lightly squeezed it: it was the way old people showed deep feeling. "So you are," she said.

"I thanked you, didn't I? For the brooch."

"Thanked me? It was yours already. Your sister . . . ?" Neither of them spoke for a moment. "You're looking particularly beautiful today, Rachel."

"Beautiful?" Rachel was tired of defending her own hideousness. She merely sighed.

"I mean your hair especially. And that's a Very. Attractive. Dress."

"Thank you, Mrs. Samuels."

Mrs. Samuels was one for the long, thoughtful pause. Sometimes. Even in the. Middle of. Sentences. Mrs. Samuels liked to say things that *mattered*. Being blind and in a conversation with her, it was like waiting for a train at an abandoned station in the middle of the night. Rachel spent the long moment remembering her number: 247.

"I think I know what you're doing," Mrs. Samuels said, finally.

"You do?"

A bird landed on a nearby branch and sang a little song. "And I think it's wonderful."

"You *do*?"

"This . . . *foray*," she said. "Into the world. Without your sister. I'd been hoping. For something like this."

"It *is* something, isn't it?" Rachel said. "But—"

Rachel listened to the bird sing. A cardinal.

"Yes, Rachel?"

"I think I should continue. With my foray."

If Helen returned and found her here she would take her by the wrist and drag her home and it would be terrible—Helen would be so upset they would spend the rest of their lives getting over it and they never would, because Helen would hold it against her forever. She could hear her now: *You said you would never leave me. Never!* And she had said that. She had lied to her sister. But this was for the best.

Mrs. Samuels didn't move.

"I think this must mean something," she said. "Meeting you here."

"You do?"

"I do." A human gaze must exert some sort of special invisible force, because Rachel felt it, Mrs. Samuels's eyes all over her face. Then Mrs. Samuels whispered a kind of secret: "*I'm just. Coming back. From your mother's. Grave.*"

Rachel pointed.

"That's right," Mrs. Samuels said, sounding a bit stunned. How could a blind girl know? It was magic! "Just over there."

Rachel had been there many times, of course. She and Helen went once a month. Helen always managed to bring up the circumstances, and how terrible it was that two people died simply because they were trying to do something good for someone—for her, for Rachel. To think they were struck down while they were only trying to help their sweet little blind daughter Rachel. *Think how much would be different now if you'd never been blind! Think about it. They would still be alive.*

Rachel didn't want to think about it.

"It's very nice, your mother's grave. A very nice place to be."

"My parents' grave, you mean," Rachel said. "My mother and father are buried side by side."

Mrs. Samuels sniffed. "Well, I don't talk to your father," she said. "We never really . . . got along. A good man, I haven't a bad word for him. But your mother was my friend. I really only talk to her."

"Why do you keep saying *talk*?" Rachel asked.

"Because I do, dear," she said. "She was never much of a talker when she was alive, you know. But now. Oh, my. She can't stop."

"No," Rachel said. "That's impossible. She's dead."

"Well," Mrs. Samuels said. "I'm certainly not going to argue with you about that. But we *do* talk. I stand by her grave and talk to her the same way I'm talking to you right now. The only difference between the way it is now and the way it was then is a cup of black coffee and a slice of Bundt cake."

Rachel laughed. "And why not bring that with you? No one would mind, I'm sure. Set up a little table beside the stone." She didn't regret saying it: why should she? Even to Mrs. Samuels, who had always been so kind. But she was thinking, *If my mother can talk, why hasn't she been talking to me?*

"She's right," Mrs. Samuels said, her friendly tone changing.

"Who?"

"Your mother. You are beginning to sound like your sister. That awful girl."

*That awful girl.* Rachel tried to slap Mrs. Samuels when she said this, but she wasn't really sure where her face was and she missed, terribly. Rachel had never tried to hit anybody in her life, and there was so much more to it, she discovered, than the act itself. Her whole body began to tremble. Mrs. Samuels took her in her arms and held her.

"I'm sorry," Mrs. Samuels said. She patted her on the back as though she were a little girl. "There now. I know, I know. But Rachel, dear, all your mother wants you to know is who your sister is. Helen is not the woman you think. You're such a beautiful girl," she said. "But you don't know who you *are*. You're a woman now, Rachel. You're all grown up. More than anything this is what your mother wants you to know. You have to start over."

"Start over?" Now she did push herself away from Mrs. Samuels, and wiped her face with her dress sleeve. "But that's what I'm doing."

"How? What do you mean, Rachel?"

"I'm leaving," she said.

"Where to?"

"To a better place," she said. "Helen told me there was a better place. Away from the Hanging Tree, the Boneyard, the House of Death. It's on the other side of the ravine. A river, and a town."

Mrs. Samuels took Rachel's hands in her own. She was crying now; Rachel could hear it in her voice. "No. *No*, Rachel. None of that—it's a story, a terrible story, and she's a terrible, hideous person," she said. "Hideous inside and out. She tells you lies and you believe her because you don't know any better, because she's never *let* you know any better. She's never let another soul near you. You *couldn't* know. But now you can, now you can. Rachel? Rachel, dear? Where are you going? *Rachel*: you have no idea what's out there."

"But I'm hopeful," Rachel said. "That's the important thing, right?"

Rachel kept walking until Mrs. Samuels' voice faded in the distance, until even the wind was louder. She didn't see anybody else on her way to the Forest, and no one saw her, or if someone did they didn't stop her, watching from a distance through the small windows of the small houses where the mill workers once lived. She felt something warm rub against her leg and disappear, and she could smell it: a dog. She could hear it running, the soft crackling of brittle twigs beneath its paws. She walked faster now as she tried to get the sound of Mrs. Samuels's voice out of her head, to forget what she'd heard. But the words felt like sand in Rachel's blood, even as she entered the woods, even as she waited for the sound of a hundred silent wings . . .

*T*here are stories in the woods, stories everyone hears and knows in their own heart to be true. Stories of darkness, beauty, life, death. Mystery. There *is* something out there, beyond the bend, before the shadow: everyone knows this. But it's not everyone who wants to find it. Rachel wanted to find it, and so did Ming Kai's Markus. He left his home just days before Rachel left hers, heading her way before he even knew where he was going, as she was heading his. Because each had been told the same story by the person they loved the most: there was a world out there better than the one they lived in now, and all they had to do was seek it.

# A PRAYING WOMAN

*I*t was getting on to a purple dusk now, so when the fog settled in so suddenly it looked like the sky and all the clouds in it had fallen into the woods and across the road, and Helen felt like she was walking through a dream. She was also lost. She didn't think it was possible to get lost in Roam, but Jonas had taken her outside of it, and the truth was she didn't have a very good sense of direction. The road split at some point a mile or so back and there was no marker, no sign, nothing; she went left and she should have gone right. The left branch of the road became a path through a multitude of tall, scrawny pine trees, and then it just stopped altogether. She turned around and retraced her steps but hadn't noticed how the path itself had bifurcated at some point and she had to make another choice and she made the wrong one again, and now there was no one in the world more alone than Helen McCallister—unless it was her sister, Rachel.

She stopped and leaned against one of the pine trees. The hem of her dress was damp and she was bleeding: some of the underbrush had cut thin red lines into her ankles. She itched all over. If she had to live the rest of her life confined to one little room somewhere it would all be the same to her; she hated the outdoors. She hated trees and grass and night and being in a place where if she died no one would ever find her.

Jonas probably would. He'd look for her. Maybe he was looking now, but it didn't matter. She was too late and she knew it.

She leaned against the tree and watched the sky darken and go black. She could feel the tree she was leaning against, and if she put her eye close to it she could see its bark, but it wasn't much to look at. She thought of Rachel. She turned away from the tree to the nothing of the night and hoped she was wrong about her sister, hoped she didn't know Rachel as well as she knew she did.

When it finally turned inky dark and thick as water, she saw a dim, white light. She walked toward it and after a few minutes saw that it wasn't a real light at all—it was her mother. Helen was in the graveyard. Her mother was pacing back and forth in front of her gravestone, looking sad and dark and grave herself. She was lost in thought and didn't see Helen until Helen was right there. Then she stopped and looked at her, not surprised at all. *"Helen,"* she said, using that same tone of disapproval she'd used before.

Helen said, "You died. I did the best I could."

"You did the *worst* you could," her mother said.

She went back to pacing, and it wasn't clear to Helen if she was even talking to her anymore, or just talking, the presence of a living ear inspiration enough.

"I imagined a different sort of life than the one I led," she said, "but I suppose everybody could say the same. That's not necessarily a bad thing, to be surprised by what you get. If the life you imagined was the life you actually turned out to live it could be boring, or un-eventful at the very least, even if the life you imagined *was* very event-ful, if you see what I mean. *Here I am in a romantic foreign land,* you could think, *just as I imagined I would be!*

"But who would have thought my first child, bless her heart, would have turned out to be so horrid, and my last child so very beautiful—but blind. This would be absolutely beyond the imagining of anyone.

"Your father and I weren't really the ideal people to shoulder the burden of our various tragedies; they seemed to swallow us up. Or you could say they defined us. They became who we were: not just a fam-ily, but a family that had suffered and endured until our deaths, which only brought more suffering to the family, to you and Rachel.

"You were so good to her once, but then you changed. I don't know what happened. If I could have screamed from the bottom of the lake I would have said, with my final words, *Do not let Helen have her.* But I couldn't say it, because I was already dead."

"I don't know what to do now, Mother," Helen said. "Tell me what to do."

"It's sad," Mrs. McCallister said. "But I can't see the future: I can only see the past." Mrs. McCallister slowly dimmed, dying again, like a candle's flame. She blended into the darkening air. And she was gone.

Helen stood there for another moment, and then walked back to-ward town, each step faster than the one before it. Soon she was run-ning, and she didn't stop running until she made it home.

# THE LUMBERJACK
# AND HIS DOG,
# PART III

When the rest of the lumberjacks went back to the mountain, Lumberjack Smith stayed behind and waited for Carla to return. Sometimes a dog would do that, he knew: go away somewhere and be a dog and then come back to the home where she lives. He missed his dog, missed her with a deep and unsettling pain that traveled through his chest and down to his stomach and then spread into his blood and to the very tips of his fingers. The tips of his fingers were the only place he could actually get to the pain, so he chewed like a rat on his nails until they disappeared completely. His fingers took on the appearance of naked eyeless snakes. He didn't understand it, an emotion of this power, didn't know what to do with it. It possessed him.

Lumberjack Smith was in love with a dog.

How could he have known? Up in the mountains for so long, for months and months at a time, he had grown used to missing her. But the idea of her waiting for him was a salve, a prize, a promise of a homecoming so fine it more than equaled the dark time away. What good is *always* being happy? Sadness hints at the possibility of a future reward. He may have loved his wife as well, but it was a different kind of love, because there were lots of women who could have been his wife, and she was as good as any other. But there was no dog other than Carla who could have been Carla. There was no blind, three-legged dog anywhere in the world, and even if there were it would have been some other dog that wasn't Carla, and there would be no more homecomings like the ones he'd had before, and there would be no more thinking of them, and there would be no more happiness. There is no greater grief than that of a man with a broken heart who only just learned he had a heart at all.

Lumberjack Smith tried to work through it. After a few months he went back to the mountain. With his lumberjack brothers he felled the mighty oaks and pine, the hearty maple, the occasional ginkgo. But there was no passion in it for him; Smith was merely going through the motions. At night around the fire, around the blazing fire that could be seen like some distant star from as far away as Roam, he rarely made a sound, and when he did it was little more than a grunt. He didn't drink whiskey and ate no more than a normal man would eat, which, as he shrank up and weakened, is almost what he became—normal. His lumberjack brothers did not save him or even try to, because there was a code among them that a man saved himself, and if he couldn't, then he wasn't worth saving anyway. It was like that old story the lumberjacks told, the one about a giant who was taken down by a flea. The story was that the giant tried to kill a flea that had taken up residence in his hair, and became so frustrated that he pulled his own head off.

One day Lumberjack Smith crawled into his hole, a cave covered with various scraps of metal and steel, a wall between him and the rest of the world, and made no plans to come out.

But then one day, one day after many weeks of darkness, one day when he was close to extinguishing the tiny flame that burned inside of him, he saw two little eyes peering between pieces of corrugated steel. He thought it was a bear at first, but it wasn't.

It was a dog.

Smith and the dog looked at each other through the slit in the steel for the rest of the day and into the night. Neither of them moved. The dog whimpered, though, and Lumberjack Smith whimpered, too. Smith's heart began to beat again. He felt the flame within him flicker. He climbed out of his hole and took the loose fur of the dog's neck in his hand, and he pulled the dog to him, wrapped his arms around it, and sobbed.

He had been saved.

He gave her (for it was a her) a name that would be uniquely hers, but would, at the same time, honor the dog who came before.

He named her Marla.

*M*arla turned out to be nothing like Carla at all. Black, feral, she growled when his lumberjack brothers came too close and caught rabbits for Smith to eat as he regained his strength. Smith had taken care of Carla; Marla was taking care of Smith. Still, Smith liked to believe that the spirit of his old dog had come down from the Great Barn or wherever it was that dog souls go and possessed this wandering canine and led her here. A formidable animal, fierce and unforgiving as a wolf, but at night as gentle and warm as any woman curled up beside him. The moments of pure happiness Smith experienced—fleeting, like the shadows of birds flying just beyond the range of his vision— made him miss his old Carla all the more.

That's when he discovered: Marla was pregnant. Soon she was the mother of half a dozen healthy pups, each one as strong and eager as the next for a shot at her milky nipples. Only one died, and when it did Smith took it out to a quiet place and dug a hole and placed it carefully within. He had never had a chance to bury Carla. This tiny body, to him, was her, and he cried like a baby.

Now he had six dogs, each as black as the next. There was no room for all of them in his cave, so he made his cave deeper, longer, wider. They huddled and slept around Smith in a circle no other living thing could penetrate. They hunted together, and brought back deer with them—once an entire herd, which Smith and his dogs shared with the other lumberjacks. One year became two. The six dogs became ten, then twenty. And all they did, down to a dog, was love Lumberjack Smith.

How sad it was, then, when Smith realized that this was not enough, that all the love from all the dogs in the world could not begin to heal the gaping wound in his heart. Though he truly believed they had been sent to him by Carla to make him happy, he wasn't; there was no substitute for the love he had for her. There was no substitute even for the *idea* of her, and it was wrong of him to think any other dog— or any other fifty or a hundred dogs—could be that one dog for him.

One night by the fire, at dinner, he told his lumberjack brothers, "I'm going away."

His brothers glanced his way briefly, then went back to gnawing venison off the bone. No one wanted to say *I'll miss you,* because being a lumberjack was a calling, and missing things was part of it—so much a part of it that if you started enumerating the things you missed as a lumberjack you could almost never stop. It was easier to name the things a lumberjack had that no one else did: the companionship of other lumberjacks. If Smith didn't want to be a part of this, he wasn't really a lumberjack anymore. Smith knew it, and that's why he was leaving.

"Where to?" a brother asked him, without trying to seem very interested. "Back to Arcadia, I imagine."

"No," Smith said. "Not Arcadia. That's where all my heartache started. I never want to see Arcadia again."

The other lumberjacks shifted a bit on the huge felled oak that was their fire-bench. That word, *heartache,* made them uncomfortable.

"No," Smith said. "I think I'll go on down to Roam instead."

"Roam," the brother said. *"Roam?"*

"There's a place to drink in Roam," he said. "And there's women."

"But no trees," the brother said. "Not like these. And no lumber-jacks."

"No," he said. "And I'll miss you, you can be sure of that."

"Don't," the brother said and spit in the fire, where it sizzled. "Knowing you're out there, missing us, isn't likely to help us much up here."

"No," Smith said, the fire illuminating a tear. "I suppose it won't."

*T*he next day he began the long walk down. He had a truck, but he didn't really need it, so he left it on the mountain for his brothers (or the men who used to be his brothers). The dogs followed him. He didn't ask them, nor did he particularly want them to, but they didn't have anyone but him and he didn't have anyone, either. He was lonely with them, but he would have been desolate without them. They ran up ahead and scared away the bears and made his journey down the mountain dull and joyless. He wanted to fight a bear. It had been a long time since he'd done that.

He'd been through Roam once before; he'd needed an axle for the truck and he'd heard of someone there who had a lot of them, and sure enough, there was an axle in Roam and he and that boy had stuck it on the truck and she was good to go. After they were done they went to the bar. It was run by a midget. He couldn't remember the bartender's name. Smitty, Igbert—something like that. The midget said he wasn't a midget but he was, not that Smith cared one way or the other. People thought Smith was a giant sometimes and he wasn't a giant at all, he was just a very big man.

As they got closer to town the dogs started barking something terrible. He'd never heard them bark like that and he hated it. He wanted peace and he wanted quiet. That was yet another reason he left the mountain. He didn't know what he'd do with these dogs if they didn't stop barking.

When he got to Roam he left them outside the bar, barking, and went in and had a drink. But the dogs were out there, barking still. He couldn't enjoy his drink. So he left and he took the dogs and walked away from Roam until he reached that point at which they stopped barking. This is where he made his home. He built what turned out to be a grandiose doghouse, with many rooms and vaulted ceilings, in which he lived with his pack. Every day he came into town and had a drink or two or three at the bar—Digby, the barkeep's name turned out to be—and then he'd return to his doghouse and read from books he found at the abandoned high school. He learned a lot reading those books. He learned about the past. Most important, he learned there *was* a past, that even beneath the dirt and rocks upon which he slept every night a thousand men had been born and lived and died, and women, too. Babies. People different from him who had been here, who were gone now, some just a hundred years ago, but some gone for a thousand, along with all of their hopes and dreams, their happiness and heartaches, their dogs. Whole worlds, all come and gone.

He marked off the days of his new life, etching lines into the wood that was his walls. Numbers allowed him to remember that along with the past there was a future, too, something he could be a part of.

He had marked his wall for the three-hundredth time on the night Rachel McCallister disappeared. That was the night he went from needing to being needed, and it changed his life.

# JONAS,
# PART IV

*J*onas admired Digby Chang, and Jonas told him this all the time. He said, "Digby Chang, I admire you. I admire you because in spite of everything you keep your head up. The fact that you're waist-high to every other man in Roam and your face looks like it's been peppered by a shotgun don't get you down. You're a lesson to me," Jonas said, but it was a lesson Jonas never learned, because Jonas was always unhappy about something, and Digby expected it every time the door opened and Jonas walked in: how no one bought scrap metal anymore, how he couldn't get gas for the cars, how—hell, there weren't even any more *nails* in the gutter.

Tonight would be no different, Digby thought as Jonas came barreling into the tavern; but he would be wrong about that. First, the lumberjack was here, too: he was sitting at the end of the bar—distant, it appeared, even from himself. His head sank into his huge shoulders as if he were trying to disappear into his own body. He had been here for an hour and had not said one word. A few old spirits—KK Munford, Caleb "Jimmy" Chi, and Fang and He-Ping of course—sat off in the corner talking about old times. That's all the spirits talked about, really, those who spoke at all. Old times this and that, how it used to be, et cetera, and so on. As much as the living were entertained by stories of what happened after death, the dead apparently didn't find much about it worth discussing.

At least Jonas was alive, Digby thought, setting up a spot for him lickety-split. Digby couldn't remember the last time he had two paying customers at the same time. Things were looking up.

Jonas started in before the door closed behind him.

"I'm going to tear the goddamn heart out of something," he said. He looked like he'd been knocked in the face with a shovel and dragged through an icy pond—worse even than usual. "I don't care who or what it is. But it's either going to be one of those dogs—who've been barking all day and night if you haven't noticed, about fifteen of 'em right outside—or goddamn Archie Yates, who shut his door in my goddamn face."

Jonas said he could see himself standing there with the heart of one of those dogs still beating in his hand, the blood dribbling down his arm like watermelon juice. He saw himself holding it up above his head and screaming like some monstrous half-human bear—the cry of victory, and a warning to those who might challenge him next. Like goddamn Archie Yates.

"Welcome, my friend!" Digby said. With his eyes he indicated the silent presence of Smith in the corner; Jonas, in his anger at the world and what the world had done to him, had yet to see anything beyond the end of his nose. Fang turned his back on them: he'd never liked Jonas.

"Oh," Jonas said to Smith. "Sorry. Didn't mean what I said about the dogs, Smith. I'm just . . . upset. Sorry."

Smith didn't indicate that he had heard Jonas either time, or that he even knew that Jonas was there. Nothing about his demeanor changed at all.

Digby climbed a stepladder and pulled a sparkling clean glass down from the shelf and let it slide down the bar. It stopped an inch away from Jonas's hand. Digby was old-school. "You look like a man who needs a drink. Actually you look like a man who needs a drink, a big steak, an apple pie, and a cup of coffee. But all I got is the drink. First one's on the house. What can I do you for?"

"Whiskey, a beer chaser, a pack of matches, and an ashtray, a cigarette if you have it, and if it's all the same to you can I pay you next week?"

"How about a hand-job to go with that?"

"Damn, Digby."

Digby pulled himself up with his elbows so he could look Jonas in the eye. "I can make that joke because I've had more women than a hundred men."

"No shit."

Digby didn't blink. "No one believes me," he lied, "but it's true."

"Include me with the no ones."

"It's true whether you believe me or not. That's the way it is with truth. You don't have to believe it. It is what it is."

"Okay." Jonas sighed. "What about that drink and stuff?"

Digby wavered a moment but served him anyway. Money didn't make as much sense as it used to, now that there was no one about to spend it. Gave him a cigarette, too.

Jonas sucked on it for a quiet minute. Digby watched what thoughts Jonas had pinging around in his brain.

"Rachel's gone," he said, as if he were talking about something of no import whatsoever. He blew a great plume of smoke toward the ceiling and watched it fill the air.

Digby took aim at Jonas with his left eye. "*Gone?* That could mean one of two things," he said. "Missing or dead."

Jonas nodded. "In this case," he said, "I reckon it probably means both."

Digby made a noise he didn't mean to. It just slipped out. It was almost a moan, a tiny moan. He had always had the feeling, watching those two girls wander around town all like they were joined at the hip . . . he couldn't say what it was, actually, but it wasn't a good feeling. A shadow seemed to follow them everywhere they went. And now the blind girl was gone. "Oh," he said. "Oh, no. Tell me the tale."

Jonas threw back the whiskey and shook his head, giving Digby the look of a thirsty man: Jonas knew he couldn't resist a good story. Digby quickly refilled his glass and left the bottle where it was.

Smith nursed his whiskey and didn't look up. Didn't even look like he tried not to look up. He was very treelike, Digby thought. Very treelike indeed.

"Well, to begin with," Jonas said. "Helen and Rachel had some sort of family dispute earlier in the day. Not sure over what because that's *private information* Helen doesn't see fit to share with one such as me." He shook his head. "I've only been there for half their lives, you know, why share anything really important with me? I'm only Jonas."

"You're being sarcastic," Digby said. "I've never heard you be sarcastic before."

"Maybe I never needed to be before," he said.

"Well, you're good at it," Digby said. "Very good. Go on."

Jonas took a look at his cigarette, sad to see that it was already half gone. "So Helen and me go for a ride. Without Rachel this time. We drive out to my shop, which is a good ways out of town, and I'm thinking, well, I'm thinking we're about to . . . you know."

"I know," Digby said. "I know what happens between a man and a woman, believe me. I have both the experience and the imagination. No need to go into details."

"But she's not in the best humor now, and she says—"

"I don't know that I've ever seen Helen in a *good* humor."

"Well, even worse now," Jonas said. "Worse than ever."

"How so?"

"She wanted me to kill her."

Digby narrowed his tiny eyes and stared hard at Jonas for a moment. "She wanted you to *kill* her? To actually extinguish her life?"

Jonas nodded. Digby, from his vantage point on the edge of the bar, peered past Jonas's shoulder: even the spirits had stopped their palaver. It was possible now that Lumberjack Smith had an ear turned in their direction.

"So. Did you?"

"Did I kill her?" Jonas said. "No I didn't kill her! What do you— Digby, I swear."

"Had to ask," Digby said, and he held the palms of his hands up in the air, as if he were turning himself in to the authorities.

Jonas went on to tell Digby the rest of the story, how all of a sudden Helen took off in the car and left him there, miles from town, and he had to walk back, and when he did he went straight over to Helen's house because you can bet by then he *did* want to kill her. But that's when he found out Rachel had gone, and when Helen got back to the house she was like he'd never seen her before, so sad and broken up and frantic, he couldn't be mad at her anymore.

"Never get mad at a woman," Digby said. "It doubles the chances of her getting even madder with you."

Jonas lost the focus in his eyes. "She looked like a ghost," he said.

The old-timers laughed. Digby couldn't help but laugh along with them.

Jonas looked at Digby without comprehension. "I just don't know what's funny about that," he said.

"Nothing," Digby said. "Nothing is funny about that." Digby poured him another drink to calm him. It worked. "And so? Then? Next?"

"She said for me to go out and get a search party together, and I said I would."

"A search party," Digby said.

"With emphasis on the search."

"And instead you came here for a libation?"

Jonas shook his head. "This is my second stop. I was over to Archie Yates's first and he slammed the door in my face. I was thinking, maybe you . . . "

"Yes!" Digby said, manufacturing a specious enthusiasm. "Yes. I will be part of your search party. I'm honored. Together we will find the blind girl."

"Honestly," Jonas said, "I don't know there's much to be done. Rachel's at the bottom of that ravine by now. Stake my life on it." Digby had seen men with their spirits crushed more often than he'd seen a sunny day, but he couldn't remember seeing a man in the condition Jonas was in right now. He was as lost as anybody, ever.

"Things have changed," Jonas said. "Used to be Helen and I were—well, we were like two dogs in the same pen. No more."

Jonas laughed, but there was no mirth in it. The two men ruminated in silence. In the quiet they could hear Smith breathe.

"I used to find nails in her gutter," Jonas said. "That's the job my dad gave me, finding nails."

"This marked the beginning of your romantic liaison, no?"

"What?"

"When you began slipping it to Helen," Digby said.

"Oh. Yeah." Jonas smiled. "We'd pick a room, a closet. It didn't matter." Jonas thought back to those times. "Rachel, we'd have to lock her out back then. She'd cry, bang at the door. But that didn't stop us."

"Sounds like heaven," Digby said and looked toward the door as if he had another customer; he didn't.

Jonas shrugged. "There wasn't much to it. I mean, usually she'd have me wait in a room where there weren't any windows and the light was off, so by the time she came in I'd have invented someone else in my head. Just do it and be done and I'd go my way, she'd go hers. Oh, people talked, I know that. About her and me and her and, you know, the others. Because there were some others for a while. I don't mean to give it any more attention than it deserves, or to think about it too much because I don't generally get along with people who *think* too much, but how is what we did any different from what every other animal in the world does? I mean *every* animal, down to the last fish in the sea? People—not you, Digby, but some of the others—have made it a lot harder than it needs to be. You got to eat, right? And you don't always eat steak. When you get hungry—"

"—you eat," Digby said. "It's the law of the jungle."

Digby poured Jonas another beer. The foam bloomed and spilled over the side, and both of them watched it stream across the dark mahogany bar as if there were a message in its sprawling amoebic shape. Jonas scratched at his chest. "I admit," he said softly, even sweetly, "in the beginning she was just a place to fix my longing, because the fact is no one else would have me. But that changed. I got to loving her, Digby."

"Loving her?"

"I know. I actually *like* to look at her. Maybe I just got used to looking, I don't know. But when I don't see her, I miss her. I guess that's why they call it love."

"I've never been in love," Digby said. It was the first truly honest thing he'd said all night. "But that is what it sounds like." He laughed and raised a glass. The two of them clinked. "To love," Digby said.

"To love," Jonas said but stopped before bringing the glass to his lips.

"What, my friend?"

Jonas forced a smile. "The thing is, the thing that makes it rough? She doesn't love *me*."

"Oh. Now that *is* sad."

Jonas drank, and for a moment his face became as blank as a baby's, without a hint of pain or sadness to color it. "I do love her," he said. "And I just . . . I just can't stop being who I am. And why would she ever want to love me?"

Digby didn't have an answer to this. Jonas stared toward the far wall, where black-and-white photographs of Digby on a series of fishing trips were hung. In each photo he was with a different customer. Some of the fish Digby caught were half as big as he was.

Jonas narrowed his eyes. "The truth is, I'm kind of glad Rachel's run off. She's always been a . . . a problem, you know? In lots of ways. Being so pretty, of course, she always made Helen feel less than what she was. And imagine having to take care of a blind girl your whole life. I was glad for a minute when Helen told me Rachel ran off. That's the truth, and I'm ashamed of it. But I figured Helen would be happier because of it. Turns out the opposite."

Digby shook his head. He could hear the dogs outside, barking like crazy: it sounded like they were about to break down the door.

Jonas's mind turned rabid circles in his head. "I had this dream, I guess you'd call it, that one day Helen and me, we'd have a family. Where do you see those anymore? Just a plain little family. We'd live in the big house on the hill there and have babies and start over from scratch. Us. This town, everything. The way he did it. You know."

"Elijah McCallister," Digby said.

"Yeah. Him. I thought we'd make a new Roam the same way he

made the old one. But *better*. She's smart, you know, Helen is, and I'm good with my hands and I don't care what anybody says, you *know* that's true. I can build anything or fix anything that's been built or broke. I thought that we could take what's left of this place, help clean it up, and make it good again. Make it *nice*." Jonas sighed. "That's what life is, isn't it? Making a world all your own inside the one that's given you, together with someone else?"

"Like what happened in my little tavern here," Digby said. He looked over at Fang and He-Ping and the others, who made their home here, living and dead. Once there was a baby born to a woman named Patricia Sing, right there on the barroom floor. A baby, at Digby's! Jonas was right. Life is about making worlds.

"I don't know what I'm going to do," Jonas said.

"My friend," said Digby. "A man is sometimes required to do things he'd rather not, in part because he is a man and has no real choice in the matter either way."

Jonas let that set, and then, after it did, he nodded. "That's true," he said. "That's really true." And then Jonas started thinking. Digby could see it happen right in front of him; he could see that something had clicked, a candle was lit, a universe of possibility born. "But if I find her," Jonas said, "if I find Rachel, everything would change. Helen would love me then, wouldn't she, Digby?"

Digby was about to say, *Gratitude and love are two different things.* He was going to say exactly that until he looked at Jonas and saw the hope Jonas had in this new plan; everything was now riding on it.

"She would love you then, yes," Digby said. "I'm sure of it, my friend."

Jonas said he thought so, too. Then he looked around at all the pictures on the wall.

"If I'm your friend," he said, "how come you never took me fishing?"

Digby clapped a hand on his shoulder. "I didn't know you fished!" He tried to seem sincere, because that was his job, wasn't it? That's how he got people to come in and talk to him and drink. That's how he made a living, by seeming to be sincere. It was the life he'd been given, and there were times—many times—he wished for more.

Jonas stood and pulled up his jeans. The stub of a pencil rested near an order pad, and he picked it up and scribbled "I.O.U." and signed his name.

"Rachel left hours ago," Jonas said. "She could be anywhere. The chances of finding her seem pretty slim, but I have to try. I have to."

"Use my dogs."

It was Smith, the lumberjack. It was as many words as Digby had ever heard him use in succession. Though the voice couldn't have been more powerful, or the words spoken with more conviction, the utterance seemed to linger in the air for a moment before being absorbed by either of the men.

"Dogs?" Jonas finally asked.

"My dogs will save her," Smith said. "I don't know if they'll bring her back, but if she's alive they will save her. They saved me."

Smith stood up, filling the bar with his gargantuan mass, as though he expanded to the size of the space he was given. His sunken eyes, nearly lost in the shadows of his face, moved back and forth from Digby to Jonas. He was wearing a long coat made from deerskin stitched together with cat guts (his dogs killed a lot of cats), and his boots were of hardened leather and bigger than Digby's torso. It was as if a new wall had suddenly arisen, turning one room into two.

"Okay," Jonas said. "We can follow them on out. But no matter what happens: it's me who brings her back. It's me who gets the credit. How's that sit with you, Smith?"

Smith didn't bother to answer. He turned and left the bar and went outside, and in a moment the dogs' howling grew more and more distant, as if Smith had told them what he wanted them to do and they were off doing it. Jonas followed quickly behind him. Then Digby hopped down from the bar, grabbed his coat and hat (the night had brought a nip with it), and turned to Fang and He-Ping.

"Don't burn the place down," Digby said.

And off they went—a near-midget, a possible giant, and one tough, reedy man—in search of a blind girl, at night, with a pack of dogs running on ahead, tearing into the darkness fearlessly, as though there was nothing they couldn't see.

# THE SEARCH

*T*he birds would have devoured her by now, removed the meat from her bones, and left the rest for the Terrible Forest Beetle, a black, hard-shelled, eight-legged animal bigger than her head, traveling silent and unseen through the piney underbrush, waiting for leftovers just like her. Each bird would have taken its favorite part: some like the arms, others the neck. *It would happen in an instant*, Helen had told her once, *but an instant that seemed to last a lifetime.* Each incarnation of the story revealed new ways to scare the living hell out of Rachel. *Their claws, sharp as broken glass. Your hair, they use to make their nests. Your eyes— they may not want your eyes at all, seeing as how they're dead already.*

And Rachel said nothing, because the story filled her heart with such fear that there were no words for it anymore. *All you could hear would be their silent wings, slashing through the air, and then a darkness even darker than the dark you live in. That's what death is.*

Now out there in the world, Rachel would be waiting for this to happen, and when it didn't, when death didn't come, what would she think? Sadder still, of course, sadder than any story Helen could tell, would be that her sister was at the bottom of that ravine, dead. But even if she were alive, Helen's life wasn't going to be the same: dead or alive, Rachel would be lost to her. A world without Rachel—and without the world she had taught Rachel to believe was real—was a world she didn't know how to live in.

"*T*wo people?" she said to Jonas when they arrived on her porch. "That's it?" She'd seen the lanterns, strange lights tethered to nothing, bobbing up the hill in the darkness, and went out to meet them.

"I tried for more," Jonas said, "but no one came. Goddamn Archie Yates slammed the door in my—"

"It doesn't matter," she said, believing it: one person could find a dead body. She could have gotten more people herself but thought she should stay at the house, in case Rachel wandered back. She looked at Digby, then at the lumberjack, who stood just behind Jonas. Digby looked like a child in the dark, especially standing next to the lumberjack—Smith, his name was. Smith.

"At your service, Miss McCallister," Digby said, almost bowing. "It's a desperate night to meet again, after so long."

So long. She hadn't remembered the last time she saw the tiny barkeep. She had never learned to drink. Perhaps she would now.

Smith didn't say anything. He looked rooted there, unmovable. Then he scraped his boots on the porch step.

"How long ago did she leave?" Digby asked her.

"Hours," she said. "Maybe three."

"She could be far," he said.

"Or maybe not," Jonas said. "She could be walking in circles. She's blind; she's never been in the forest. She could be close."

"The dogs will find her," Smith said.

"Dogs?" she said.

"Lumberjack Smith sent his dogs on ahead," Digby said.

"How could they possibly help?"

"Dogs know," Smith said. "These dogs, they know."

"He has complete confidence in their abilities," Digby said. "Our job will be to follow their lead. In a way, then, we're not merely four, we're much, much—"

"It doesn't matter," she said. "We should go."

"We talked about it," Jonas said. He was trying to be the leader now. "We'll split up. You and me, we'll go out past the graveyard. Digby and Smith will cross the field. We'll meet up at the ravine."

"Fine," she said, stepping off the porch. She took a lantern from Jonas and began walking, and the rest of them followed her until they came to the end of the drive, and then two walked one way, and two another, into the dark forest.

$S$he could hear the dogs now, howling. They'd been howling like this all night, and maybe she hadn't heard them because she was thinking about Rachel so intently, or maybe because it seemed that, since Lumberjack Smith moved here a year ago, there had always been some sort of howling, some dog always seemed to have something it wanted to say. Now that she was listening, it sounded like the dogs were talking to one another. One howled and another answered, and then another. They were everywhere.

Jonas trailed a step or two behind her, then caught up and matched her gait. He'd push the branches out of the way, or hold one up for Helen to walk under, and she could feel him looking at her, waiting for a glance, a nod, something. But she wouldn't give it to him. She blamed him for what happened today. She knew it wasn't his fault, but there was so much rage and anger and sadness and hopelessness and shame banging against one another in her heart, she had to have someone help her with the burden of all these emotions, and that was Jonas.

"I saw the car," he said to her as they walked. "By the tree. I could have fixed it and driven here, but it needs a part. Must have fallen off. Would have had to go back to the shop to get it, and it was getting on dark, so I figured I'd go back and fix it later. Maybe tomorrow."

Helen kept walking. She didn't say anything, because there was nothing to say. She wasn't in the mood for small talk, but then she never was, especially with Jonas.

"Why'd you leave me there?" he said. Twigs snapped beneath their feet in the absence of an answer. As Jonas was looking at her, he ran into a tree. Pitiful. She kept walking. He caught up with her again. "I don't know what I did."

"Nothing," Helen said, finally.

"Nothing? Then why—"

"It doesn't *matter*," Helen said, and realized she'd said that a few times tonight already. "You didn't *do* anything. I had to get back. I knew something like this was going to happen. It's like leaving the house and thinking, *Did I blow out that candle? Is the house going to burn down? Should I go back and make sure?* I had to go back. You . . . you didn't do a thing."

"Good," he said. "Because if I did do something and you told me what it was, I wouldn't do it again."

"*Rachel!*" Helen yelled as loud as she could. "*Rachel!*"

"*Rachel!*" Jonas bellowed.

In the distance they heard Digby crying out the same.

There was, of course, no answer, because she was likely dead and she couldn't answer. But even if she were dead they needed to find her body. Helen was not going to leave it out here for the buzzards. To think of her sister facedown at the bottom of that ravine tore a fissure through her own heart. They called again and listened to the dogs and were quiet for the next few minutes.

"How far is it?" she said.

"To where?"

"To the ravine, Jonas."

"Oh. Not far." He stopped. "You think that's where she is, don't you?" She looked up at Jonas. The lantern made his face appear solemn and shadowy, his green eyes reflecting the light like the moon. She leaned her shoulder into his chest and he draped an arm around her, pulling her closer, tighter. She shook, but she didn't know what it was that was making her shake, whether it was the tears or something else. He had never held her like this, not in all the years they had been with each other. She felt like she had just met somebody new in the dark woods, someone she had mistaken for somebody else.

"Look," he said.

He gently pushed her away and turned her to one side and pointed at the straw-covered ground, and she held the lantern outstretched for a better view.

A shoe. Small, white, taped together—Rachel's shoe. Helen picked it up and brought it close to her face, as if it might yield a clue; maybe there would be blood on it. There was no blood. It was just her shoe, and Rachel had lost it as she walked and couldn't find it when she went back for it. Or maybe she was running from something chasing her. Helen's mind kept spinning the darkest tales—but then that was Helen, who she was, the kind of tales she told.

"I made up a place," she said to Jonas. "A river. I told her it was across the ravine. And then those boys, talking about the bridge. That's why she did this. It's my fault. Everything is my fault."

"No," he said. "You just made up a story. You didn't tell her to come out here. She did that. We'll find her, Helen. Don't worry."

She'd never heard Jonas use that tone of voice before: it was so warm, so comforting, a voice she wanted to believe in. She almost took his hand. Instead, Helen held on to the shoe with one hand and the lantern with the other, and they kept walking, calling out Rachel's name, following the howls.

They weren't too much farther when a dog up ahead started barking like crazy. Helen had never heard a bark like that before. Wild—and beckoning, or so she wanted to think.

"Jonas, do you—"

"I hear it, too," Jonas said. "I think it means something. I think it means—"

Helen looked at Jonas and saw the hope on his face. He was squinting into the patch of woods before them. "I see something," he said. "Do you see that?" He pointed straight ahead.

Helen looked. She may have seen something; it was hard to tell. She may have just told herself she did because she wanted to so much, wanted to see Rachel standing there in the woods before them. She did see Digby and Smith, the light from their lantern anyway, floating in the dark some five hundred yards away. It looked ghostly.

"Rachel?" Jonas said, and when there was no answer he walked ahead, toward whatever it was he thought he saw, saying, "Rachel, Rachel?" over and over again.

"Hold up," Helen said to his back. "Take the light."

Instead of stopping he began to run. "It's not far," he said, then called, "If she's here I want to find her for you," and just like that he disappeared into the inky black woods, invisible, not even a shadow anymore. She heard him, though, the branches cracking beneath his boots. "It was just right here," he yelled. "Can you see anything? It's just—"

Then something happened. He didn't scream, but there was the sound of surprise, like the sound you make when you accidentally drop a glass, say, or forget your hat and have to go back inside the house for it. Sort of like, *Whoops.*

"Jonas?"

Nothing. Helen took a few steps, and with each step the light broke through the darkness a little more, but beyond it there was only more darkness and the trees, the branches scraping across her cheeks and pulling her hair as she walked faster, calling out his name, and still nothing. She took one more small step and was fortunate to have had the lantern, because she had come to the ravine, and there was no light bright enough to show any more than the edge of that: beyond the edge was black like the night sky.

"Jonas?" she said, the word barely passing her lips. She couldn't call for him, because she knew he couldn't call back, that he had fallen and was a puddle of meat and blood at the bottom, alongside Rachel.

"Helen?" Jonas said.

His voice was just as soft as her own and came from the ravine itself, and she carefully held the lantern outward, above the abyss. All she could see was his face, shining, looking up at her. It was as if there were nothing left of him but his face, three or four feet away.

"You fell," she said.

"I didn't fall," he said. "I tripped and slid over the edge and lucky for me there was this—I don't know what it is. But I'm standing on it."

She lowered the lantern a bit and saw that he was standing on what appeared to be an outcropping of slate, or shale. He could fit on it only by turning his feet sideways. He was holding on to a thick vine rooted to the red clay walls of the ravine, and that's all she was able to see: everything else around and below him was black solid dark. His whole body was shaking, vibrating, as if from cold. But it wasn't cold.

"I'm lucky," he said. "One step left or right and that would have been it for me."

Only Jonas would think that. "Very lucky," she said. But she heard the tremor in her voice, the fragile breath the words were borne on. They didn't have much time here.

"Dead," he said. "I would have been dead." He laughed. "I thought I was falling all the way down, but even when I didn't, I started missing things I would have started missing if I'd fallen and died."

"Jonas. Not now."

"Like seeing your face," he said, looking at her the same way she was looking at him. She couldn't argue with him now, or dismiss him, or laugh at him the way she always did—laugh at him not because he was funny, but because he was an idiot. Things changed when you were looking at a man standing in midair, suspended in darkness above a ravine.

"Please don't talk," she said. "Give me your hand."

The space between them was the length of their arms. She put down the shoe and the lantern and with her right hand took Jonas's hand and with all the strength she had in her body pulled him upward. But he didn't move, not even a little. She pulled again until she felt like her arm was going to leave its socket. She let go of his hand and picked up the lantern and held it over the edge of the ravine to see his face, and he was smiling now, though it was a different smile from any she had ever seen on his face before.

"This is like my life," he said, "being here. I can either go up or down. That's how it works for everybody, I guess. And I've been going down for such a long time. But I want to go up now, Helen. Up."

She stood and looked down toward the field edge and saw the light and called out as loud as she could, *"Digby!"* As loud as anybody could. *"Digby, Smith!"*

The light stopped moving: they had heard her. She didn't have to say more; already she could see the light hurrying toward her, toward them.

"It's going to be okay," she said. "They're coming. Smith—he'll be able to fish you out of there, no problem."

"Hand me the lantern," Jonas said.

"Why?"

"Just hand it to me. I want to show you something."

She gave Jonas the lantern, and he showed her what he wanted her to see. The shelf he was standing on was thin, and fragile, and the vine he was holding was pulling away from the clay strand by strand.

"I don't know where they are," he said, "but I hope they're close."

"They are," she said. "They're coming."

"Good," he said, and he seemed to believe her. He shook his head and considered things for a moment. "I really wanted to find her," he said. "For you. Or maybe . . . for me. So I could show you I wasn't who you thought I was. Or that I was more than who you thought I was."

"I know," she said.

"Give me your hand," he said.

"I can't pull you up."

"That's not why I want to hold it."

He let go of the vine and took her hand. He'd never held it tighter. "I like this view," he said, "with the light coming up like this from me to you. Where are they now?"

She looked. They didn't appear to be much closer. The lantern light was just as small as before, just as distant.

"Coming," she said. "They'll be here soon."

Then the shale cracked, and she could see one half of it drop away; he only had room for one foot now. She looked into his eyes, and it was as if he had already fallen. His eyes had a nervous excitement to them, like he was taking a trip to a place he'd never been before. It was just like he was thinking about what came next, and wondering how things were going to be different in this new place.

"Oh," he said, "oh, shit," knowing before it happened that the rest of the shale had broken and below him was nothing but a long way to fall. *Oh, shit*: his last words. He let go of her hand, but he held on to the lantern, and for a long, long time—a lifetime—she watched him recede into the depths of the night, unable to scream or even move, as if he were falling into the mouth of a monster. He watched her, too, but she would have disappeared long before he did. All he could have seen were the stars, their ancient light, cold, distant, remote, dead.

$\mathcal{T}$hey would never find Rachel. Not that night and not the next day. Though they were sure she would be at the bottom of the ravine, probably not far from Jonas, she wasn't: only his body lay broken, horribly broken, on top of a boulder beside the stream. Smith climbed down and put him in a bag and hauled him back to town, and they buried him behind the church, the church doors that hadn't even been opened for the last fifteen years.

A couple of days later, Jonas came by the tavern, as Digby hoped he would. He was the same as he had been in life—reedy, skin stretched taut against his bones—except that he had the same smoky grayness all of the spirits did, the same passive acceptance of this permanent change. Jonas was there in the morning when Digby opened up and there in the evening when Digby locked the doors. He sat at the bar and listened to Digby tell his stories. One day Digby asked Jonas about Helen, and whether he'd seen her. But Jonas just shook his head. "That's something I can't do just yet," he said. "For me to see her and her not to see me, I don't know if I could stand that. Because I was never happier in my life than when

I was falling, because I knew she loved me then. I could see it, the way she couldn't stop looking at me. She never stopped looking, not until I disappeared."

Smith went back to his encampment at the edge of town. All of his dogs had left that night but for one. He liked to think that this was the first dog, the dog that had started it all, but he had no way of knowing. Smith and the dog slept in the same bed, and in the morning Smith would find himself holding her against his chest. Waking early, he watched the rising sun burn past the tops of the trees on the mountain. He tried to count how many trees were there, but he couldn't count that high. He could hear the trees calling out to him: *Cut me down!* they seemed to be saying. *Cut me down!* He heeded their call. That very day he left Roam and went back to the mountain, where he resumed his life as a lumberjack with his lumberjack brothers. He was almost happy after that, or as happy as a lumberjack could be, which was never as happy as other people sometimes were.

For the next month, Helen looked for Rachel every day. She looked for the other shoe, some article of clothing Rachel had been wearing, her skirt, her blouse, but Helen never found anything, no clue to what happened to her sister at all. Not finding her allowed Helen to imagine sometimes that Rachel could still be alive somewhere, but there was no way that could be true. To believe in that was a lie, and Helen was giving up on telling lies, to herself or to anybody else.

She kept to herself—not that there was anyone to keep herself from anymore; only a few dozen scattered families remained, faces and names she knew but didn't need to know any better. The grocery store was still open, stocked with food people grew, which others bought or bartered for. When she went down there, she'd say hello to people, but not much more than that. It was a dark and dreary town, and living in it was like living in the windowless basement of an abandoned house. She supposed this was the way it was with the world, the coming and going, the rise and fall of people and places. Roam was no different in that way from anywhere else.

But she didn't think about these sorts of things very much. Instead she thought of Rachel, and of Jonas; she thought of birds and dogs and the other shoe. She thought over and over again of that night, of holding Jonas's hand before he fell. Digby and Smith didn't get there for another minute or two; they might as well have taken forever. Later that night, after Digby walked her back, she had him leave her at the bottom of the drive, because what was there to rush home to? Nothing.

But as she got closer, she saw that every light in the house was on. Every light. She hadn't left it that way, had she? She couldn't remember. Her house was the brightest place in Roam. Maybe Rachel had come back, she thought, maybe while they were out looking for her . . .

But Rachel wasn't there. Rachel was gone: Helen felt that, literally, in her bones. Their life together had turned them into one thing, that *girl,* and a part of Helen was missing now: this is how she knew. She made it to the porch, where a tear caught itself on an eyelash. She couldn't breathe. The bright, empty house loomed before her, bigger than it had ever seemed before. She couldn't go in. She stood there, staring at the house where she'd lived with her sister, with her family, a house built by the man who had built everything else in Roam, and suddenly there were ghosts, ghosts all around her, slowly converging. No: that was just the fog. The fog was as white as smoke. She watched it curl around her ankles like manacles, slip up her legs and under her dress and all around and over her. The fog crawled into her mouth and down into her body. And she fell. She fell to her knees on the rocky drive, and without knowing how or to whom, or what good could possibly come from it, she began to pray.

PART II

# MARKUS

e found the body in the woods behind the Peach Blossom Motel, the first motel he'd seen in his whole life. He thought the hotel was going to be better than it was, but it was mostly wretched, so wretched that seeing a body in the woods behind it did not shock him as much as it should have. The room itself was like a crypt, small, dark, and dank. The mattress was no more than a piece of pressed wood with a sheet stapled to it. A hole in the ceiling oozed some sort of syrupy brown liquid that pooled in a corner and (no matter how many times he soaked it up with the bathroom towels) streamed malevolently toward him across the floor. He slept with the light on because he knew that the dark would prove to be no more than an invitation to the vermin he heard inhabiting the walls, and he declined to remove his suit, uncomfortable enough during the day (it was a hand-me-down), which that night in the motel seemed to gradually shrink

further, especially around the area of his crotch. But he wouldn't remove a stitch: there was no lock on the door, and if someone were to come in and try to kill him in the night he wanted to be dressed for it. He didn't want to be discovered dead and half-dressed, his hairless body splayed across the floor, his bony chest a figure of fun to the awful men who would remove his carcass with all the care they would take with a bag of flour.

Oh, how he hoped he didn't die in the night!

Frankly, he had expected more from the outside world than the Peach Blossom Motel, and yet what more that was, what he hoped for exactly, even he couldn't say. His name was Markus Kennerly. He was nineteen years old.

In the Valley, people talked about the outside world all the time, and when they did it was with a mixture of reverence, fear, and revulsion, as though their own impossibly remote dip in the earth was the only completely good place one could be. No, his people said, the Valley didn't have much to offer. Electricity hadn't come that far; there were no telephones. A hard day's work was a hard day's work, no matter which way you cut it, and there was no getting under, around, or over that. But what the Valley did have was a real community where the load was shared equally and the people were honest and if you needed a chicken there was always a chicken, no questions asked. All you had to do was kill it.

But you still had to wonder, looking at the mountains looming over this dark place, how your people ended up in the Valley at all. Many of the homes were built at weird angles to the rise of the hills, and when it rained, great sheets of water came rushing down the mountain, sweeping away your hut, your food, the occasional loosely tethered youngster. The summers were scalding, the winters cold and damp, spiders grew hideously large and insidiously aggressive, and a thick green moss covered everything left too long unattended. Women too old to do anything else became moss-scrapers, and when someone became a moss-scraper you knew it wouldn't be long before she was gone. His mother was a moss-scraper right now.

So why the Valley? Why settle in this dark sad place?

It was the place where his great-grandfather's horses had died. His great-grandfather, Ming Kai.

# ROAM:
# A SHORT HISTORY,
# PART IV

A s Elijah McCallister lay dying, firing shot after shot into what he hoped was Ming Kai's head or back or both, he did not miss by much. But it was enough for Ming Kai to know that there must be a reason fate would not allow him to be killed that day. The bullets came too close to miss, and yet they *did* miss: for a few brief moments, Ming Kai was immortal. With his hand on the jeweled doorknob he paused and waited either for his friend to stop shooting at him or to die. Neither happened. The gun kept clicking even after all the bullets were gone. *Click click click.* It was that pathetic sound that touched Ming Kai the most, Elijah's desire not to see him go persisting long after he had already gone. He heard it even after he left the room, and took a deep breath, and left his best friend behind.

He had already packed a wagon with all of his belongings and food, including flour, bacon, rice, coffee, sugar, dried beans, dried fruit, honey, salt, vinegar. His replacement family sat in the wagon, patiently waiting. They had been a good replacement family. He had learned to love them. He climbed up, took the reins and snapped them, and without looking back even once slowly rode away.

They rode in silence for an hour until Ming Kai abruptly stopped. There didn't appear to be a reason—they were in the middle of no-where—but he stopped and stared ahead into nothing.

"Ming Kai," his replacement wife said. "What is it?"

"Oh. Nothing," he said. But it was something. He stopped because he realized he had no idea where he was or where he was going. He wasn't sure how far this road went before it stopped being a road at all. Then what would they do? And what would they do if it *didn't* stop? What if this were one of the roads Elijah had begun and then abandoned?

No matter. He snapped the reins again and off they went, into the mystery.

*T*he horses died on the sixth day.

They had paused at a small stream for water. The horses drank. One of his replacement sons had climbed down to fill a canteen, and when the first horse keeled over it fell on his son's right leg, break-ing it in two places. The boy let out a cry that echoed through the Valley and came back to them sharper and stronger than when it left his mouth.

His replacement wife would never forgive Ming Kai for what hap-pened next: he attended to the horse first. Not because he didn't love his replacement son; he did. But even if his replacement son were to lose that leg and live his life out as a one-legged Chinese man in some faraway American city, selling potions from a wooden cart on the cor-ner of a busy sidewalk, it was better that the horse live; if it didn't, the chance that his son would ever get to that city, with or without his legs, was very slim. So he looked first at the horse.

It was dead.

"Locoweed," Ming Kai said, pulling a green stem from the horse's mouth. "Must have eaten it on the trail."

The last few miles, the road had become narrower and narrower and the going slower and slower, and the horses had been pulling up weeds growing at the edge of the forest and eating them. Ming Kai hadn't worried about it because he was worrying about so many other things, mostly having to do with his own life and the life of this family and what would happen to them. He wanted to give them a better life than the one they were leaving behind, and now he had serious doubts as to whether this was going to happen. He was feeling less and less sanguine about his decision to leave Roam, and yet, at the same time, he couldn't imagine going back. And now here they were with one dead horse and a boy with a broken leg, in a steep, densely wooded valley as distant from any one place as it was from another. How could things get any worse?

The other horse died then, and when it fell it turned the cart over, spilling all of their supplies along with Ming Kai's replacement wife to the damp and mossy forest floor. She was fine, though, and scrambled to her feet to save what she could of their food, while the boy continued to cry out as though inch by inch his skin were being removed from his body and his naked flesh covered in pepper flakes.

It was at this inopportune moment that Ming Kai had an epiphany: he had never really *done* anything, had he? Everything had been done *to* him. He was knocked out and put on a boat and brought to America. He was given this second family. And he was forced into doing McCallister's bidding for the last twenty-five years. (Or was it fifty? It seemed like forever.) He'd done nothing on his own—nothing.

He wandered off to investigate the parameters of their new world, one thought before all others in his mind: if McCallister could make something out of nothing, so could he.

But he couldn't. In fact, they would have died within the week if not for the other families who, also fleeing the end of their lives in Roam, followed Ming Kai's trail, hoping that he might know where he was going. When they ended up in the same situation, dead horses and all, what could they do but agree that this was where they'd make a new home and start their new lives?

A home never materialized—ever—not in the sense that Roam was a home. Not in the sense of a real community, with a main street and shops and like-minded women who met every Thursday night to knit and talk about their children while their husbands went to the bars and caroused and on Sunday rested, sleeping late into the morning. No. By the time these families arrived they were worn-out, nearly hopeless. America had proven to be a huge disappointment, and not just to the Chinese who had come here, but even to the white people. The Chinese would have returned to China if they could've, but they had no idea how: they could no longer even smell the ocean in the Valley, and the Chinese could smell the ocean from a long way away. In every way there was, they were lost.

Ming Kai wanted to take all his people from this dark land, but without horses, how far could they go? Elijah would never have allowed the world to stop him from achieving his dream—yet this was the essence of Ming Kai's dilemma: his only dream had been to leave Roam, and he had achieved that. Now what?

Ming Kai paced the Valley, thoughtful, melancholy, like a king without a kingdom, and tried to find something good, something he could point to and say, *Here. This. This is why I have chosen this place instead of another.* But there was nothing like that to point to in the Valley. Were they to forge ahead, surely they would discover a better place; he had seen such places himself, many years before. But the truth was simply this: Ming Kai was afraid.

"No," he muttered to himself. "No. We must leave, today."

And it was then, the moment he decided to dream a new dream, that he found the cave.

The entrance was blanketed by vines and was just big enough for a single person to slip through. A sound had drawn his attention, an intimation of the familiar amid the mysteries beyond. He knew the sound well; he'd heard it as a child back in Nanking when the rains would come and everything would flood. It was the sound of a river, a powerful river.

He pushed the vines away and stepped inside the cave.

As his eyes adjusted to the gloom the cavern walls appeared to glow in starry patches on the surface of the rocky walls—white, green, blue, gold. It was like being inside the mind of a dreaming man. The river had carved a giant hallway through the rocky earth, a natural path on a gentle slope leading deeper and deeper into the underground world. He followed it down to the river. He could see the cave dust enter his own mouth and disappear; his skin *glowed*. He moved carefully down the rocky path, deeper and deeper into the underground world, the river becoming louder and louder in his ears, until finally he saw it. It was like a monster, tearing past him, moving from the darkness behind it to the darkness ahead. It looked like an enormous snake, with no end and no beginning—a never-ending river. Were he to step into the river he would have disappeared into it, without even a moment to take a breath. And he thought about doing just that.

But there was a small pool adjacent to the river. He knelt, and touched it. It was cold, and full of those starry sparkles floating in it like effervescent tadpoles. He cupped his hands and brought a bit of it to his lips. He had never tasted water like this: he could feel the bright granules on his tongue, but after a moment they melted into a sweetness. Following the slope of the soil he could see the bottom of the pool. It was enough for a man to bathe in it. Ming Kai let the water drip from his hands until all of it returned to the pool. A source of water, he was thinking; perhaps a place to bathe. Good.

But then he looked at his hands. They had changed. All of the scars and calluses and wrinkles were gone. He had the hands of a young man, soft and smooth. He was not imagining it, or hallucinating in the dim light. It was real and true. What was this water? He had cut his arm on a branch that morning, not deeply, but he could see the dried blood and the open wound, and so, in thoughtless wonder, he applied the water to it like a salve, and he watched as the wound disappeared. He took a quick step away from the pool, suddenly afraid of what might happen if he let the water touch him again. He didn't trust it. Magic is dangerous: it's neither good nor bad, right nor wrong; it can be both a blessing and a curse. It takes strength, the strength of a man, to make the magic his own, to make it serve him, and not the other way around.

He had much to think about as he turned and made his way back to his world.

*A*s he walked out of the cave, waiting for him were his replacement wife, his replacement sons, and some of the others, about ten of his people altogether. They stared at him.

"What happened?" his replacement wife said. "I thought you were dead."

She seemed neither happy nor sad to see this was not the case.

"What's down there?" she asked him.

"Hear that?" said one of the others. "It sounds like a river."

"And look," one of the others said. "Ming Kai's hair glows. What is it you found inside the cave, Ming Kai? Tell us."

Ming Kai wiped the last of the glittery cave crystals off his arms and spit. "Nothing," he said. "Nothing but the bones of the dead."

*T*hey did not leave the Valley. They grew some food and they killed some squirrels and sometimes something even bigger like a bear. But there were no schools and there were no stores. Little was created; objects just moved around from shack to lean-to, depending on who needed what, when. When it rained, most everything got wet, and when someone died they buried them in the grove in a plot close to where Ming Kai buried his horses. Where Roam had forced the forest out, Ming Kai's settlement appeared to wedge itself uncomfortably within it, day after day asking for permission to exist.

The people there had children, and their children had children, and before long it was difficult to remember who belonged to which family, or why that was so important, and there were times when a man and a woman came together who shared the same bloodline and whose children proved it. Whole crops of these offspring wandered through the Valley, some disappearing into the mossy dark, others hovering like ghosts behind stands of trees. They'd broken or buried all of the mirrors they'd brought with them, because no one wanted to see what they'd become; they carried within them the image of what they might have been had things gone differently, had Ming Kai taken a different road out of Roam, or taken a right turn instead of a left, or if doubt hadn't made him pause briefly so that his horses could eat a bit of that locoweed.

But Ming Kai was a good man. His people would follow him anywhere. As little as they liked the place they had ended up, they followed him, because over time he proved to them that he knew things. Magic, spells, potions that cured them from sickness and kept them from pain. The old magic the rest of them had forgotten or never knew, Ming Kai kept *up here*, he said, pointing to his head. *I keep the magic up here.* They loved him for that; they respected him. They came to Ming Kai for his miracles, brief moments of wonder punctuating the infinite dreariness of their lives. It was the water from the cave, of course, bowls of which he kept in his hut, to help soothe the souls of the people he had doomed to this dark, dank life.

He never told them about the water. He wanted to believe that one day they would leave the Valley, and if he told them about the water he knew they never would. But a secret like that was too big to live inside just one man; he had to tell someone. So he told the old woman Liling, who in turn told Markus. Markus had yet to tell anybody. But then he had yet to know anyone he wanted to tell.

*M*arkus was the product of the marriage of Ming Kai's grandson Norton and a white girl named Kelly. Kelly had long, stringy yellow hair and dark brown freckles, and had worked at the silk factory all of her life. Norton had fallen in love with Kelly years ago, when he worked in the factory, too. He was too shy to even talk to her in Roam, but when he saw her arrive in the Valley on the back of a cart his heart flew to her. Her face was blank, and she'd not bathed in weeks. But Norton knew the woman asleep inside her, and he was determined to awaken her. They were married two weeks later, in one of the first formal ceremonies of its kind in the Valley. On their wedding night he took her to his lean-to and she lay on a bed of straw and he made love to her. He made love to her often, but it took her ten years to become pregnant. This was Markus. She died in childbirth, and Norton died, too, not long after from a snakebite. Markus was raised by an old Chinese woman named Liling, whom he would know and forever think of as his mother.

In spite of this, Markus thrived. He was slight, but strong. After

Ming Kai's replacement wife grew tired of taking care of her slowly dying husband, Markus took over, turning him in his bed of sticks and straw twice a day to guard against bedsores, and feeding him, and cleaning him with a wet rag dipped in the magic water. The tales Ming Kai told Markus! By the time he was twelve—nineteen years after Ming Kai had taken to his deathbed—Markus could recount the entirety of his great-grandfather's life, year to year, month to month, almost day to day. Ming Kai's early life in China, his adult life in Roam, the love and hatred (each in equal portions) that he had for Elijah McCallister—Markus knew this all so well he could have told the stories himself, verbatim. He could feel his great-grandfather's grief and disappointment, that he had been given but one life and that this is the way it had gone for him, and his heart broke for him.

But when Ming Kai told Markus about Roam, something inside the boy sparked. It was as if Markus were born with the idea of what the ideal world might look like, and Roam coincided with that idea perfectly. Markus dreamed of Roam—not as something created but as something *discovered,* a place that had existed forever, and when Ming Kai and Elijah McCallister built it they weren't really making something new, they were carving out of the earth and the air the eternal design of Home. Roam had real streets, and on the streets there were shops, and on others there were houses, and in the houses were people who had hopes and dreams and a chance of making their dreams come true. They didn't always come true, but at least they had a chance.

The sad stories Ming Kai told were not about the past: they were about the future. They always began, *When I go home. When I go home I will build another small cart, and I will sell what I make in the marketplace. Our home will be small, but dry, and warm. Perhaps I will have another child? Perhaps. I say this because with my wife there has always been such love. Such love. To walk again in the land I came from. I would swim there if I could, but I can't. All I need is a boat. A small boat, enough for me and one other—you, Markus. You. You and me in a boat going home.*

Markus said, *I will build you a boat.*

So Markus built a boat. Markus gathered the men of the Valley together and told them Ming Kai's sad tale. He stood on the hillside, on a tree stump, looking down on them all; they stared at one another blankly, and kicked at the dirt with their feet. There was a routine in the Valley, and the routine had much to do with doing nothing. They lived without the will to live. Ming Kai had brought them here, to this place, and now Markus expected them to build him a boat? Why? The ocean wasn't even within smelling distance.

Markus saw all this in their faces.

"He is a good man," Markus told them. "He was knocked over the head and kidnapped, and was brought here against his will. You followed him to the Valley on your own! It's not his fault you're here. You could leave at any time. And yet you don't. None of us do, because we're scared that something even worse is on the other side of the mountain. The least we could do is build a boat for him."

"I will help you build your boat," Chang Perkins said. "But only if he takes me with him."

"You're not from China," Markus said. "Why would you want to go there?"

"My mother is from China," he said. "She says there's no place better."

Edwin Corn said, "I'll help, but I want to go, too. I've heard good things about China."

Huan Stone said the same thing.

"Then we will build a boat big enough for Ming Kai, Chang, Huan, and Edwin, a boat big enough and strong enough for us all."

●    ●    ●

$\mathcal{I}$t took five years to build the boat. Five years as Markus and the three men cut and hewed and nailed and pounded and cursed and laughed. They made a clearing just fifteen yards from Ming Kai's small hut and they worked on the boat every day, even if some days it was just a little, just a nail or two. Edwin Corn knew something about boatbuilding. He'd made a canoe once, many years before. He carved it out of a tree with a knife, a spoon, and a whole lot of muscle—but it worked. He and his father paddled around the Big Green Lake in it. Then he built a raft by tying together a bunch of tree limbs with silk, and the raft floated well. He put his dog on it for a practice run and the raft floated around the lake bend, out of sight, and when he finally found it lodged against the bank and a gnarled bunch of tree roots his dog was gone, and he never saw him again. Then he built an actual boat, with a hull and a bow and sails and everything—everything a boat needs to be a boat. It was a miniature boat; he couldn't have even fit his dog in it, if he still had a dog. He could only fit a palmetto bug. So he put the palmetto bug on the boat—tied it there with some silk— and launched it into the green. It floated away, moved quite nicely across the water. He could imagine, he said, that if the lake were the ocean and everything else was relative to it, his boat would be about the right size. Then the palmetto bug escaped, and when it jumped into the water the boat capsized, a fish ate the bug, and the boat sank.

These were some of the stories that were told while they were building the boat in the Valley.

At the end of the day, Markus would report to Ming Kai on the progress they were making. *Today we cut the mast from a giant tree*, he might tell him. Or, *We're working on the hull, to make sure no water can get through the planks.*

Ming Kai nodded. Even with his eyes open he appeared to be dreaming of the boat. He was dreaming the boat into existence. *There should be a bed on the boat*, he said. *And a kitchen. There will be,* Markus said. *I want a window in the hull, a place to watch the fish swim by. That we have already done,* said Markus. *I want a carving of a beautiful woman on the bow,* he said. *Of course!* Markus said. *Naked,* Ming Kai said. *With lovely breasts. With lovely breasts too big for my hands. Yes,* Markus said. (He would leave that part to Huan.) And then Ming Kai would close his eyes, and sleep.

Markus had no intention of finishing the boat. Whenever they were almost done Markus would find some problem that needed to be addressed—the bed wasn't big enough, the masts insufficiently strong—and they would have to start over. Two years after they'd begun, Huan Stone died (he fell and hit his head on a rock) and Edwin Corn changed his mind, deciding he'd rather stay in the Valley than take a chance on the high seas. Chang Perkins just got tired. But by that time, four years into the project, Markus had learned enough to finish—or not to finish—the job himself.

Finally, however, almost by accident he did. Markus hammered his last nail, smoothed his last plank, framed his last bulkhead. Though he had never seen a boat before, he could tell that this one could withstand the long journey to China, braving every wave and any harsh wind. The boat was perfect. With a piece of burnt wood he wrote the word *HOME* on the top of the hull, wiped his hands on his shirt, and walked the fifteen yards to tell Ming Kai the news: his boat was ready.

But Ming Kai already knew. Ming Kai knew everything. He lay on his bed of sticks, a silk blanket pulled up to his chin, shivering. He had never been a big man; age and illness had made him even smaller. His replacement wife knelt beside him, spooning water into his mouth, letting it drip all over his body. She had loved Ming Kai, though only grudgingly, because she had never forgiven him for going first to the horse when her boy had broken his leg all those many years ago.

When Ming Kai saw Markus, he smiled.

"So you are done?" he asked him.

"Finished," he said. "And it's very beautiful. I believe it is seawor-thy. I believe it will get us to China."

"I never said China."

"What?"

"I never said I wanted to go back to China. I said I wanted to go home. China is too far away in time to be my home anymore. I meant Roam."

"Oh," Markus said. "Then why—"

"A boy like you, he needs something to do with his hands. He needs to keep busy. And now look: you are a man!" This pleased Ming Kai. "Do me a small favor," he said.

"Anything."

"Make a world all your own. A new one. A world no one has seen before, no one has even imagined. Make it beautiful. Make it good."

"Only that?" Markus said, as if there were nothing easier.

They both smiled, and then Ming Kai closed his eyes.

His wife sighed. "It's okay, Ming Kai. It's okay. You said your peace. Now you can die."

That sounded like a good idea to Ming Kai. As he felt the life ebb from his body, he spent what he believed to be his last few moments thinking of his friend Elijah McCallister. It surprised him how much he missed that man, even after all the terrible things Elijah had done to him. He had kidnapped him, shipped him to a foreign country, lied to him repeatedly, and then, in a final act of friendship, tried to kill him. Ming Kai hated him, and yet he also loved him. Elijah McCallister was his father, his brother, even his wife. Not in all ways, of course, but in most. McCallister was his one true family. Together they could do anything, but apart they were doomed.

"*Die*," his replacement wife hissed. "Die and be with your pre-cious horses!"

He couldn't believe she was still thinking about this, after all these years! As he lay here dying, this is all she could think of?

But he smiled.

"Not with the horses," he said. "Not with the horses, no . . ."

Ming Kai gasped for air, a breath he didn't seem to exhale, and his eyes fluttered shut.

"He's dead," his replacement wife said, not without a little sadness. "He's dead."

A moment passed, that silent moment when the soul leaves the body. Or, rather, when it's supposed to. "No," Ming Kai said, eyes still closed. "Not dead. Sleeping so I can dream."

"Damn you," said his replacement wife. "Damn damn damn you."

*M*arkus left the hut and walked out into the night. He stood before the *Home* and knew that he would leave the Valley soon, just as Ming Kai had asked him to—not by boat, of course, but by foot. He knew who he was enough to know that he couldn't become the man he wanted to, the man Ming Kai wanted him to, by staying here. This is what the building of the boat had taught him. It had kindled inside of him a fire to see the world. He stared at the beautiful woman on the bow. He had never seen a naked woman before, but it was her eyes, not her body, that claimed him. Her eyes reflected the moonlight, bright, open wide—brave—staring hard at what lay ahead.

*T*he dog found the body, not him. He heard it barking outside the bathroom window. *Look!* That's what the bark sounded like. *Look! Look what I've found!*

The dogs had been following him since the day he set out. One or two, then more. Now there were at least six or seven. They were hard to count because all of them were black, each and every one of them, head to tail, built like wolves but smaller, mixed breeds, wild. Not a one got close enough to touch, but they were always there, darting through the woods, appearing and then disappearing again. He thought they were waiting for a good time to eat him, so he stayed close to the road, hoping the possibility of passing cars and the long flatbed trucks of the lumberjacks might deter them—the strange logic of hope and youth. Walking by the road only made him wish he had a car. One day he thought he would, but for now he was on foot, and the dogs followed behind and around him on every step. Soon he stopped being scared, because the longer he went without being killed, the more he came to believe that's not why they were there. They were there to save him.

They had saved him twice so far.

The first time the dogs saved him was three nights ago when Markus was lost in the woods. Night fell. He had nothing with him but a small sack made of silk, in which Liling had packed a blanket, a pound of dried beef, and a sour apple. He curled up beneath the overhang of a boulder, hoping he might be able to sleep and wake the next day knowing where he was. But he couldn't sleep. The night made too many sounds. It was as if he could hear the trees growing, their wooden veins straining against the bark, and ghosts pushing through the branches. He felt something crawling up his leg and he had to take his pants off to flush it out. Lying beneath a boulder with no pants on, brushing off whatever happened to be crawling up his leg, he could not imagine how life could be much worse.

That's when the bear came.

He knew about bears, of course. He had seen many in his life: there were plenty in the Valley. But this one was like nothing he'd ever heard before: each step fell like a bag of rocks, crushing everything beneath it with a predatory ease, like a hint—a promise—of what was going to happen to Markus when it found out exactly where he was. Getting eaten was not the worst that could happen, though: getting *half*-eaten and living, living somehow with only half your body—that would be the worst.

He slowly stepped away from the rock under which he was hiding, pants-less, and saw the night was not as dark as he had imagined, not black at all, but blue. With the low moon and high stars, everything around him was almost like the day, just turned inside out. He could see everything. He could see the shadow of the bear on one side of the rise. He could see its eyes just as its eyes saw him. He thought, *This is what it's like to know you're about to die.*

A dog appeared. Then another. Suddenly there were three of them, rocketing right at the bear's head. A terrible melee ensued, full of growling and dog yelps and angry bear sounds. The dogs were no match for the bear; its huge paws knocked them off, and they sailed away into the night. But the dogs weren't the least bit discouraged. They came back and went right at it, this time taking little chunks of fur and maybe more from a leg. And the bear, wondering what it did to deserve this, fell on all fours and ran away.

*T*he second time the dogs saved him was just yesterday. He had come upon this sign:

THE PEACH BLOSSOM

COOL AIR.

FREE LIGHT.

This sign excited him. The Peach Blossom itself, however, did not inspire the same enthusiasm. Five rooms in a low brick building. One big truck, its long flatbed loaded with scrap metal and rubber, was parked in front—probably a lumberjack. The office was a green door at the back of the house with the word OFFICE painted on it. Hidden in the trees, Markus cased it out for a while, because as much as he wanted a room he wanted just as much not to pay for one. He wasn't sure, but he thought that the last of his money might have fallen out of his pocket when he took his pants off the previous night. He watched a man come out of the office, one of the fattest men Markus had ever seen. Balder than bald, not a hair on his head, and no evidence there ever had been. The man went from room to room opening the doors, peering inside. He left the doors open—to air them out, maybe. Markus could see the rooms. Beds. Tables. Colorless nubby rugs. The fat man walked from one room to the other as slow as anyone had ever walked. Then the man made his way to the small house through the door marked OFFICE and was gone.

Markus slipped into one of the rooms—#3—and hid in the shower, and after the man came by just before dark and shut all the doors, as Markus had thought he would, Markus came out of the shower and watched the man disappear back into his house.

He was hungry. It was dark now. There was a light coming from the fat man's house—a moving light. He left the room and went to the man's window and saw him leaning back in a big chair watching the box Markus knew was called a television. There was a big brown television in the Valley—Markus's cousin had brought one back with him, carried it ten miles or more in his arms, and he had told them all what it would have done if there had been electricity. Markus watched the man watch the television, and then watched a bit of it himself. The man was watching a show in which cars chased each other through streets and crashed into things, but no one ever really got hurt. Many of the men were able to get out of their broken cars and make a run for it, shooting guns. No one got hurt then, either. After a minute or two someone did get shot in the arm, but you could tell he'd be okay.

Markus tried to come up with a plan that had some food in it, when the fat man leaped up from his chair and before Markus could take another breath the man was out the door and had the muzzle of a shotgun digging into Markus's chest.

His little black eyes were even less loving than that bear's two nights ago.

"Freeloader," he said. "Don't think I haven't had a bead on you since you was cowering in the woods like the jackal you are."

What could Markus say? Nothing. That's exactly what he was: a freeloader. A jackal, maybe not, but a freeloader certainly.

"I am missing my show," the man said, "which—if I didn't have reason enough—makes me feel even less kindly toward you. Look at you: no more than a boy. If I don't shoot you now what does the world have to look forward to but more of the same, a lifetime of freeloading from one such as you? Killing is wrong, but letting you live is wronger. It's a favor I do mankind, snuffing out the bad before it moves on to cause more of the same. Saying all this not for you incidentally but for me and for God, who's listening. So He knows why your life is no more worthy to continue than a—a—"

He stopped talking as his eyes turned toward something behind Markus. No time even to lower his gun before the dogs were on him.

Markus ran back to his room and shut the door. He didn't want to witness what the dogs were doing to the man: he had seen too much already, the moment their jagged teeth clamped onto his bulging neck vein. It wasn't Markus's fault—there was nothing he could have done to stop them—but even so, the image haunted him. He felt unclean, calloused, well on his way to becoming the man he had never meant to become. The next he looked the man was gone, and all that remained was a purple stain in the gravel.

•     •     •

*I*t was the next day when he was washing his face in the mirror and heard the dogs and saw what was surely yet another dead body. It was a woman: he could tell it was a woman because of the long orange hair that fell back behind her head and brought a strange and lovely hue to the forest floor. He splashed his face with water and stared at himself in the mirror again. *That is me*, he thought. It was new to him, being able to see who he was, what he looked like. The day before he had stared at himself for close to an hour. But enough of that. He walked out behind the low brick building and gingerly stepped over the puddles, careful as he could to keep the mud off the edges of his shoes, until he made it to the girl. Nothing could have prepared him for what he saw: so beautiful, so perfect. He felt like he should shield his eyes.

"What happened to you?" he said, as if she could tell him.

He brushed the dirt off her face.

She was still warm.


*M*arkus picked her up from the forest floor and carried her back to his motel room. The dogs watched from a distance, then vanished into the trees. She was light, almost impossibly so, and in carrying her he felt as though he were also holding her down, as though if he hadn't come when he did she might just have floated away. He placed her on the bed and then brushed the dirt off her face and pulled the leaves and twigs from her hair.

He looked at her for he didn't know how long. He watched her breathe. He studied her features. There was a cut above her left eye, the blood a thin red line. His eyes traveled the part in her hair as if it were a map itself. Every so often her right hand would shiver. She made sounds—small, sad sounds—as if she were dreaming. He sat down on the edge of the bed and touched her hair—nothing else, just that. Even so, he felt as if he'd done something wrong.

Finally she opened her eyes. He let her take him in, get used to the idea that a man was sitting on her bed, looking at her. He showed her his friendliest face.

"I'm Markus," he said.

She didn't tell him her name. She didn't say anything. Her eyes wandered past him.

"I found you out there in the woods," he said. He pointed. She didn't seem to care. Her eyes were open, but she wasn't looking at anything. She wasn't looking at anything at all. "Are you okay?"

"Am I alive?"

He nodded. "I didn't think you were at first. I found you," he said again, as if he were claiming her, as if having found her meant she was his now. A part of him hoped it would be that easy.

"Where am I?"

"I don't—I'm not sure," he said. "Where did you come from?"

"Roam," she said.

*"Roam?"*

She said it as though it were nothing special, just another place to be from, when to Markus it was the end of his exploring, the beginning of everything else.

"I will take you there." He said it as though he were taking a pledge.

"No," she said.

"But it can't be far. It can't be."

"No!"

"Okay," he said. "All right. It's just . . . that's where I was going, where I've always wanted to go. My great-grandfather's told me about it, and he . . ."

She still hadn't really looked at him, and he wished she would. He wished this was going to be like one of those stories, of two people finding each other in the middle of nowhere because they had to find each other *somewhere*: something that was meant to be.

"The birds," she said. "The birds didn't get me."

"The birds?"

"I made it through the Forest," she said. "The birds didn't get me. I knew they wouldn't."

"Birds?" he said. "What kind of birds can get a person?"

"Flesh-eaters," she said, with such conviction he didn't dare contradict her.

"You do have a little cut above your eye." And he reached to touch it, and that's when he noticed: she didn't blink or flinch the way most people would. "Here," he said, touching it. "That's all, the only thing." He passed the open palm of his hand back and forth before her eyes—still nothing. "But . . . are you blind?"

"Last I checked," she said.

$\mathcal{S}$he needed some food, and he did, too, so he went into the house where the motel owner had lived and figured out how to use a stove (it was just a machine that made fire) and cooked up some eggs and bacon. She sat up in bed and ate it, but then she went to sleep again and didn't wake up until the next day. He went back inside the man's house and found a shoe for her, a brown one, and while she slept he slipped it on her bare foot, and it was too big, but it would do. He slept on the floor beside her. Every time she moved he woke, so he didn't sleep that much at all, but that was okay with him. He was in a motel room with a blind girl. What a thing that was. It was like being in a dream you didn't know was a dream. One dream bled into the next and then she moved again and when he opened his eyes he saw she was standing above him.

"I don't want to go to Roam," she said.

"Okay," he said, as much as he had always wanted to go. As much as Roam had been his only hope. And even though his compass had been set for half his life pointing toward this singular destination, he would have said okay to anything she asked. There were, he discovered that day, other worthy goals. "There's only one other place I know."

"Then take me there," she said.

"I will."

He thought she needed him: he was the one who could see. But it didn't feel like that. It felt like *he* needed *her*, and that she knew it somehow and the fact that he had eyes was secondary to the rest. He thought this a kind of magic.

Markus stood up and brushed himself off. He peered outside. The day was warm and the sun was shining—a good day for traveling back the way he came. Looking on the bright side—Markus was good at that. He picked up his hat and turned it until it felt right on his head, and then he stood there, looking at her for a long moment before something occurred to him. "You haven't even told me your name."

And she said, "Rachel. My name is Rachel."

*Rachel.* He had never heard a more beautiful name in all his life.

# PART III

# A SERMON
# FOR THE DEAD

So much light flooded through Helen's bedroom window in the morning that it was impossible for Digby to sleep past eight. It was as if his eyelids were being pried open by the sun itself. A barkeep never woke before noon: this was a lesson—maybe the only lesson—he learned from his father, who taught by example. But there wasn't much bar to keep these days, and Helen liked to greet the day early, to attack it, as if there weren't going to be another one coming tomorrow: she was up and gone before he had finished his last dream. He admired her energy, but sometimes he wished she would keep it to herself for an hour or two more.

Not even a year had passed and the entire world had changed.

His shirt and pants were hanging off the back of the red butterfly-backed chair in the corner of the room. She had placed them there, as she did every morning. At his place, where he never was anymore, his clothes were always where he had left them the night before: on the floor. But Helen picked them up, folded them, and sometimes even washed them, all while he was asleep. He insisted that it wasn't necessary, and that he rather preferred his clothes strewn across the floor, but this wasn't true anymore, and both of them knew it. Digby liked being tended to, having tended to so many others for so long. If he never said as much, it was only because he wanted to maintain the fiction he had brought into this house with him: that he had been a happy man alone. And maintaining fictions, after all, had been his job.

He lay in the bed and listened to the house, but it was silent. She must already have gone to the church. His breakfast—a boiled egg, one green apple, and a roll—would be waiting for him in the kitchen, and he would eat it and then go join her, walking alone down the near-deserted streets of Roam. Life was good: he actually felt this. It was very strange to think he had lived so long without being able to articulate this simple idea.

Helen McCallister and Digby Chang. Who could have seen this coming? Not Digby. Not Helen. Not even the best fortune-teller there ever was.

*A*fter the night one year ago when they went looking for Rachel, the night Jonas died, Digby stumbled back to the tavern in a daze. He felt as if he had been ripped out of his own world and taken to another one, a world he didn't know and couldn't understand. None of it made sense: a blind girl running away from home, and Jonas—poor, poor Jonas. No one should have been out in those woods after dark; the odds were that something terrible was going to happen to somebody. They should have waited until first light, but Helen wouldn't have it. He probably wouldn't have been able to wait, either, if Rachel were his sister. Still, cooler heads should have prevailed. Cooler heads never prevailed, though; that was the thing about cooler heads: they only made good sense in retrospect, and by then it was too late, and that's when the cooler heads said *I told you so*. Even the leftovers, the spirits who crowded his tavern, were preternaturally quiet that night. They knew what had happened—they sensed it.

But even then, even after everything that had happened, Digby had been gripped with a sense of the inevitable: he and Helen McCallister were going to be together. It was like a vision, and it stunned him. How could this be? He had no surreptitious affection for her. In fact, he hardly knew her at all, and what he did know of her—her face, primarily—he did not care for. That same evening, not three hours before Jonas died, Digby went on and on with Jonas about it. *How did you manage to maintain yourself, keep the fire of your desire alive, when you knew that on the other end there was . . . that . . . face?* And Jonas gave him the only right answer there was: he loved her. Digby had pretended not to care much for love, and instructed his patrons in the whoremonger's approach to women—not because he believed in it himself, no, far from it—but because it relieved the pressure on a man's heart.

He'd never felt such relief himself.

Digby told his patrons otherwise, to make them feel less alone, that they were talking to someone who knew whereof he spoke, when in fact he had only been with one woman in his entire life. She lived in the house next door to the one he grew up in (as much as he was going to grow up). She came from somewhere else—China, perhaps, or someplace like it. He could spy the girl from his bedroom window. She saw him, too. They were both fourteen. Every night before blowing out their candles they would give each other a long look. He watched her brush her long black hair. Neither waved, and it's possible that not even a smile or a nod of the head was exchanged. Everything happened in that look. It really felt to Digby then that if a person paid intense and discreet attention to another person they could say anything they wanted to with their eyes, have an entire conversation, share their deepest feelings, and he wondered if there were tribes somewhere in the world that did that, whole tribes where people didn't speak at all but only expressed themselves in a look. He tried it with other people to see if it worked, and it didn't: everyone thought he was odd, and one boy punched him, and that's when he realized it wasn't a language just anyone could speak.

It was, literally, the language of love. He loved the girl and the girl loved him. They'd never met, never exchanged a word—he didn't even know her name—but none of that mattered: he knew who she was the moment he saw her. They said things with their eyes they never could have said with their lips. *Oh girl you are so beautiful and your life has not been easy and the future is unknown but now let us be together we are meant for each other at least in this moment in time.* And she said *I want to know what it's like to be loved.* And finally that singular night came when he left the window and walked out into the dark cornfield behind his house and waited for an hour and then she was there, and she kissed him, and they brought each other as close as they could, skin to skin, and still only spoke with their eyes. Then it was over, and everything was different. He couldn't say if it was he or she who changed, whether it was he who wanted more or she who wanted things to stay the same. But he didn't understand her in the same way. And then—almost overnight, it felt like—she grew, while he stayed the same. Not another inch did he add to his fourteen-year-old frame. Not a midget—never a midget—but just a very, very, very small man.

As he grew older he listened to the men around him tell the tales of the women they'd had, or been had by; to memory he committed the vocabulary, the *dialect,* of the womanizer, and made it his own. He took great care not to mimic any single story but instead to take the woman of one and combine her with the situation of another. No one believed

Digby could possibly have done what he said he had, because if his numbers were accurate the chances were good that he'd not only slept with your wife, but with everybody's wife. Still, he told a good story, and if he'd only done half of what he said he did, that would have been something. The truth, of course, was that he had done precisely none of what he'd said he'd done. And later he wondered if the men from whom he had lifted those details—the soft contours of a woman's hips, her pleasured cries, that warm vortex—had been lifted by them as well.

But the way it was with that girl was the way it was with Helen. They didn't have to say anything. They didn't have to talk at all. They just looked at each other and they knew, even though with Helen it would take some time for her to admit it, to accept it. He knew her name and she knew his. This is something he wanted to talk about with Fang and He-Ping, those two old souls. But when he got back to the tavern that night they were gone, and he hadn't seen them since. It was as if they had died—again. But it wasn't like that at all, and he knew it: they were starting their second life, in their new home.

$\mathcal{H}$e dressed, ate his breakfast, and walked down McCallister past the darkened storefronts and piles of discarded furniture, and when he passed the abandoned houses the old-timers came to the windows and waved. He waved back. They were always so happy, happier than most of the living he knew. They wanted for nothing, now that most of them had their homes back. Maybe that's what contentment was, not to want anything anymore. Or maybe that's what it meant to be truly dead.

It had been a rough year, truth be told, for him, for Helen, for the whole town. But mostly for Helen. He'd visit her, after Rachel disappeared, once a week, then twice a week, then every day: he worried about her, not able or willing then to admit to himself that worry and love were not that much different. She didn't eat, she lost weight, until her clothes hung off of her like drapes, and whatever light there was behind her eyes dimmed and darkened and died.

He'd seen this happen before. Not with people, but with animals. He'd never tell Helen this story—he would never tell anybody—but he'd had a goat when he was a boy, and the goat fell in love with one of the wild cats that lurked around the barn, and the cat fell in love with the goat. They ate together, slept together, went everywhere to-gether: they were a couple, even though they couldn't have been more different.

Then the cat died. Run over by a thresher out in the field. It was awful. Worse, after a few days of being alone in the world, the goat killed himself. *Suicide.* Digby saw it happen. The goat hurled himself in front of a team of horses, pulling a carriage with some dignitary in it—one of the last horse-drawn carriages in Roam. Digby had never seen anybody kill themselves before or since—until now: Helen really was giving it her best shot.

She'd have done it, too, if it hadn't been for Digby. He kept her alive. He brought her water and milk. He gave her food; he made her eat. He sat in a chair and talked to her. Then he sat on the edge of her bed. Then he slept with her—just slept, being a warm, living body, ready proof that someone in the world cared for her, that she wasn't alone. Slowly, she came back, and when she got back she wasn't the way she was before. It was as if she'd gone to a foreign country and learned things there, new customs, ways of being she had never imag-ined were possible. For starters, she was kind to him, and grateful, and she never mentioned—even once—what a small man Digby was, how close to being a midget without being one, and every night she made sure he had a fresh case on his pillow, because a fresh pillowcase was insurance against having bad dreams. And she *prayed.* She prayed all the time: when she woke up, before she went to sleep, and then three or four times over the course of the day. Why she did this was a mystery, but he didn't ask because he didn't want to rock the boat.

Then, one night, she told him everything—the whole story, from the beginning, from that rainy day Helen was brushing Rachel's hair to the day Rachel left and Jonas died. A month had passed since he'd come to stay with her, over three since her sister had gone, and she told him what had happened, what she'd done, her words hovering like moths in the bedside candlelight. And finally he understood her.

A long quiet passed between them, and then he said, "It was raining, you say?"

"What?"

"The day you—um—traded faces with Rachel. It was raining, and the two of you were sitting on the bed listening to the rain?"

"Yes, why?"

They were leaning back against the headboard, the tops of their heads exactly even, and he couldn't help but notice, as he noticed every night, how her toes, which gently jutted upward from under the sheets, were about two feet closer to the far edge of the bed than were his own.

"Do you ever wonder what would have happened if it hadn't been raining that day?"

"Ah! It's the rain's fault!"

He moved closer to her. "Imagine," he said. "Imagine if it hadn't been raining. You wouldn't have been inside, bored, and she wouldn't have asked the question. You wouldn't have answered it. And we wouldn't be here in this bed, talking."

He touched her on the cheek.

"That's how it is," he said. "In a moment, everything can change. And we can change everything in a moment. One life is this far away"—he held his thumb and index finger a hair's width apart—"this far away from another one, a different one, a new one."

•   •   •

$\mathcal{T}$he church hadn't been opened for twenty-five years. The tall, heavy wooden doors—big enough for a bear to walk through—had been locked by some long-gone caretaker and forgotten. But the locks were unnecessary: no one wanted to be there. Church had never caught on in Roam. There were weddings, and funerals, and a preacher came through town once and tried to explain to whoever would listen all the good things a church could do for the town. But it didn't take. It had been built to fill the void left by the death of Elijah McCallister, but it turned out that nothing could fill that void. Whatever meaning Roam had was attached so firmly to its creator that, once he was gone, meaning was gone, too, and no amount of invention was going to bring it back.

But one day Helen passed the church on one of her walks with Digby (she took the same walks she used to take with Rachel, but there were no birds or Boneyards anymore: just the empty old town), and she stopped, turned, and stared at it. She stared for a good five minutes. Then she walked up the stone steps and tried to open the door. There was a large metal lock clasping the door handles, and she turned to Digby and said, "Can you help me get this lock off?" He returned a few minutes later with a crowbar.

"This item was often used on the skulls of the more cantankerous tavern patrons. It has served me well."

Then he put it to the door, and in a moment the lock swung loose and fell to the stones with a thud.

Inside the dark vastness, the air was thick with dust, and in seconds both Helen and Digby were coughing more than they were breathing. Digby gave Helen his handkerchief, and he pressed the sleeve of his shirt (which was too big for him, as almost all of his shirts were) against his mouth. Light barely penetrated the stained glass, and what light did eke through was colored thick shades of red and blue. Unable to see where he was going, Digby tripped over a wooden pedestal, and the flowerpot on top of it crashed to the floor.

"That's an omen," Digby said. "Maybe we shouldn't be in here."

She took his hand and squeezed it. "Or maybe you should watch where you're going."

They made their way down the aisle until they came to the altar. There were two candelabras on either side of an ornate podium, and as they stood in silence Digby thought he could read Helen's mind. He removed a box of wooden matches from his pocket and lit one of the candles. Suddenly the immensity of the church was clear: it was as if they were standing inside the belly of a whale. The ceiling was higher inside than it was outside, if that was possible. The rafters appeared not to have been cut from trees but to be trees themselves. Behind the altar was a mural of an angry god, robed in silk, with his eyes gazing heavenward; in his right hand he held fire and in his left ashes, which were falling from his hand like black snow. The face, Digby and Helen both recognized from the hallway portraits in their own house, was that of Elijah McCallister. The candlelight flickered; a bird left its nest in the rafters and fluttered past their heads. Digby had a moment of spiritual awakening during which he was able to sense the presence of some greater power living coexistent with him in the world; then he wanted a drink. He wanted a drink in the worst way.

"I guess we should get out of here before something falls on our heads," he said and tried to turn, knowing there was no way it was going to be that easy. It wasn't.

Helen knelt and pulled him down with her.

"Are we praying, Helen?" he asked.

She nodded.

"Do we have to?"

"We do," she said.

And, for some reason Digby was unable to fathom, they did.

• • •

$\mathscr{I}$t took them a month or more to clean the church, and they spent every single day doing it, just the two of them. There were still some people left in town who might have helped—there were probably two dozen warm bodies in Roam, fewer every day—but there were none who had any interest in improving a place they had every intention of leaving just as soon as they found another place to go to. Helen didn't ask them to help, though, and neither did Digby. Digby didn't even ask Helen why they were cleaning it, or for whom, because he knew. It was for Helen. Every moment she spent absorbed in the rehabilitation of this pointless structure was a moment she didn't have to think about Rachel, or herself, or about what had happened and what she'd done. She'd given herself to something greater than herself, and that gave her a chance to escape herself.

He just wished she wouldn't make him pray so much. Helen had a limitless enthusiasm for prayer. It could happen at any moment. It got so he was afraid to walk past her while they were working for fear she would grab some part of him and pull him down to the floor. He wasn't against it, but he preferred to know why he did what he was doing. He preferred to have a reason, something tangible, like a bottle of scotch and a glass of potato vodka. But then he'd feel a hand on his shoulder, and that was all she wrote.

"I think I've prayed for everything I can pray for, Helen," Digby finally protested.

"There's no end to praying, Digby," she said. "Especially for people like you and me."

"Why people like you and me?"

"Because of all the time we spent *not* praying."

Together they lowered themselves to the floor. He let her start, because it was her idea and because it took her twice as long to get there.

"Figure it out yet?" he asked.

"What?"

"Who we're praying to, and what good it's supposed to do. That sort of thing."

A shaft of sun highlighted the sea of dust between them. "You want a name," she said. "You want a name and a face and a story. I understand that. You want to know if we're praying to a him or a her or something else altogether. You want to pray to someone who's going to help you. Someone who is going to do you a favor. Make it rain, make the sun shine. Bring my sister back. Pray to someone who's going to look down and give us, of all people, some special attention.

"But there isn't anybody like that, Digby. I'm not praying like that. I'm praying because I've done nothing my whole life but hurt the people around me. I'm praying because I'm sorry. I'm praying because I don't know how to make things better, or if there's even any *way* to make them better. But I have to try. So what I'm doing when I pray is to make a place in myself and in the world where I can change—an opening where the good can rush in. Even if it's too late. If you *have* to know, then, that's what it is: I'm praying to the good, for the good; I'm looking to another world for help in this one. Because there has to be another world. *Has* to. You said that yourself. You said we could have another life, and that's the same thing. So that's why I'm doing it. And you're doing it with me because . . . I want to do everything with you." She kissed him on the cheek. "No harm in that, right?"

Digby shrugged. "No harm in that," he said. "It does pain my knees, though."

Being close to her, even on their knees, was worth it to him. Just feeling her skirt edge against his skin made him tremble a little, he had such feelings for her. It was worth bruised knees, and a whole lot more. And the thing was, sometimes she surprised him: he'd sigh when he felt her hand on his shoulder and realize it was time to go down to the floor again, but occasionally—more than occasionally— it wouldn't be for praying.

Helen was complicated like that.

*T*hey were almost done now. Today he was going to ascend the ladder and scrape the last bit of grime from the stained glass windows. He had to admit, the way the light flowed through the colored glass and made the room virtually glow was stunning. He could imagine that a man who was sitting in a pew with an empty mind and an open heart could sense that glorious something, that invitation to another world, that escape. At the very least, he could indulge himself in the mystery of life, and there was a lot of that to go around. Old-timers stood in the windows of every abandoned home he passed. They waved, he waved. Digby wondered if this was something peculiar to Roam, or if it were a regular occurrence all around the world, unseen and unknown by anyone other than bartenders. Because Roam was weird. One morning when he was a kid Digby woke up to find the streets choked with deer, hundreds of them, wandering around as if they lived there. They were gentle creatures, gone in a week. And there were the birds that one time, sparrows that every night at dusk flew through open windows and down chimneys and perched on the walls of every home, the gentle way they lightly rustled, making the walls look alive, pulsating, feathered. A month or so later they flew away and no one saw them ever again.

He turned the corner from McCallister to Ming Kai Lane and stopped, because he saw something there he'd never seen before: two old-timers, out for a walk. He recognized them: the one on the left was Chen, and the one on the right, Kelly Neighbors. He hadn't seen them since they left the tavern, when their houses opened up. The sun shone straight through them; they glowed like the last embers of a fire.

Up ahead he saw six or seven others, some of whom he knew—Daisy Chow, Kepler Cosgrove, Melanie Grinney—strolling down the street as if they didn't have a care in the world. (He guessed that, in this case, that was probably true.)

"Digby."

It was Jonas. After he'd fallen into the ravine and appeared at the tavern, he'd stayed for a couple of days and then left without saying good-bye.

"Jonas, my friend," Digby said. Jonas had that same starved quality about him, like a dog who'd been abandoned on the side of the road and hadn't eaten in a week. He stared up at Jonas and smiled. "You look—"

"—the same," he said disconsolately. "I look the same."

"Where'd you go? We missed you down at the tavern. Everyone spoke fondly of you in your absence."

"Nice to hear," Jonas said.

"Yes," Digby said, suddenly discomfited and—just as suddenly—realizing why. It was only the strangeness of the circumstance that had kept him from immediately understanding the import of this moment. Helen.

"And so," Digby said. "Where are you—where is everybody off to? It appears to be an exodus. Don't tell me even you folks are leaving."

"We're going to church, Digby," he said. "Everyone is going to church."

"The church? You and . . . the rest? But why?"

He shrugged. "It's nice," Jonas said. "Some of us went over there last night for a look. It's nice. And big. Not many places like that around here, you know. And then there's Helen."

"Helen?" Digby said, as if the name rang a bell, but only a small one.

Now Jonas looked Digby hard in the eye. When he wasn't smiling, his face went slack and flat as a fence post. "You and Helen," he said. "You two are together now. That's what I heard."

"Yes, well, that's true," Digby said. "If by together you mean—"

"Sleeping together," Jonas said. "Living together and sleeping together. In love."

"Then most certainly yes. I hope that's not . . . an issue with you? You are dead, after all."

Jonas shrugged. "I have to admit, when I first heard about it I felt like I'd swallowed a hornets' nest. But it's okay now. More than okay. Is she happy?"

"After all that's happened," Digby said, "I don't know if she'll ever be happy. But as happy as she could be under the circumstances. I think it would be fair to say that."

"I'm good with it, then," Jonas said. He dragged the tip of his shoe along the sidewalk. "Can't wait to see her, though. I guess I'll—"

"You do that," Digby said. "I'll be right along."

Jonas caught up with the rest of them as Digby hung back. Had someone seen him—the few people left in town to be seen by—he would have looked odd, odder than usual, dressed in his coat, hat, and red-and-gold-striped tie, with black boots and a pocket watch strung across his vest—the clothes Helen had laid out for him. He looked like a toy man. He accepted that. To be that man and to be seen standing talking to the air, though, was perhaps too much.

By the time he got to the church himself, no one was there but Helen, standing in front of the big wooden doors alone, waiting for him, her arms at her sides, her dark hair lifted by a burst of a breeze, the hem of her blue dress rippling in it as well. He took off his hat as he mounted the stairs and stood before her.

"Look," she said, and she moved aside so he could.

Digby peered through the open door: the church was full, every seat in every pew. He'd never seen so many dead people in one place before, and their collective milky essence glowed like a wave of pure light. In the very first pew he saw Fang and He-Ping. He stared at them until they turned to him, smiled, and waved. Digby took a deep breath and held it for a second or two, then turned back to Helen.

"You never told me you could see them, too," he said.

"You never told me, either."

"I didn't want you to think I was crazy."

"My mother and father are in there," she said. "Jonas is in there. *Elijah McCallister* is in there, Digby."

"And Rachel?"

She shook her head and scanned the crowd again, probably for the hundredth time. "I don't see her," she said. "But everyone else— they're waiting, Digby."

She sounded like a girl about to go onstage for the school play. Stage fright, that's what it was. But it still took him a moment to get it. Waiting? He liked to think of himself as the kind of man who got things, but he was slow on the uptake today. Tired. He was tired, plain and simple. The road to now had been a long one. But they'd survived the worst, and here they were.

"For you, you mean?" he said.

"For me," she said. "To hear me say something, and I don't know what. What do I do? What do I tell them?"

He thought about it. He felt real for the first time in his life: the woman he loved had asked him what to do. She needed him the same way he needed her. In that moment—not yet even in the church— they were married.

He took her hand. "A woman is sometimes required to do things she'd rather not," he said, "in part because she is a woman and has no real choice in the matter either way." He stood on his toes and whispered in her ear. "Tell them the truth," he said. "Tell them that everything is going to be all right."

"But is it?"

"Sure it is," he said, and hoped she believed him. "One day."

And that's what she did, that day and the next, and the next, and the next, days becoming weeks, the weeks a month and more. For anybody and everybody who came, whether it was one or a hundred, she told them—she told herself—that everything was going to be all right. And hoped they believed her, too.

# THE DOGS

*T*he dogs came first: two, three, then half a dozen at least. There hadn't been a single dog in Roam for a long, long time, not since Lumberjack Smith left, and their absence, while never consciously noted, was something deeply felt by those people who remained behind. There was an emptiness—when even the dogs give up, you know things are pretty bad.

But then they crept on back. All black, one no different from the next, they wandered up and down the streets of Roam as if they owned it. No one touched them; no one even got close to them. On the one hand, they didn't cause any trouble, but on the other, if you tried to shoo them or didn't step aside they confronted you with a fiery malice in their eyes until you backed away and went about your business. Not that there was much business to be had in Roam anymore.

After just a couple of days of this, the few citizens who had been on

the fence about leaving now had no doubt at all. The remaining population was halved. No putting up FOR SALE signs, of course; the truth is
that anyone could have come and taken possession of a nice home and
made it their own through no more effort than it took to move in. On
a Main Street that once boasted a dozen stores selling everything from
the most elegant feathered hats to rare Chinese noodles, eventually
there was only one: a general store selling whatever was left over and
behind. You were as likely to find a brass commode there as you were
a bag of flour. Old Man Cummings manned the register, his half-inch-
thick eyeglasses reflecting the light from the huge, ancient candelabra
hanging from his ceiling, smoking incessantly. If he was awake he had
at least one cigarette going, sometimes two or three. And he drove
a hard bargain—he wouldn't take a penny off the price of anything.
Sometimes he'd raise the price while you were looking, just because
he wanted to. But when the dogs came, he locked the doors and never
opened them again.

The dogs ended up gathering around the McCallister house, there
beneath the dying magnolias, the withering pin oaks, the relentless
kudzu winding around the porch columns. Oh, this house! Just two
years ago it was a rotting hovel held upright by nothing more than
hope, one strong wind away from collapsing entirely. But it had
been transformed, saved by the labor of the smallest man in Roam,
Digby Chang. He'd sealed up all the holes in the floor and installed a
banister the length of the winding stairs. He'd painted almost all the
rooms, most of them in soft colors—Helen loved peach. He cleaned
the windows, removing years of cobwebs, leaves, and dirt. Helen
cleaned the kitchen ("Scour for an hour every day and all the grime
will go away," her mother always said) until, one day, it began to
gleam. There was something magical about order, Helen had come
to believe. Something happened when everything was *just so,* when
every piece of the puzzle fit and perfection—fleeting perfection—was

achieved. Was that happiness? Satisfaction at the triumph over disorder?

This is the house that was surrounded. Helen was inside. So was Digby. Eight or nine times a day one or both of them would be standing at the living room window, pulling back a curtain and staring. It was like this going on three days. Digby had tried to go outside once and had almost lost a finger.

"Still there," Helen said, not even needing to say it. The idea that the dogs would ever leave now seemed impossible, unimaginable.

"I keep waiting for the lumberjack," Digby said. He sat on the couch with his hands on his knees, his knees pressed together, and his feet flat against the floor, as if he were a spring-loaded mechanism that might at any moment pop up. "They're his dogs. I keep thinking he's coming off the mountain and they know it and they're waiting here for him."

"Well," Helen said.

"What?"

"Remember the last time we saw them?"

Digby was silent. He remembered and was hoping Helen wouldn't. "I remember," he said.

"Smith said they'd save her. Jonas told me he said that. His dogs would save her."

"True," Digby said. "That was said by Lumberjack Smith. I didn't understand it then and I don't now. But those words were spoken."

"And we haven't seen them since. That's all I'm saying."

Digby gazed into a middle distance, somewhere between himself and the living room wall.

"Do you remember the birds and the deer and the bears, Helen? The way they used to come and take over the entire town. And then they left, and it was ours again. I think this is the price one pays for living in the wilderness."

"So you think the dogs will just go away?"

"We'll wake one day and they'll be gone and we'll go about our lives as if they were never here, and then, soon, we'll forget they ever came."

She walked over to the couch and sat beside him. He kissed her on the cheek.

"I know what you're thinking," he said.

"That's because I told you what I was thinking."

"But even if you hadn't, I would know."

He kissed her on the cheek again, in the same spot, or thereabouts, where he had planted a thousand of them in the last year. "He sent his dogs away to save her," she said. "He said they would save her, not that they would bring her back."

"And so now that they're back—"

"I haven't seen her in church," Helen said, "with the others."

Digby was silent.

"You would think she would come," she said.

Helen's services, which were held three times a week (twice on Sunday and once on Wednesday night), had become standing-room-only affairs, as more and more of the old-timers were drawn to her sermons of hope and redemption. Helen had the sense that, even though they were essentially without the ability to change themselves or anything that had happened through the course of their lives, the dead still had a stake in life itself, the same way the Chinese who came to Roam so long ago still had a stake in China. The fact that they didn't live there anymore didn't change anything for them.

"So what you're saying is—and this is something I can't quite fathom—you believe there's a possibility, however slim, your sister is still alive."

"No," she said. "I don't. But it's not *completely* impossible."

"But that's what possibility is, Helen, the absence of *complete* impossibility." He sighed, as if readying himself to perform a task he'd performed many times already. "One year," he said. "Twelve months, Helen, three hundred and sixty-five days she's been gone and not a word."

"All we found was her shoe," she said.

"She's at the bottom of that ravine—"

Helen closed her eyes and placed a hand on Digby's knee, squeezing it. "No. Don't. I see her in my dreams every night. I know what must have happened. Still."

"Still," he said. "It's important to accept it. So we can move on."

Neither spoke now. For a long time they sat together on the couch like two old lovers. That's all Digby wanted: fifty years from now if they were still together, sitting on the couch holding hands, he would be happy. Or anywhere on any couch. How long could they hold out in Roam, the way things were going? Even before the dogs came, Digby had been trying to convince Helen to go away with him, it didn't matter where. Arcadia wasn't far, he said, but there were other places beyond Arcadia—who knew how many? An infinite number. And out of all of them, all they needed was one. But she wouldn't go. Helen thought about it—it was impossible to watch the exodus and not want to join it—but she wouldn't. At first Helen stayed in the hope that Rachel might return; then she stayed for fear that she never would.

So Helen remained and discovered in her sister's absence what love and the loss of it is; she discovered both at the exact same time. It's not just a feeling: it's a real thing inside of you made of a paper-thin glass, and when it breaks the shards move through your blood and cut you to pieces.

Helen missed church. She missed church more than she missed freedom and food. Had the dogs let her out that's where she would have gone first. She missed her flock, the attentive dead who hung on her every word as if she had something important to say, as if there were something she *could* say that would help them, though all she could do was tell stories, the same thing she had done all of her life. Different stories now, though: good ones. And they were more powerful than any lie she ever told her sister. She felt like she was finally becoming human, because out of all the life on Earth this is the one thing only people do. What other animal tells stories? Or more important: what other animal listens?

Helen felt like she'd died, too. There was a Helen, another Helen, whom she'd buried when Rachel left her, and like the spirits who were her congregation, the leftover Helen was a vaporous shadow, gray as a cloud—the only difference between her and the others being that she was growing into her new self, and they would be the way they were forever. That's why all eyes were on her. No one even blinked.

"Welcome," she had begun that first day, and she said exactly what Digby had told her to say. But after that, she hit a wall. It was a kind of stage fright, but more than that: she was scared of herself. She stood there for an entire minute, silently staring back at them, until one of them—James Harding—stood and said, "Tell us about yourself, Helen."

"About myself?"

"Tell us what you've done with your life."

Another minute passed before she spoke.

"Well, I did some things," Helen said. "Some terrible, terrible things."

"But *what exactly*?" he asked her. "I think we've all done terrible things"—and a murmur of agreement spread through the pews—"but just saying it isn't enough. Cat of mine had a litter of kittens I didn't need. So I drowned them in the river. Six of them, in a bag with a rock in it. Watched their bodies struggle against the silk until . . . well, until they stopped." He sat back down and popped back up and said, "That's what I'm talking about. Get it out and let it go."

Jeddy Wong said from his seat, "Slept with my wife's sister once."

His wife looked at him and said, "Once?"

Others followed them, and more followed the others. It wasn't confession as much as it was admission. Not that there was anything wrong with what they had done, but that wasn't the point. The idea was that there was no one who hadn't done *something*.

"So now," James Harding said, about half an hour after he'd opened the floodgates. "What is it *you* have to share with us?"

Helen stood, feeling protected behind the pulpit. But this was no time to feel protected. She moved away from it and presented herself fully to the congregation.

"I let my blind sister walk into a bees' nest," she said. They stared, waiting. "I mean I walked her into it. She was stung all over, head to toe." Helen wiped the palms of her hands across the front of her dress. "I rearranged the furniture so she'd run into it and hurt herself. That made me happy, to do things like that. I told her she stood a good chance of being hanged one day because she was a blind girl. I told her . . ." She let her words trail off into silence. Why was what she wanted to say now any worse than anything else she'd done to Rachel? Was there even a scale on which these things could be weighed, and judged? Helen thought: yes, there was. "I stole her face," she said, "and I gave her mine."

Digby watched her from the back.

There was too much to say for just one service. The next Sunday, Mrs. Cravens, the sixth-grade teacher (when there was a sixth grade in Roam), stood and told Helen and the spirits gathered there, "Everything I did was an accident. Everything good and bad. I floated on the surface of the river of my life and held on to whoever could keep me from drowning." She blushed. "I don't know what happened. I don't know what's happening now."

Then Jonas stood up. He lowered his head toward Helen in a

gesture suggesting love and respect and sorrow. They had spoken, once, on the first day the church was open, the first time she'd seen him since he'd died. He'd been shy with her, the way old boyfriends were with the girls they still loved. He'd said, "I appreciate everything you did for me, Helen. I wasn't easy. Especially when you tried to help me—you know. That last night. I appreciate that."

*That last night.*

So today when he stood she thought he was going to talk about that. But he didn't.

"I killed my father," he said. He paused, looked around. "Still—I don't know. I don't have a feeling about it. I don't feel much of anything about that."

He shrugged, looking all around, as if for help. Then he sat back down.

The meetings had become a time of healing for her congregation, though she suspected they were there, in part, because they had nothing else to do. They were stuck here the same way the living had been stuck here, only the dead had no reason to go anywhere else. They were stuck in Roam forever, even as it succumbed to the rapacious and, now, relentless onslaught of greenery engulfing the homes and stores. They were always there, and would always be there, and if there was a reason she and Digby could see them when no one else could, she wasn't sure what that reason was. But it would have been lonely had only one of them been able to, and this was reason enough for her. All she knew is that every Sunday she left the church a better person, changed for the good, while they all stayed the same. This was how she came to realize that she wasn't there to help them, but they were there to help her. They did more than that, though: they saved her.

•     •     •

$\mathcal{T}$he quiet, inside and out, was unsettling. When the dogs stopped howling there was nothing to hear but the wind edging in through the windows Digby had yet to repair—a high whistling sound.

"We're running out of food," she said.

He looked at her, but she kept her gaze fixed on the door. Dust motes like a million miniature fish swimming through the lighted air, reproducing too fast to clean, a woman with her hands on her thighs, torturing herself with her past; and the man who really loved her not a few feet away, ready to do anything he could to make her happy.

"It feels a little like the end of the world, doesn't it?" he said. "What preachers preach about it. *Know thou that dogs will come and . . .* and I don't know, surround your home so you can't even go out to get a drink? Can't get much worse than that."

But she didn't smile at his little joke. Instead she said, "I've been thinking about that, too. But the end of the world's not dogs, Digby. It's plagues. Plagues, floods, locusts, fires. And miracles. Lots and lots of miracles."

He took her hand and held it tighter now, and she held his tighter back.

# ROAM

arkus fell out of the woods as if he'd been thrown out of them, his coat and pants torn and ripped in half a dozen places, light red stripes across his cheeks and even deeper cuts on his arms, where there was some serious blood, dirt smeared like camouflage around his neck and chin, gasping for air, looking behind him, ahead, as if at any moment something could come at him, from anywhere, and he had to be ready for it. Somehow, his hat had stayed on his head. Finally he either felt safe or gave up on feeling safe, brushed his pant legs and shirtsleeves off (as if that did any good whatsoever), and ran, ran just as fast as he could without falling. His shoes were mostly poster board and string now. With his face clenched from the blistering pain, he didn't stop until he came to a sign. It was hard to assemble the letters into words because they were worn away by weather and time. He had to study it for a while.

WE COME TO RO    M
THE SILK N      ARADISE
AND    ND
OF ALL EXP ORIN .
EL JAH MCCALL      TER. OWNER

So he had made it for sure. In his rush to get here—and to escape
the dog that was chasing him—he wasn't sure where he was. When
he got to that bridge over the ravine (so old and worn and fragile he
wasn't sure it would support him), he ran across it as fast as he could,
at the very least hoping that if it fell it would fall behind him, that he
could stay a step ahead of the dog. But it didn't fall. He wasn't sure,
but he thought the dog was just behind him and that it might be a good
idea to cut the bridge down (it was hanging there by a single thick,
fraying rope) but decided (the way such things are decided, in less
than a moment) that he might need it if he were to go back.

Now he was here, the place he'd been moving toward one year
ago. Ming Kai had told him stories about it since he was a small boy.
How there had been nothing here but nature, and how two men made
their way through the nothing of it all and created a world, a world so
closely tied to the men who made it that when they became dead to
each other the town itself began to die. From Markus's small home in
the Valley, remote from everywhere, Roam was never real. It was just
a story. And now here it was.

He took off his hat and gave a look around. Even for a man who
had never seen a real town before, Markus knew this one was dead.
Empty, overrun by the forest, broken really—a lot like the Valley. But
the Valley had never been much of anything, while Roam—according to Ming Kai, at least—Roam had been something. Markus closed
his eyes and tried to see it the way it must have been, streets so busy
you had to slide past the tide of people going the other way. Stores

bright with colored boxes from all around the world. And silk. Silken curtains, silken tents. Silken kites for the children. Silken everything. A soft, cool place to be . . . and now, but for a few lonely places, shuttered and dark.

Markus put his hat back on and started walking until he heard the crack of a twig somewhere behind him, a stifled growl. Without looking back again he ran, ran toward the dark house he saw looming above the desolate and decaying town.

# THE BROOCH

There were three dogs prowling around the front porch, so Markus slipped around the side of the house. He didn't have time to knock. He threw his shoulder against the door, and when it didn't open he tried the knob, but it was locked. He slammed his hand into the window and it shattered, but the opening wasn't big enough to do him any good. He knew the dogs were coming. Inside he saw someone, what he thought at first was an old woman and her little boy, but then realized he was a man, just a very small one, and a young woman, just very homely. When they saw him they froze, in a kind of shock. He held up Rachel's brooch, which he had kept with him all this time, and when the woman saw it she went straightaway to the door and opened it, and he fell in the house just as he felt on his ankle the nip of a dog's sharp teeth. She closed the door and he lay there, not sure he could get up, and not really wanting to, for having made it to his final destination he was spent, even though he had yet to do what he came to do.

The little man said, "Who are you?" And the woman: "Where did you get that brooch?"

A whole minute passed before he was able to lift his head, to stand, to sit in a chair and breathe. He raised his head and looked at the woman. He had never seen an uglier woman in his life, and coming from the Valley that was saying something. He turned away, not because he couldn't stand to look but because he didn't want to hurt her feelings, for surely she could see in his eyes his wonder at her remarkable face and she would know what it meant. But she was kind. She poured him a glass of water from a pitcher and handed it to him. He took it and swallowed and just that quickly felt his strength returning, his breath, the power to speak.

"I need to see Helen McCallister," he said.

"I'm Helen McCallister."

He looked at her again. *Couldn't be,* he thought. He said, "Helen McCallister, Rachel McCallister's sister. That's who I mean."

The little man stared hard at him, not in a threatening way really, but protectively. Markus felt like he needed to move slowly, to speak carefully, or he might do something to set the little man off. Markus was not a fighter, and little men were the worst; they were tough and mean as rusty nails.

"I'm her sister," the woman said.

Markus blinked, thinking. Her sister. It kind of made sense, with all he knew about Rachel and her sister. Helen McCallister and the little man, though, they looked like they'd been hit in the head by a rock and were standing frozen the second before they fell.

"You're Helen McCallister," Markus said. He shook his head.

"What?" Helen McCallister said. "Why are you looking at me like that?"

"You're just not what I expected," he said. "The way she described you. I thought you looked different, that's all."

Helen took the brooch from him as though it might crumble at her touch, cradling it in the palm of her hand, studying it. She looked back and forth from him to the brooch, and he could see her putting it all together but not believing it. "Because she told you I was beautiful," she said. Markus realized Rachel was right: Helen thought she was dead. All this time.

"That's right," he said. Then: "She's alive, Helen."

She swiveled her head toward the little man, no words necessary now.

"We looked for her the night she left," Helen said. "Digby and I looked. Jonas, too. Smith. Some time had passed. We didn't know where she'd gone. How far could a blind girl go? That's what I was thinking." She laughed, and just as quickly stopped. "Where could a blind girl go?"

"Turns out, pretty far," Markus said.

"What's your name?" the little man said.

"My name's Markus. You Jonas?"

The little man shook his head and frowned. "Digby. Jonas is dead. He died the night Rachel—"

"—disappeared," Helen said. "She was nowhere. Nowhere. We sent out word to Arcadia, in case someone delivered her there, in whatever shape. We wanted to know. I *needed* to know. I had nightmares," she said. "But then, you know, one day you just stop and try to accept it. That she's gone and she's not coming back. And that's when it gets even harder. It's just really, really hard to know what to do then. I pray about this every day."

"You pray about it?"

She nodded. "Why?"

Markus was confused. "No reason," he said.

"She's alive," she said, somewhere between a statement and a question. She was catching up.

"Very much," he said.

His gaze didn't waver, even a little.

Finally the two of them sat, Digby in a chair at the edge of the room, as if he were more of a guard than anything else, Helen closer. Markus looked all around him, at this room so perfectly arranged, so clean. Then he looked over his shoulder, as if he expected somebody to be there, and when there wasn't he leaned in close to speak in a softer voice near Helen's ear.

"She's alive," he said, and he looked behind him again, and then to her, still speaking in a voice weirdly hushed. "But that's not even the most important part," he said.

Outside he could hear the dogs rustling, growling, barking, and howling. Rachel was getting closer.

"Not the most important part? But what could be more important than my sister being alive?"

"That's just it," he said. "Your sister, she's . . . not your sister anymore. She's not the girl you remember, or even the one I used to know. And she's on her way."

"Here?" Helen said. "She's coming here? But that's good. That's a good thing . . . "

He shook his head. "No," he said. "No, it's not." Helen didn't get it. He didn't blame her. Her eyes were as soft and uncertain as Rachel's had been when he met her, but that seemed a long time ago now. "Helen," he said. "She knows what you did to her. Everything." He let this settle until he saw she knew what he meant, until she *had* to know what he meant. He reached across the table and touched her hand, not to reassure her—because this wasn't that kind of news. He did it to be sure she heard what he had to say. "She's coming *to make things right.*"

And this is what he told her.

# FINDING RACHEL

*G*oing always took longer than the coming back. Even though the idea of leaving had been tumbling through his mind, for years and years, Markus's first steps out of the Valley had been hard going. He wouldn't look back. He'd have to see Liling if he did, his friends and family—all the rest. His life. He thought it would get easier, but each step was harder than the one before. Who up and leaves their life behind like that?

Well, a lot of people. Because a lot of people think there's something better than home and friends and family—a lot of people, like almost every man who'd come to or been born in this valley. One day they'd go and they'd never come back, and later you'd forget they had ever even been here. They'd become just another lost thing, accompanying all the other lost things, until you lost more than you ever knew you had. The journey wasn't even about being happy, or happier, here or there. It was simpler than that. It was more like, *If there's something here, there's something there, and I've been here, now let's see what's there.* It's how people came to the Valley in the first place. It's how anybody gets anywhere.

He went back with Rachel the way he came, the dogs following along. For a blind girl with only one good shoe, Rachel could walk pretty fast. It helped that there were no bears this time. She didn't talk. Markus hoped he'd get her story, because he knew there had to be one. How often does it happen that a beautiful blind girl with one shoe ends up facedown in a forest close to the middle of nowhere? If there was a story anywhere, there was a story there, but she wasn't telling. Maybe it was too big to tell all at once. Or maybe she was shy, like him. That was okay. He could wait.

The night of the day they first set out he waited too long to build a fire and the dark bled through the air and every tree in the forest and it settled all around them. Rachel found more wood than he did, and he scraped a flint against a dry stack of twigs and warmed up some chicken meat they'd taken from the fat man's cabin. The fire crackled. Night birds sang. But Rachel didn't say a word. Finally he couldn't take it anymore and he just started talking.

"My grandfather told me a story once, how a long time ago there was no light in the world at all. Then fire came, and there was a great battle between the dark and the fire, and darkness won. But before the fire died it whispered its secret to a man, and that man told another man, and soon fire was everywhere, and darkness gave up trying to kill it. They had to make a deal."

He stopped, and watched her as she chewed the last bits of chicken off the bone.

"Don't you want to know what the deal was?" he said.

"I guess," she said, so softly he could barely hear.

"It doesn't sound like you really want to know."

"No. I do. Tell me."

He poked the fire with a stick. "It's just a story," he said. "He probably just made it up."

"Or maybe it's true," she said. "We don't know."

"We don't," he said.

He tried to smile. She couldn't see him try to smile, of course, and he realized that people smiled so that other people could *see* the smile, instead of just smiling for themselves. It had less to do with being happy than with showing someone else you were happy. He didn't have to do that with her. Things changed when you sat around a fire with a blind girl.

"I know you want me to tell you," she said.

"What?"

"Everything," she said.

"Well," he said, "only since the moment I found you."

She moved a bit closer to the fire. It was impossible to tell where the fire ended and the red of her hair began. Her face glowed white. She didn't speak.

"All I know is your name," he said. Which, he didn't say, would still be enough, if that's all she gave him.

"I didn't know I'd be alive now to tell anybody anything. There was the ravine, first," she said. "I thought I might fall into it. And then the birds."

"The birds?"

"In Roam they're everywhere," she said. "In the trees, in the forests. You've never seen them? You've never . . . ?"

"No," he said, when he saw the fear and doubt on her face. "I think—sure. I mean, I've never heard of them coming this far, this far out."

This seemed to satisfy her, but it was impossible to tell what she was thinking. She was holding a stone in her hand, which she dropped and picked up, over and over again.

"I didn't leave Roam because it's a terrible place, though. I left because of my sister."

"What did she do to you?"

"To me? She didn't do anything to me. She did everything *for* me. After our parents died she could have . . . she could have done anything she wanted. Put me somewhere. Gone away. But she stayed. She stayed because she loved me. She gave up her life to take care of me. That's why I left, on my own. She would never have let me go."

"I see," he said. But he was more confused now than when he didn't know anything at all. "So she doesn't know where you are?"

She shook her head. "She thinks I'm dead. It's hard to believe I'm alive myself. But I would have given up my own life so she could have one of her own."

He looked away from her briefly, hearing something in the forest behind him. There was a dog out there, for sure.

"Now I am putting my trust in you," she said. "All I want is to live long enough to go back to Roam one day and show my sister. *Look*, I'll say. *Here I am. A woman. A woman who has learned to take care of herself, your sister, who now you can freely love, without responsibility or worry.* And I will thank her for everything she did for me. Everything." She paused. "Maybe you can help with that, Markus," she said.

"I think I can," he said.

"I know you can, Markus," she said. "At least, that's what I'm going to believe, until you prove me wrong. I've been lucky so far. I have to be thankful for my life. Some blind girls have no real life at all; and blind girls who look like me—" She laughed. "They may as well have died the day they were born."

"Look like you?" Markus said. "What do you mean? You're beautiful."

Rachel threw the stone at him and it flew past his head.

"This fire must not be as bright as it is warm."

She held her legs up close to her chest and rocked back and forth in front of the fire. But she was still shivering, so he gave her the blanket he'd taken from the dead man—after you die everything you ever owned is returned to the world, free to those who find it—and Markus curled up close to the stone circle—it was where the dark had told the fire to stay—and slept. Already he knew he would do anything to keep her.

*T*he next day they walked up a mountain and then across a long wide-open plain and then back into the thickness of the forest, where the trees were so tall you couldn't see the tops of them or the sky above them. Occasionally he would take her hand and lead her over a rough spot, but for the most part she was okay walking on her own, even though as far as he knew it was the same as walking with your eyes closed. He couldn't do that, but maybe with practice he could learn to, and she'd been practicing most of her life. Then they came to what was the Fallen Wall, a stone field Ming Kai had told him was once a great wall separating the Valley from the rest of the world, a wall he'd had to break to get there, but even Markus knew it was really just a big pile of rocks. He didn't need anyone to tell him what stories were for.

As they came to the ridge above the Valley, Markus saw some of his people, as if they were on watch, a little ways away. He didn't know if somehow they knew he was coming or whether they'd waited there every day, hoping he would be. One of them raised his arm from his side and held it in the air for a moment, then let it drop. Then he and the others turned and disappeared below the sightline.

"Almost there," Markus said, without much enthusiasm.

Rachel seemed more excited than he was. She stopped, and took a sudden, quick breath.

"What's it like, Markus, your home?"

She touched his arm, lightly. He wondered if this touch for her took the place of the connection that happened when one person looked into another's eyes.

"Does the sun come up in the morning," she said, "and paint the town all yellow, warming the porches and the windowsills?"

"Windowsills?"

"Does the dew cling to the soft green grass before it spirits itself into the air, the air that smells of pine needles and down?"

"Well . . ."

"Is the sky a milky blue, and at night does every star come out to shine on the perfect little houses and—"

She stopped, too excited to go on. He watched her breathe: she had come to life. Markus didn't think he could stand her becoming any more beautiful than she was already was, but she was becoming more beautiful by the second, and he was enduring it. Somehow.

"Like that?" she said.

"Something like that," he said. "I mean, I can sure smell those pine needles sometimes."

He took another step, but she didn't move.

"And is everybody happy?" she said.

"Happy?" How far would he go to please her? This is how he thought about it then, in the beginning. He was pleasing her by telling her things she wanted to hear. Why she wanted to hear them, Markus didn't understand. But isn't that the way with everybody? We all have our own ideas about things. Was it his place to tell her she was wrong about them? And she looked so expectant and bright. "I'd say so," he said. "Yes. They're happy. But I don't know how they'll be when they see you. You're . . . different."

"Different how?" she asked. Then, before he could make anything up, she said: "Wait, don't say it. It's because I'm homely, isn't it?"

"Homely?" Markus laughed. "No, Rachel. I told you—"

"*Don't,*" she said, turning on him. "Don't lie to me. Don't be like everybody else. I know who I am. My sister told me."

"Your sister told you."

Even Markus was able to start putting it all together. *It's the sister who has done this to her, told her these stories. The sister she loves, the sister she left.*

"But I'm more than just an ugly girl, Markus," she said. "So much more."

He waited for her to go on, but she didn't. She smiled, smiled as though she were happy to finally be able to share this news with someone. Her right hand enlaced his wrist and sort of tugged at it. She brought him close and whispered: "Do you know about the river?" She was so beautiful. He could understand her now, a little. He was coming to understand the sister, too, and of the two, he thought—unfortunately—he knew the sister better.

"No," he said, before he could stop himself. "I don't."

*N*othing had changed since he left the Valley ten days ago, though Markus felt like he'd been gone for a long, long time. He wasn't surprised: nothing ever happened here, nothing but the slow and steady exodus of one man after another. Some took their families with them, others left them behind and took their chances on their own, but it was a certainty: one day everyone would be gone, one way or another, and then the moss would grow and the rain would wash everything away, even history. Maybe the boat would be here for a while, and some lost traveler a long time from now would come upon it and wonder whether the oceans had once come this far in. Balanced on logs on a flat stone outcropping, the boat dominated the dim valley like an abandoned temple. And even after five days it was mossing up, the deck covered in leaves and branches, vines hanging off the bow.

Now the Valley was still as Rachel and Markus walked down the rocky slope and arrived in the middle of nowhere. Rachel did whatever she did to understand where she was. She tilted her head back, then to one side; she sniffed, she listened, she sensed. Markus was watching a blind girl see. Like him, she was waiting. Then, slowly, as if finally deciding it was safe, his people came out of their huts and lean-tos, stepped out from behind wherever they were hiding, and the old people, the moss-scrapers, whose backs were hunched and rounded from bending over all day—including his mother, Liling—they rose and joined the circle of people who had come to see the new human being Markus had brought with him back to the Valley. When had this happened—ever? It had never happened. And so everyone (all fifty-three of them) came out to view this phenomenon. Markus and Rachel were completely surrounded, and Rachel could feel it, holding tight to Markus's arm, whispering: "What's going on?"

"Nothing," he said, though he could only imagine what this must have felt like to her. He wished he could show her, make her see: they were only people. People like her, like him, only . . . different.


Night fell fast, edging through the Valley like a fog. Rachel needed a safe place to sleep. Not that anyone in the Valley would hurt her, but some of them were curious—overly so.

He decided to put her on the boat.

He walked her to the deck, and then into the small room Markus called the cabin; there was space for some bedding in it and not much else. His head bumped against the ceiling, though she slipped in just fine. He watched her try to understand where she was.

"It's a boat," he said. "The cabin of a boat."

"A boat? But—"

"Long story," he said. He thought about how much of his life he left within these planks, how ridiculous it was, and how ridiculous he was to have ever started building it. But maybe this is what it was meant for all along. "There's a bed for you, and a roof if it rains, which it does quite a bit."

She fell asleep before he was even able to go. He watched her breathe, her chest rising and falling in soft, shallow breaths, like a sheet lifted by the wind. He covered her in silk and took the liberty of brushing the hair from her face——brushing it perhaps more than it needed to be brushed—back off her forehead. But that was all.

She stayed in the boat for two days, eating, cleaning herself up, getting her strength back. She listened to the Valley from the prow. She had never been away from her sister before. Three or four of the dogs settled in on the ground beneath the hull. Markus brought her food and sat with her while they talked about what she wanted to do. She said she wanted to learn about everything: to be in the world no differently than anybody else, to see without seeing. To be able to take care of herself, without the help of anyone. These were not his goals for her—his goal was to keep her as close to him as possible, so that one day she would see that she *could* in fact do anything, be anyone she wanted to be . . . as long as he was beside her.

On the third day, Rachel and Markus descended the stairway and joined the Valley people in the one small flat clearing there was, a field where some food was grown (a little corn, squash, tomatoes) and where goods were exchanged, and where the moss-scrapers gathered with their old knives, scraping moss off of whatever they were asked to: chairs, clothes, the family silver brought from Roam.

Markus cleared his throat. "Everybody," he said. "Everybody? This is—"

Rachel pulled on his coat sleeve. "I can do this," she whispered.

She smiled tentatively and looked around; she almost seemed to see everyone. "My name is Rachel McCallister," she said. "I come from a place called Roam. It's not far from here, but . . . far enough, I suppose. Markus saved my life, I—I'm indebted. I hope to learn whatever it is you have to teach me."

One of the old combos gently touched Rachel on her arm, took her hand, and said, "We have corn. I'll show you." And Rachel went with her, casting not even a blind glance back at Markus, who watched her go, suddenly, inexplicably bereft.

His replacement mother, Liling, the old moss-scraper, saw what was happening. She was pure Chinese, though she had never seen China. But the way she walked, her slow, tiny strides, the old threadbare kimonolike wrap she wore day and night—even her pidgin English—made her seem authentic, directly from the mainland.

"Why you bring her here?" she asked him.

He ignored her: he was watching Rachel, who was on her knees, in the garden, digging into the soil with her fingers. How could she do that and still be so beautiful? Liling didn't go away. "I told you. She was lost in the woods. She was almost dead."

His mother stared at him until, defeated, he looked away. Liling looked at the moss beneath her nails, the scabs across the side of her hand.

"No good will come of this," she said.

Markus didn't answer. What could he say? Maybe she was right, maybe not: he was willing to take any chance, every chance, for the good.

"Ah," she said. "I see."

"See what?"

"You want her to be wife!" She shook her head. "All because she pretty."

"Not that. Not *just* that."

"So, if she not so pretty you bring her here and make her wife?"

Markus decided it was best not to say anything further to his replacement mother. She would only twist his words to make them fit into the story she was telling herself.

"About her, this is what we say," she said, tossing a handful of moss over her shoulder. "We say, '*She like a seashell washed up on shore. Pretty on outside, but inside—empty.*'"

"Maybe," he said. "But how do you know what's inside if you never look?"

Liling scoffed. "You think she will want this? If she knew where she really was?"

"She's blind, Mother."

"Yes, but for how long?" She glared at him, and then looked away, toward the cave. "If you love her, you know what to do."

Markus knew what she meant. But is that what love was, really? Was it something floating around out there, like a cloud, something everyone could see and agree on? Rachel would have died without him, facedown as she was on the forest floor, blind: didn't that mean something?

But that's not how it worked, and he knew it. And he wasn't built like that. It was only a matter of time before he would do the right thing.

"Maybe we'll go away together," he said. "Maybe to Arcadia. Maybe somewhere else."

He surprised himself. He had no idea he had planned this far ahead.

She shook her head. She was old; she knew better. "You lie to her, you lie to me, you lie to yourself. Blind girl blind you."

And she went back to her moss.

• • •

$\mathcal{T}$he rest of the Valley welcomed Rachel, and not a week had passed before she became a part of life there, such as it was. No one cared that she was beautiful; no one cared that she was blind. Her beauty and her blindness were the same to them: differences, distinguishing characteristics. They put her to work in the morning—stacking stones for walls, gathering wood, patching up the lean-tos, digging rainwater ditches—and at night she sat beside the fire, where the old ones remembered the past, and told stories about it, because they knew the past was all they'd ever have. Rachel didn't say very much, but Markus could see her listening, taking everything in, as if she were more than a visitor to just the Valley: she was a visitor to the world. She was learning how to be a human with other humans. He could almost hear her mind thrumming, like a bird trying to get out. Then, as the fire died down, he'd take her back to the boat and say good night and she'd disappear inside the cabin until the next morning, when he would be there, waiting for her again. He was never far. "Maybe you shouldn't work so hard," he said to her one day when she was working so hard. And she said, "Maybe you shouldn't tell me what to do." But with a smile.

She bathed in rainwater and dried herself with silk. The women made her dresses; they braided her hair. When he heard her laugh for the very first time, he knew he would never live long enough to hear that sound too much.

Weeks passed like this, then months, and Markus only fell deeper in love with her. How could he not? The more he saw, the more he loved. There was nothing she could do he didn't love. The gentle way she held a river rock in the palm of her hand; the way her lips curled when she smiled; how every word she said was considered so thoughtfully before she spoke it, and how it was spoken, softly, beautifully, as if no word were more important than the one passing her lips: each deserved the unreserved attention of her tongue.

Her tongue. All her parts. Thoughts of her filled him up, constantly. Even her hair possessed him. He dreamed of it. He dreamed of climbing through it, naked, getting lost in it; of crawling inside her body through her mouth. He dreamed of what it would be like to kiss her. He could feel it in his heart, his blood; his hands trembled. And once he thought of kissing her, he couldn't stop thinking about it. His lips were pressed to hers in his mind forever. She exhausted him with her kisses. They had no time to eat, and barely had time to breathe. If it ever actually happened—if in real life she actually did kiss him—he thought he would probably die.

All day long, day in and day out, he was close enough to touch her shoulder, or hold her slender wrist, but he never told her how he felt, and he was sure she didn't know. But he wrote her a love letter. The same one over and over and over again.

*Rachel,*

*I love you.*

*Markus*

He kept twenty or thirty in his back pocket, and when he was with her he'd press one into the palm of her hand.

"What's this?" she'd ask.

And he'd say, "Nothing."

"It's always nothing," she'd say, and smile.

"Keep it with the others, just in case."

"In case what?"

"In case it becomes something."

It was their own joke, that single thing they shared that no one else would know or understand, like people did when they were in love, even if one of them didn't know it yet.

But she was happy. Look at her. That is something everybody knew.

$\mathcal{H}$e tried to avoid Liling, but there weren't that many places to go in the Valley, so he often found himself in her company. And here they were again today, together, Rachel out collecting firewood with one of the old men.

"She is so happy," Liling said.

"Yes, she is."

"I think for a girl who cannot see, she is *very* happy."

"Please. Stop."

"Stop? Stop what? I only say I think for a girl who cannot see, for blind girl, she is very happy."

"I know what you're saying."

Liling was a foot shorter than he was, but it never felt that way, even when she was looking up at him, the way she was now. "What, Markus?"

"You know," he said.

"Then why you not hear me?"

He looked around, made sure no one was listening. "And what makes you think it will be so much better then? She's happy. You said so yourself."

"This not about her being happy. It is about *you* being happy. Is all about you."

"No. It's about *you*. You don't like her because I like her. Because I love her. You don't want me to love anyone but you."

"I raised you wrong," she said. "Why can you not do right thing?"

"She thinks the world is . . . different than it is. She believes things.

If she knew how things really were I think she might . . . I think she might change. I saved her life."

"No prize for picking beautiful girl up in woods. It's for after; that's what you get prize for. For doing hard things. But you don't even take her to Ming Kai!"

"He's sick."

She slapped him. She had never done that before, but it seemed to come quite easily. "You lie to me again, I hit you again. In case you don't know when you do it. Okay?"

"Okay."

"Ming Kai show her things you don't want her to see. You only want her to see you."

He shook his head, but when he saw her raise her hand he nodded. Everything she said was true.

"You tell her about river," Liling said. "So she decide on her own."

"I'll tell her," he said. "Soon."

She studied him, gauging his heart. "Yes," she said. "I believe it. Soon, she will know."


The problem now was getting Rachel alone. She did so many things, and everyone loved her so much, Markus didn't have the chance to talk to her the way Liling wanted him to, the way he knew he should. But as the weeks passed he felt his replacement mother watching him, waiting for him to do the right thing. Finally he saw his chance: Rachel was washing her hands in a water bucket. She had been sweeping leaves all morning, and the leaves had continued to fall, and she had continued sweeping them . . . but now she stopped, and Markus approached her.

"Markus," she said, without turning.

"How do you know when it's me?"

"Your footsteps are apologetic."

"What does that mean?"

She turned, smiling, wiping her hands on her long, black skirt. "It doesn't mean anything," she said. "Everybody else here just does what they want to do and doesn't think twice about it. But you're never sure."

"And you can hear that—"

"In your feet."

"Oh."

He asked her to go for a walk, and she said yes, and for the first minute of it he listened to his feet. He couldn't tell the difference between the sound of his footsteps and anybody else's. The sun broke through a sheet of gray, and a sunbeam landed on her face, then faded as the clouds smothered the light. They kept walking, farther from the others but not far enough, in a sweet silence.

"Look at me," she said.

"I am."

"I mean look at me: I'm walking. No one is telling me where to go. No one is holding my hand or guiding me. Not even . . . my sister."

"That *is* good," he said.

She nodded. "I can gather firewood and plant a garden. I can clear a trail. I know everything about the Valley, Markus, where every tree is, every rock. In my mind there's a map, and I can walk it, going anywhere I want to, without anyone to help me."

She stopped and curled one arm around his neck and the other around his back and hugged him, pressing his body so close he could feel her ribs, the top of her hips. She had never done *this* before. He didn't know how long he could endure it.

"Thank you," she said.

"No," he said. "You did it."

Her face was so close to his he could feel the air move when she breathed. He breathed, and when he did he breathed in the air that had just left her, and in the same way she took in his. He was staring into the eyes of a blind girl, and she was staring back at him.

"Helen is going to be happy," she said.

"Who?"

"When I go back to Roam she'll see that I'm alive, and that will make her happy enough. But then she'll see that I'm alive in a different way. She won't have to take care of me anymore. We can just love each other, as sisters, and friends."

"Helen?" he said, bewildered. "But I thought you were happy here."

"I was always hoping to go back to Roam, Markus," she said. "You know that. The Valley is—was—practice. I think I've practiced enough, don't you?"

He couldn't look at her any longer. He stared at the forest floor, at the impression of her footprint in the dirt. "I understand."

She must have heard the forlorn and bitter sadness in his voice, and touched him lightly on the arm. "You'll go back with me," she said. "I want you to see Roam, meet Helen. I need to go, Markus."

"I won't try to stop you," he said. "But we were lucky to get past the birds once. I don't think we could get past them twice. I mean, it's possible, but do you want to take that chance? You know what they could do to us." It was not easy for him to lie, but he had never wanted anything as much as he wanted Rachel. She was worth lying for.

"I was hoping you would say, 'I know a secret path. I know how to get past them.'"

"I don't," he said, shaking his head. "I don't. We were lucky."

He couldn't bear to look at her now, so disappointed. He looked down again, blinked, concentrated on bringing the ground into focus. When it did, he saw something protruding from the soil, something unnatural and foreign. He dug it up with his fingers, cutting one on a surprisingly sharp edge; a thin stream of blood dripped off the tip of his index finger. It was a piece of glass about half the size of his hand. Then he wiped the dirt off its surface and saw that it was more.

It was a mirror, or a shard of one. The first time he had seen one was at the Peach Blossom.

"Markus."

Liling, walking in her mincing steps down the path toward them. He slipped the mirror into his pocket and stood. He knew why she was there in an instant: she was carrying the empty wooden bucket. Her face was flat and humorless. She looked from him to Rachel and back again. "Ming Kai is sick," she said.

Markus nodded.

"What's wrong?" Rachel said.

"He's thirsty."

Liling held out the bucket. He took it, but didn't move.

"I wish you would let me meet him," Rachel said.

"He's sick," he said.

"You always say that."

"Because he's always sick. He's very old. Isn't that right, Mother?"

"Oh, yes," she said. "Older than old. When he's better, he tell you so much about Roam. He was there, you know, at very beginning."

"I know," Rachel said. "Markus told me. I hope Ming Kai gets better."

"He will," Liling said. She glared at his great-grandson. "Why you wait? Go!"

Markus went, turning back every few steps to see if Liling had left Rachel alone. She hadn't. When he came to the entrance of the cave she was still there, next to Rachel, watching him, waiting.

Later when he came out of the cave they were gone.

$\mathcal{H}$e found her on the boat an hour or so later. She was standing with her back to the door, her thick red hair falling halfway down her back.

"I was looking for you," he said.

She didn't turn. "Your mother and I had a talk today."

"When I went to see Ming Kai," he said.

"That's right. I realized it was one of the only times I've been alone, without you somewhere around, since I've been here."

"I don't think—"

"It's true," she said. "Maybe the first time."

"I just want to help you, Rachel, take care of you. That's all. You know how important you are to me."

She turned to him. "My sister was like that," she said. "She always wanted to take care of me. She never left me alone. That's one of the reasons I left. To show her I could be on my own and that she—" For the first time since he'd known her, Rachel began to cry, just one tear, glistening on her perfect cheek. "And that she could be on hers."

Markus held the mirror he'd found in his right hand, hidden, as if she could see it. He'd been looking at himself a lot since he'd found it.

"So what did you and my mother talk about?"

"What do you think we talked about?"

"I don't know."

Rachel shook her head. "We talked about the water, Markus. The river water. The water you took to Ming Kai."

"Oh."

"She said it was a kind of medicine. A kind of magic."

"It can be."

"She said that I might be able to see again. That the water could make it happen. Why didn't you tell me, Markus?"

He hesitated a moment. He wasn't sure whether to tell some of the truth, or all of it.

"I was going to," he said.

"When?"

"When I thought it was time."

"When *you* thought it was time?"

Markus tried to find a way to say what he meant. He looked into the mirror. "The world," he said, "*your* world, is different than you think it is, Rachel. In so many ways. I didn't want to upset you."

"Different how? What does that even mean?"

"You don't want to know what it means."

"You're wrong," she said. No tears anymore, just anger.

"You're not ready."

"No," she said, her voice rising to a harsh crescendo. "*You're* not ready!"

He couldn't look at her anymore, and so he looked at himself, at the face of a man he never imagined becoming. So ashamed. He had always admired the old men who told stories around the fire, and one day he thought he would become one of them. Instead, he'd become a liar. A storyteller makes up things to help other people; a liar makes up things to help himself.

He looked up from the mirror, but he was too late: she was out the cabin door and off the boat before he could even move.

"Rachel! Rachel, wait!"

By the time he made it out the door she was already halfway down the hill, running wildly, but running directly toward the cave: clearly, Liling had even told her where it was. She was fast, unbelievably so; she had memorized every rock, every root and branch, and navigated her way down the hill. He wasn't going to get to her in time. How could she be so eager to get away from him, after everything he'd done for her?

But then she tripped, and fell hard, cutting her hands as she tried to break her fall, one side of her face scraping across the rocky embankment, rolling twice before she stopped, her chest heaving, her face contorted, wincing in pain.

Markus pulled her to her feet, and not gently.

"I'm sorry, Markus," she said. "I'm sorry. Take me back to the boat. I don't want to go to the cave. You're right: I'm not ready. Later . . ."

"No," he said, gripping her by the arm: he would leave a bruise. "I'll show you. I'll show you what I was protecting you from."

She struggled against his grip, but he wasn't going to let her free of it, no matter what. The Valley people watched them, watched them as though they were witnessing a play that they had no reason or desire to interrupt. When Markus came to the thick sheet of vines hanging over the cave entrance, he stopped, knowing that nothing would be the same after this.

"Markus!" she wailed. "Take me back to the boat!"

He pulled her through the opening and down the path he'd taken so many times. Rachel cried and kicked, but Markus had the strength of his anger, and there was nothing she could do now, nothing, that would free her from his grip.

He walked her waist deep into the cold pool, the river rushing by just below them. One last time she struggled. But she was spent. She was shivering, no fight left in her.

"Markus," she pleaded. *"Please.* I'm afraid."

"You want to know, Rachel? You want to know? So *know.*"

And with that he pushed her under, all of her, holding her by the back of the neck for far, far too long. Her arms and legs tore at the water violently—no doubt she thought he was trying to drown her. And he almost did. But at the last possible moment he pulled her out, and she gasped for her life. The rainbow dust fell like rain from the cave walls, fell on her wet hair and her face, until she herself glowed. She didn't struggle; her chest rose and fell, slower and slower. She stood like that for a minute or more.

Then she turned to him. He had loved her from the moment he saw her, and now he loved her even more—now that he knew he would lose her.

"Oh, Markus," she said, gazing at the glittering world around her, wide-eyed in wonder, "why would you ever want to keep this from me?" She threw her arms around his neck and hugged him.

She let go of him too soon, and took his hand and started to pull him up the embankment. He didn't move.

"Wait," he said. He knew that as much had changed for her, more change was coming, and he wanted to hold this moment for a moment longer. "I did this for you," he said.

"I know," she said. "Thank you."

And since he still wouldn't move, she let go of his hand and walked to the cave's entrance, pausing before the vines, where the sun slipped through in raw, thin beams, and then pushed her way past. He waited for a moment, imagining what she was seeing now: the gray trees and rocky soil, the leafless branches veining hopelessly into the sky, the primitive huts and painfully lethargic people, all of them turning now to stare at her. Even the dogs stood and stared. He wasn't brave enough to be with her as she took it in. But he was close enough, just on the other side of the vines, to hear her horrified whisper: "Oh," she said, "oh, my God."

$\mathcal{H}$e would have stayed in the cave forever if he could. He wasn't angry at her anymore and wished he'd never been. He wanted to take it all back now, because he knew that nothing was going to be the same. And no, it hadn't been perfect before, but it was good enough, and now all of that was gone. He stepped through the vines and she was there, an arm's length away from him, but he didn't reach out to her: she was rigid, so transfixed on what was before her he thought that if he touched her she would crack and shatter like a sheathing of river ice. She looked so small now, her thick red hair matted wet against her blouse, water still dripping from her fingers. "You wanted to know, Rachel," he said. "You told me—"

And Rachel, softly but clearly: "I know what I said."

He took half a step closer and saw her stiffen. He walked around until he faced her, until there was nothing she could see but him, and still she wouldn't look at him; something kept her from it. Finally, though, she did, and she almost smiled.

"So you're Markus," she said. She lifted her right hand—out of habit—to touch his face, then dropped her arm to her side and studied him instead, gathering him into her eyes. "You're . . . pretty. Or hand-some. Girls are pretty; men are handsome." She saw his confusion and said, "I don't think it matters: even if you've never seen it before, you know what beauty is, and what it's not. It's amazing how quickly—how quickly I see it, and know the difference."

She blinked her eyes. She looked like she'd been asleep for a very long time.

"I'm sorry," he said. "If I hurt you."

"You almost drowned me."

"I'm . . . sorry."

He could tell she didn't care whether he apologized or not. Her eyes—beautiful even when she was blind—burst with light, like a pair of suns. "It's not what I imagined it would be," she said. "But you knew that. You knew I had a different picture of the world. Because you helped make it for me. It's awful, isn't it, even for you?" She waited for him to answer; he only nodded. Seeing her so disappointed made him almost unbearably sad. But how could she be otherwise? "I wish I were back in the cave," she said. "No—I wish I were still blind. Just like Helen said: it's better not to see at all."

"Don't say that."

"Don't tell me what to say," she said. "Don't tell me what to think. You've done that enough already." She turned away. The damp earth, the gray sky: she took all of it in. "*This* is where you brought me?"

He didn't answer. She knew everything she needed to know about the Valley, all from a single glance. "I don't know what to do now," he said, though he did know. He knew what he had to do as he gripped the mirror in his hand. He would finish what he started. He had hoped—and it was a ridiculous hope, he knew that now—that this moment would have marked the real beginning of their life together. That he would be able to name the world with her, for her. *Tree,* he'd say, *this is a tree.* And she'd look at it from every angle, piecing its parts together, first the sprawling grandness of it and then closer, examining a branch, bark, the mystery of a leaf. They could spend a day on a tree—two on a shoe. He looked at her shoes now, thinking of them. They still didn't match. She still wore the one she had when he found her, the other from the man at the motel the dogs had killed. She raised her arm again, and he wanted her to take his hand, to forgive him, to say everything was going to be all right. Instead she pushed him aside, and took a step toward the people, who still hadn't moved. They were stunned. Even though all of them knew what the water was capable of, they had never seen such a thing as this; they had never seen such a thing as Rachel.

"Rachel, wait," he said, and when she didn't stop he said, "Please."

"What is it, Markus?"

"There's . . . more."

"More what?"

"More for you to see. More I have to show you."

He pressed the mirror into her hand. He pressed it there so hard it cut them both. She winced, and opened her hand. The mirror angled away from her, toward the gray and misty sky, and, as if being directed to, she looked up toward the sky as well. So she knew what it was. She had to. *Mirror.* He watched her lips move around the word, but she made no sound. *Mirror.* Then, slowly, she turned it on herself, and for the first time saw who she was. Her cheek, chin, her lips. Her eyes. Then all of her, her entire face, a face that had no equal in the world as far as Markus knew, as far as Markus could even imagine. With her fingertips she traced the curve of her cheekbones, and then the shallow hollows beneath her eyes. She touched her lips, and watched herself touching them, and then her nose, and her chin. She blinked: for some reason, this almost made her smile.

"So," he said. "Now you know what real beauty is."

She nodded. Rachel knew. She couldn't stop looking at herself and the face she had lived behind without even knowing what it was. The curse her sister had laid on her was lifted in that instant, but the curse was replaced by a mystery. By more than one mystery—by many, too many to count. And as the mysteries filled her up the blood drained from her face, and her face turned the pallor of death. Her perfect beauty was still there, but all that was lovely about it, and sweet, and hopeful—and whatever scrap of love she had for Markus, or for the world—melted away.

She couldn't stop looking in the mirror. When she spoke it was as if she were talking to herself.

"Not having to see myself—my face—was my only blessing in this life. Helen told me that. She said, *As hard as it is to be blind, if you had to see yourself every day, to know the face you really wore: that would be worse.* But it's not—I'm not—like that." She looked at Markus, bewildered as a child. "She said I was so ugly my face frightened people. Why would Helen say that if it wasn't true?"

"I don't know," he said, knowing full well why. "I don't know."

She nodded. Then she dropped the mirror to the ground and crushed it beneath her shoe. Rachel remembered what Mrs. Samuels said, the day she was leaving Roam: *She tells you lies and you believe her because you don't know any better, because she's never let you know any better. She's never let another soul near you. You* couldn't *know. But now you can, now you can.*

*Now I can.*

"And you," she said coolly. "Why didn't you tell me? When you knew who I thought I was, all this time. You waited an entire year."

"I told you," he said. "I told you the day we met, but you didn't believe me. I tried, Rachel."

"You should have tried harder."

"Yes, yes . . . But, Rachel," he said, desperately. "It doesn't matter now. I love you. I've always loved you. And I think you love me. I saved your life."

And now she touched him, touched him the way he always dreamed she would. The tips of her fingers traced his cheeks, his nose, his chin. He closed his eyes so she could touch them as well and felt her fingers touch the deepest part of him. She pulled him closer, his mouth so close to hers he breathed her breath, and closer still, until the dream he had nurtured every day since he met her became too real to believe: she kissed him, a kiss so light and brief it almost may not have happened at all. But it did happen. His whole body felt it.

"Thank you for saving my life," she whispered in his ear.

Then she slapped him with all the strength she had, and he fell back, stunned, holding his face in his hands. It was as hard as he had ever been hit in his entire life, as hard as he ever would be.

"What else haven't you told me?" she said. She took a hard step toward him, and he flinched. "What else?"

He shook his head from side to side without conviction. He was a liar. He had become the man he never thought he could be. His desperate need to love her had made him so. A secret doesn't feel wrong until it's discovered, and he felt it, every dark scrap of shame. One last glance from her, knife-sharp, and she pushed past him, knocking his shoulder to one side with the power of a man. He stumbled, but it was his grief that made him fall to his knees.

"Rachel," he called after her. "Stop, please!" But it was pointless: she wasn't listening to him anymore. "Where are you going?"

"Where do you think?" she answered. "To see Ming Kai."

*M*ing Kai's hut was at the top of a rocky incline, just before the Valley ended and the next world, whatever it was, began. Beyond that lip of land was the mystery so many of the Valley people had journeyed into. Ming Kai's hut was propitiously situated to encounter the least amount of runoff during the heavy rains (the hut at the bottom suffered most; its inhabitant, Jerrod, the slow boy, lived ankle deep in mud, not that he seemed to mind much), but its distance from the rest of his dwindling tribe also insured a privacy no one else could claim.

Rachel hadn't known where Ming Kai was until she got her sight back. She knew where everything else was in the Valley because she'd been taken everywhere else, and she'd taken it all in. She'd mapped out the Valley the same way she'd mapped out Roam, step by step. Ming Kai's hut was in a blank spot in the topography of her mind. She knew now, though. No one stopped her, and no one followed her but the dogs; even Markus hung back. He had known how this was going to play out. Maybe it was for the best; maybe she would understand why he had done what he'd done . . . though he doubted it. Because Ming Kai wouldn't lie to her; he didn't know how.

# MING KAI

No one had ever known a man so old, or even *believed* that any man could live to be so old, as Ming Kai. They had stopped counting the years years ago. His body was shriveled, shrunken by age, the skin so tight around his bones she could see every one of them, a skeleton covered by a thin leathery sheaf. She could see his heart beat; she could see his heart. There were two old women on their knees on either side of his bamboo cot spooning water on him—his head, his chest, his arms, his stomach, his thighs, the thin and fragile remnants of what used to be a man. They were humming to themselves. He breathed four or five times a minute; all he had to do was skip one breath and his eyes would close forever.

He was sleeping when Rachel pushed through the skein of weathered silk that served as his makeshift door.

"Ming Kai," she said.

The old women glared at her and shooed her away. "Sleeping," one said. But Rachel paid no attention and pushed past them until she stood over him. "Ming Kai!" When he didn't stir she shook him by the shoulder until his eyelids creaked open.

"Ah," he said as his eyes fluttered open to see her. He even smiled. "Rachel McCallister. Pretty Rachel McCallister."

"You know me?" she asked.

"Oh," he whispered. "Oh, yes. Markus tells me everything. I knew your great-grandfather, too. I knew Roam before it was Roam. I know almost everything. Live long enough and so will you."

"Then tell me," she said. "Tell me everything."

He opened his mouth to speak, but as he did his eyes closed, and he fell back asleep.

"Ming Kai!"

"At your service." It was less than a whisper: the words almost died before they found the air. "So, what is it you want to know?"

"Listen to me."

"I am listening."

"When I was younger, when I was blind, my sister told me things. That Roam has a Boneyard where the dead were thrown, and a tree where they were hanged, and a house where a door opens and blood flows into the streets, and in the forest all around it are flesh-eating birds that will kill you in seconds and eat you before your shadow disappears."

He listened, his smile fading. He stared, his eyes as sharp and clear as any man's.

Rachel was desperate. She needed her past; as wretched as it was, without it she had nothing. But somehow she knew it was not to be. She knew, and still she said, "Tell me. Tell me that's what Roam is."

"If it is," Ming Kai said, "why would you ever want to go back?"

"Because my sister is there," she said.

"I see," he said. "But no: it is not so. It sounds like something out of a book, this Roam. A fairy tale meant to scare children." He breathed again, with some difficulty. "No, this is not Roam. Roam was just . . . a simple town. A small town, where people lived and worked. But beautiful. There were streets, and on some of them were shops, on others . . . small houses where people raised families. There were cats and dogs—not like these dogs, your dogs, but sweet dogs who slept by your feet on a cold winter's night. It was . . . our home. And together its people made the softest most wonderful thing there is in the world. Together." He took as long and deep a breath as he could. "But there is nothing so beautiful it can't be ruined by man. And Elijah McCallister ruined everything, including my life."

"Mine, too," she said.

"Yes," Ming Kai said. "Yours, too."

Markus was behind her now, edging into the small hut. She stood and turned to him. Even the fire in her eyes was cold. "You were right, Markus: the world is different than I thought."

"Rachel—"

She held up her hand.

"Don't speak to me. If I never hear your voice again it will be too soon."

How still the world became as the truth coursed through her. Everything she knew was wrong—everything. But she didn't know what to do with the truth; all it could do was destroy her. She shuddered, and for the first time in a long, long time, she looked like the girl he had found behind a motel in the woods, blind, nearly dead, and missing one shoe. But not for long. Slowly, she began to walk away.

"Where are you going?" Ming Kai asked her.

She stopped, and without looking back at him said, "I'm going home. To see my sister. To thank her for everything she did for me—to make things right."

"Rachel," Markus said. "No."

Ming Kai looked on, too, as the old Chinese ladies continued coating him with water. The old Chinese ladies didn't look at Rachel anymore; somehow they were able to pretend none of this was happening. They continued spooning water onto his head, his chest, his stomach, his legs. He wished he could tell them to stop, but he couldn't: even though he had led them here, to this dark valley, he was their leader, and they would have been even worse off without him. As long as he was alive, there was a chance that next time he might get it right. *The next time he leads us somewhere*, his people thought, *maybe he'll lead us someplace good. As long as he's alive, anything can happen.* He could never tell them the truth—that he was done with leading, done having ideas, done with it all.

And he had always blamed Elijah, for Roam, the Valley: everything. But now, as he came face-to-face with her, he knew it wasn't Elijah alone who made Rachel into the woman she was: Ming Kai had a part in it as well. It was at the very beginning of their journey into America. He remembered how after many days of riding horses through the forbidding wilderness, Elijah had made the trade he had no doubt planned on making from the very beginning—he would bring Ming Kai's family here if Ming Kai would just tell him one simple thing: the name of a tree. And Ming Kai told him. But then Ming Kai said to Elijah McCallister, *No good will come from what we do. No flower grows in a poisoned field. We may not see it now, but our children will, and our children's children. They will be the ones who finally suffer.* How many years had passed since then? How many lifetimes had come and gone? He had meant it when he said it, but he never thought it would actually happen—that his curse would land on this girl, and her sister. Ming Kai was just a man, after all, and they were just words, words like *silk, worm, mulberry tree, wife, family, love, friend.*

Home.

"Yes," he said. Now he knew how this would have to end. "Home." *A small town, but beautiful, where they made the softest thing in the world.* "You must go home."

"Ming Kai!" Markus yelled at him. "What are you saying?"

Ming Kai's voice was weak. Rachel looked down at him as if she heard the sounds he made but not the sense. He held her in his gaze. He was so old, he *did* look like he knew everything there was to know. He looked wise. Only he knew that being old taught you only one thing: that being young is better.

"She must go home," he said again. "There is no other way."

Rachel nodded, and took a quick step away, as if to leave this very moment.

"But wait," Ming Kai said. She stopped and looked back at the old man who, for the first time in thirty years, actually had something to live for. "I will go with you. We will all go with you," he said. "We will all of us go back to the place where we belong. Everybody."

"Why would I want you with me?"

"I know the best way there," he said. "I remember."

"I can find my own way," she said.

"And your sister," he said. "I will take you to her."

"You don't know where she is," she said. "How could you?"

"Not where she is," he said, cryptically. "But where she will be. I will show you—but only if everybody goes."

She studied him for a moment, then nodded. "Yes," she said. "Everybody." Then she turned to Markus, her voice as sharp as a knife to his throat. "Everybody but you, Markus."

"Me? But Rachel, please. I—"

"I don't want you near me. Not after what you've done."

"Rachel, please—"

"You stay here. See what it's like to have nothing, nobody."

"You can't make me stay here, Rachel."

Behind them, one of her dogs began to growl.

"Rachel," he said. "I'm sorry. I only did what I thought was right. Because I love you. Don't leave me. Please. Let me come with you."

There was nothing in her eyes now—nothing. "It must be hard to take someone's life away, day after day after day. The way you did mine. The way she did mine. Even I know that's not love, Markus. No: that's just evil, pure and simple."

She turned and walked away, and disappeared into the falling darkness. Markus looked to Ming Kai for help, for direction, but Ming Kai's eyes were closed. Markus would never see them open again.

The next morning, everybody—every man, every woman, all the children and dogs, and of course Ming Kai, carried on his cot by his two attendants—began their trek up and out of the Valley. Rachel was at the front: she could find Roam all by herself, she could taste it in the air. Bringing up the rear was Liling. She could not forgive Markus. She waved good-bye to him as they set off, and he waved back. He was a good man in his heart, but what could she do for him now? She took one long look and followed the others over the rocks and up the hill. When she came to the top of the ridge and was about to take her first step into the other world, she couldn't help it: she turned to see him one last time.

But he was gone.

# THE JOURNEY BACK

*T*hey walked until dusk. Rachel moved through the forest as if she were following a well-worn trail, as if she were following signs that said THIS WAY TO ROAM; the rest of them stumbled along as best they could, because she wasn't stopping—that much was clear. Around midday Jerrod, the slow boy, stopped to pee behind a pine tree. It took him a while, and by the time he finished up, everyone had gone. Someone told Rachel he was missing, but she didn't even turn her head. No one ever saw him again.

When the last light of the sun shot through the army of pine around them and cast shadows as dark as ditches across the forest floor, Liling hurried, one quick small step after another, to get close enough to Rachel to touch her elbow. Rachel shook her off and kept walking. Liling touched her elbow again—she wasn't scared of the blind girl (which is how she still thought of her)—and then grabbed it and pulled. Rachel wheeled around and pushed her, and if she'd had a knife in her hand she probably would have cut her wide open.

"What?" Rachel said.

"Dark now," she said. "We rest."

"Dark or light," Rachel said. "What difference do you think that makes to me? I'm not stopping. I know what I need to do."

Rachel gave her one last hard look before stalking away.

"Why you leave Markus back in the Valley?" Liling asked.

This stopped her. "You left him, too," she said, turning to her. "And for the same reason. Because he's a liar."

"He give you everything," Liling said. "He show you everything." Liling grabbed Rachel's wrist and yanked her close. "He save your *life*."

"No," she said. "He didn't save my life. The girl he found in the woods that day—and he killed her. I'm done with him."

By then everyone else had caught up with them—worn-out, exhausted. Rachel drew on some vestigial kindness and relented. "We'll sleep here."

*T*he night was so black that even a fire wasn't enough to crack the darkness, the sparks from the fire rising and dying, swallowed up in it. Everybody slept but Ming Kai. He lay on his side in a small puddle of the magic water, staring into the nothing of the darkness ahead—until a glowing appeared, like a hovering cloud of insects, and coalesced into the figure of a man.

"Elijah McCallister," Ming Kai said to the spirit. "See what you've done."

On the outside Elijah looked like he did in the days before he died: all hollowed out. But now he had been filled up with the peace of death. "It's not what I intended, Ming Kai. And please don't say *I told you so*."

"I told you so!" Ming Kai said. "You've cursed us! And the girls most of all."

"I'm sorry," the ghost of Elijah said. "I'm sorry for every terrible thing I did. I don't know what else I can say."

"One word cannot change the past."

"But that's just it, Ming Kai," he said, his ghostly translucence moving closer to his ear, to whisper: "This isn't about the past: it's about the future. You know that now."

"Future." Ming Kai sighed. "There is no future for you, Elijah. Or even for me." His old eyes, dimmed now, reflected on his ruined life. "But for them? Maybe."

"So," Elijah said. "What are you going to do?"

Ming Kai smiled. "You know so much, you tell me."

But Elijah fell back into the night and soon was no more than a fire's spark himself.

The next morning he was back. Ming Kai was being doused with the water as usual—he felt as if he had lived the last years of his life underwater—and when he looked at one of the old women there instead was Elijah.

Ming Kai sighed.

"You haunt me," he said, "when it is I who should haunt you! What is it you want!"

"Remember?" Elijah said. "Remember what you said to me? About the worms."

"No," he said stubbornly. Though he did remember.

"*A worm is born a worm*, you said. *Then it becomes a moth. It is born twice. It has two lives.*"

Then, almost in unison: "We should all be so lucky."

Ming Kai closed his eyes and rolled his head back and forth against the wet cot, and when he looked again, no Elijah. It was the old woman. He had forgotten her name.

"What you saying, old man?" she said.

He didn't answer, but with his remaining strength he reached out and knocked the bucket from her hand. The water soaked into the loamy soil.

"Ming Kai!" she gasped. "What are you doing? Now you know what will happen? Without water, you will die!"

"I know," he said.

Everyone stopped, even Rachel, who turned to see what the problem was. She pushed her way through the ring of people until she was standing beside Ming Kai.

"What's this?" she said.

Ming Kai shook his head, but Rachel wouldn't leave without an answer. She was glaring at him, waiting for a reason she had been held up.

"I saw him," he said.

"Who?"

"Elijah McCallister. We talked."

"Really? About what?"

"Worms," he said.

He looked at her rusted copper eyes, her drawn cheeks. Not so beautiful now—or beautiful in a different way.

"You hate him, don't you?"

"Yes," he said, with great affection. "I do."

She laughed, once. "That's why you wanted to come back with me: to see what it's like to have revenge on the person who destroyed your life. We're the same, you and me."

Ming Kai shook his head. "No," he said. "But we used to be."

Rachel smiled at him, her lips tinged with malice. She rubbed his sunken chest with the palm of her weathered hand, as if she loved him. And she resumed her trek to Roam—all of them did. It wouldn't be long now, not long at all. Ming Kai could feel it in his bones.

# A PLACE FOR EVERYTHING

*D*igby wanted a drink—not for him, but for Helen. She didn't drink, though, and as far as he knew never had. But now would have been a good time to start. For a man who thought he had seen and heard everything there was to see and hear, he'd never heard anything like this. Best to just sit there, he thought. Best not to say or do anything. It just wasn't his place.

Markus looked down at his hat and turned it three full times before looking up again. Outside there was a commotion. They heard one dog howl, then another. Soon it became a song, a canine chorus. Markus turned toward the window.

"She's almost here," he said.

Digby waited for Helen to say something, anything, but she seemed lost.

"Why did you come here?" he asked Markus.

Markus shook his head, still looking toward the outside, and shrugged, as if he weren't really sure anymore. "She doesn't have much use for me," he said. "After what I've done . . . " Markus looked up at Helen, and Digby saw how it was with the two of them, how they lived in the same world, with the same guilt, born of loneliness and love. "I saved her life, but it didn't work out the way I wanted it to. I messed up. I thought maybe if I could save you, I could save her—one more time. And maybe that would be enough."

"She would never hurt me," Helen said. "Never."

Markus turned away. "Oh, Helen," he said. "She would."

"Where is she?"

"By now she's at that bridge. Just barely made it across my-self—looks like it's about a hundred years old and held together by spiderwebs and spit. She could make it over, maybe. But not the rest of them. Not that the rest of them need to. She's enough for whatever she means to get done."

"Then I have to go," Helen said. And Markus and Digby both nodded, relieved. This is what they wanted to hear. "To see her, I mean," she said. "I have to go see her."

"Have you been listening to this man, Helen?" Digby asked her.

"Of course I have, Digby," she said. "That's how I know what it is I have to do."

"I won't let you."

But Helen, as if she didn't hear him or it didn't matter if she did, moved toward the door. Markus blocked her path. "You won't be able to stop her," he said.

"Who said I wanted to?"

He walked to the window and pushed back the shade as outside the dogs made a sound that filled up the world, baying and singing. "It's the dogs I worry about, more than anything."

"Helen," Digby pleaded with her. "*Please.*"

They met in the middle of the room and embraced. She kissed him, and again he took her in his arms and pressed her close, his head resting just beneath her breasts.

"I love you, Digby," she said. "Don't worry: I'll bring her back here with me and she'll see, see how things have changed . . . "

But even she didn't believe this. The house was lovely. She tried to keep it clean. *A place for everything and everything in its place.* Cleaning a house was a way to show how much you loved it. She and Digby had rescued the house from time, but she knew it wasn't enough. She'd wake up in the middle of the night, listening to the silent dark, knowing it; she'd told the whole dead world it wasn't enough. The past never left her; there was nothing she could do to erase it.

On the way out she stopped and looked at herself in the mirror. Older now, she'd softened, the edges smoother, the eyes open and kind. While she didn't have a face anybody would ever pick out of a catalogue, she didn't feel the need to hide it from herself, nor did it cause her to shudder when she caught a glimpse of herself. *This is me,* she thought, *what I am.*

*You're more than just a face,* Digby had told her. *But that face I love, too.*

Digby was the best thing in the world.

She wished she had more time to fix her hair, but she felt like she should go. She brushed it back behind her ears and let it fall down around her shoulders. That would have to do. All of this happened in a moment, but it felt like time had slowed to a crawl now. It was as if she were memorizing her life.

She looked out the window. She could have been looking at a painting: no movement at all, nothing, not even a bird. The dogs were gone. They'd filled the yard for so long (only a few days, really, but it felt like forever) that their absence made the view a lonely one.

Then something did move. She saw it now: a single dog. It sat at the edge of the field, waiting. The dog caught her looking, and in the moment their connection was made it raised itself up on all fours and ambled away. Looked back just once to make sure she was still watching. A little farther on it stopped, sat, and waited again.

She opened the door and stood by it for a moment: she knew exactly what came next, and wasn't sure whether she was up to facing it. But then she decided of course she was. Her life had been practice for exactly now. Markus and Digby watched her from the window as she walked through the yard, through the vast and empty field, and disappeared into the forbidding forest beyond.

# MRS. MCCALLISTER

rs. McCallister knew Rachel was coming. She heard it the way one hears things when you're dead: news just blows past your ears, and if you're listening you can pick it up.

She'd been there on the other side of the bridge for an hour, waiting. Then she saw her daughter, pushing through the woods, a crowd of the oddest-looking people behind her.

Mrs. McCallister waved. It had been a long time since she'd been anywhere but the church. Sometimes she visited her own grave, because it felt like home. Kids would come down in the middle of the night and gather around her stone while one of them told the story, in hushed tones, of how she died, how Mr. McCallister drove off the bridge and into the lake in pure daylight. *No one knows how or why it happened,* they said. *Maybe they saw a ghost themselves!*

*It was a bird!* she wanted to tell them. *A bird flew into my hair!*

But she didn't want to give them the satisfaction. One time they gathered in their spooky little group on top of her grave and a twig snapped somewhere out in the woods and they ran for it. Chickens. She remembered being scared like that; it was how she spent most of her life, actually. Death turned out to be quite a relief, for her and her husband both. They still cared about things, of course, cared a great deal. But they didn't *worry*, because what could they do? They were dead.

Rachel had changed. Mrs. McCallister could see that. She was a woman now, all grown up, but the change went deeper than that. Rachel looked as though she'd died, too. She looked like a statue carved to honor the girl she used to be. Even her hair was different. Once it glowed a gentle orange, like a late setting sun; now it blazed a fiery red.

"You knew, didn't you?" Rachel said, getting right to it. "What Helen did to me."

Mrs. McCallister smiled. "You know me," she said. "Even though—"

"I know you," Rachel said. "I imagined you just like this."

"So not even a hello?"

"Not even that."

In the forest Mrs. McCallister saw more of those dogs slipping in the shadows between the trees. They were a nuisance. One of them had defecated quite near her grave.

"Did you know?" she asked again.

"No," Mrs. McCallister said. "No. Not until it was too late. And when I found out it broke my heart. But back then? Of course not." She paused, let this sink in until she had a feeling Rachel believed her. "A man came by here," she said. "Earlier."

"A man?"

"Young. Dressed in black. With a hat."

"Markus," she said. She shook her head. "It doesn't matter. Nothing he does matters anymore."

"He skittered across the bridge like a little bug," Mrs. McCallister said. "But it doesn't look safe to me."

"Don't worry about me, Mother," she said. Something in the way she said it hurt Mrs. McCallister; the suggestion was that she had never worried about her much, or enough. The opposite was true—she had worried about her daughters too much, both of them.

"I wanted to see you, Rachel," Mrs. McCallister said. "And for you to see me. You never really have before."

"And so your job here is done."

This girl, she wouldn't give an inch. "I also wanted to talk with you," Mrs. McCallister said. "To tell you that, as I see things, you should forgive your sister. That's the only real power any of us have—to forgive. We make mistakes and we're forgiven for them. That is what happens. Otherwise, we can't go on . . . "

"These wounds don't heal by themselves," Rachel said. "It's only right she suffers the same way I did."

"What are you going to do to your sister?"

"I don't know," she said, though her mother could tell this was something she'd been thinking about. "We'll see."

"Oh, Rachel: she told you some stories—that's all. And they were terrible. I'm *not* defending her, because she was awful. But she was just a girl, and she's changed—changed so much—and, in the end, what is she really guilty of?"

"We've all changed," Rachel said. "You, me, Helen."

Mrs. McCallister moved closer to her daughter. She reached out to touch her, but she couldn't, of course: her hand went right through her.

"What have you become, Rachel, that you would want to hurt your only sister?"

"I just want things to come out even," she said.

Mrs. McCallister cried. Now she knew how this was going to end. She saw it clear as day, and she couldn't bear it. Rachel turned away for an instant, toward the crowd behind her, and Mrs. McCallister took that opportunity to leave. When Rachel turned back, Mrs. McCallister had vanished; all there was to see was a church spire against a gray sky.

Like a good mother who loved all of her children equally, Mrs. McCallister went to the one who needed her most.

# THE CURE

*H*elen stopped at the edge of the forest. It was a bit warmer than she expected, so she removed her shawl and folded it into a square and placed it on the ground. That's something she could say to Rachel when she saw her, just to start a conversation. *It's a nice day, isn't it? Warmer than I expected.* Best to start things off with something trivial; the rest would come on its own.

The dog was gone now, so she walked into the forest alone, following the old trail first walked by Elijah McCallister over a century ago. The shadowed path was crowded by trees, tall and thick and ancient; looking up, she could see the sky in only small patches. All she could hear was the sound of dried and brittle twigs breaking beneath her feet. She had been here before, looking for Rachel—the night Rachel left, and then the day after, and the day after that and again, until it was clear to her and Digby and Smith that she had died the way Jonas had died, or worse.

Helen should never have given up.

Then she heard something: wings. A bird, screeching. She stopped, held her breath. But it was just a bird. She kept walking into the forest's darkness. The trees seemed to lean toward her until she had to turn one way and then the next just to slip through them. But then, just beyond the last dense canopy, she saw a pool of yellow light. She broke through the smaller branches (it was like breaking out of a tree-lined prison) and emerged into the suddenly bright and iridescent day.

The sunlight burned into Helen's eyes, and for a moment she couldn't see: it was as if the forest had filled with fog, the trees draped in spiderwebs. She squinted, held a hand up to block the sun, and that's when she spotted her sister, impossibly close and impossibly far away, on the other side of the bridge. Dressed like a spinster.

"Rachel."

Helen stepped closer, but the ravine scared her, its cavernous darkness so deep and mighty it threatened to swallow her if she got too close. How far away was her sister now? Close enough to look into her eyes, close enough to see her being seen. But Helen didn't look away, and neither did Rachel. It was as if there were nothing left in the world but the two of them, and everything depended on them and what they did here. Helen didn't even see all the people and the dogs just a few feet behind her sister on the other side.

How long were they like this, silent, staring? It felt like forever. But it was probably just a moment or two until the tips of Rachel's lips became a dark, sly smile. "You," Rachel said. "Look at you. You and your terrible, terrible face."

"Rachel—"

Rachel kept staring, as if she were still not sure she could believe her eyes. "You're everything I thought I was."

"Rachel," Helen said again. "Sweet Rachel."

"Not so sweet," she said. "Not anymore."

And Helen could see that this was true.

"*Why?*" Rachel asked her. "Why did you do this to me?"

"You must know," Helen said. "Now that you can see. Now that you can see who I am, what I am."

"And you thought that, since I was blind, it wouldn't matter who I thought I was. And not just me—but the world. You made up this terrible place for me to live in. Did you ever tell me anything that *wasn't* a lie?"

"It just came out; I didn't know what would happen, that I would keep doing it, what kind of person I would become. I was just a girl, Rachel, the—"

"I don't want to *hear* it," Rachel said. Her trembling voice echoed in the ravine. "I think you're evil. You hurt me, Helen. So much. And you should pay for that. Why shouldn't you pay for that?"

Then everything was quiet. Her people, hovering close behind her, moved a step backward and huddled together. They looked lost and frightened—all but an old Chinese man who sat up from the cot where he was lying. He was so old. His bones looked like they had turned into dried little twigs, his face wrinkled and lined, like the skin of a dead animal. And yet, shaking, he stood.

Rachel took a step onto the bridge. Then another. It swayed and creaked, unsteady beneath even her thin frame.

"I'm not that person anymore," Helen said. "I've changed."

"So have I," Rachel said. And then, as if it were the saddest truth she knew: "So have I."

Rachel took another step, then another, down into the curve of the sinking ancient bridge. The hundred-year-old twine uncurled around a supporting branch, and the branch dropped into the ravine. No one heard it hit the bottom.

"I love you," Helen said. "I didn't then. I didn't know how. But I've learned."

A single tear drew a wet trail down her face. Rachel saw it, watched it fall with a child's heartless curiosity.

"Wait," Rachel said, as if she'd just understood. She laughed once. "Of course: you want me to for*give* you. After everything. That's what you want from me."

"No," Helen said. "I would never ask for that. Never. But—"

Helen wept. Her voice was so soft, Rachel had to strain to hear it across the ravine. "I don't know what else to say."

The bridge was slipping, inch by inch. Helen could see it shudder and then catch itself, as if falling were the last thing it wanted to do. Rachel didn't seem to notice, or care.

"Come off the bridge, Rachel," Helen said. "Please."

Rachel didn't move, not forward or back.

"Look," Helen said. Helen reached into the large pocket stitched to the front of her dress and removed a small shoe. An old white shoe, worn and torn, held together with string and tape. She lifted it into the light. "It's yours. The shoe you lost the night you left. I found it not far from here. I've kept it with me every day since then. Every day."

She held it out for her sister. "Here," she said.

But still Rachel didn't move. She looked down at the shoes she was wearing: the one brown shoe Markus had found for her at the motel, too big for her, heavy and hot. And on her right foot the match to the shoe Helen was holding, its mate.

Behind Rachel, the old Chinese man was hobbling toward the bridge, stopping to summon more energy. He looked at Helen, and smiled. A lovely smile, wide and toothless. Helen had never seen a kinder smile. His hoarse whisper was carried through the air like a feather.

"Can't you see?" he said to Rachel. "Your sister loves you."

Rachel shook her head. "All I see is a shoe," she said.

"*Forgive her,*" Ming Kai said. "Forgive her as I have forgiven Elijah

McCallister." Ming Kai took a deep breath. He looked to the heavens and as loud as he could, he shouted, "I forgive you, Elijah McCallister! I forgive you for everything! For everything!"

"It's too late for that," Rachel said.

"No," he said. He could barely talk: shouting to a dead man had taken his breath away. "No. It is never too late."

Rachel's eyes softened, and for a moment she looked like the girl she used to be, sweet and loving. But then the bridge shifted and fell half a foot, trembling and swaying, and Rachel had to take hold of the guiding ropes to keep from falling. When the shaking stopped, she took yet another step toward her sister. She was in the very middle of the bridge; the risk of moving forward or going back was the same now.

"*Come off the bridge, Rachel,*" Helen said. She held out the shoe again. "Quickly. You can do it. The bridge will hold if you hurry."

Rachel didn't move. There was a fiery light behind her eyes, but it was dying. She wasn't bitter anymore, or mean: she was resigned.

"No," she said. "Bring it to me."

"What?"

And Rachel held out her hand. "If you love me," she said, "bring me my shoe."

Helen knew what this meant before she took the first step onto the bridge; she was resigned as well. She heard her name: it was being whispered by a hundred people, and she felt them, the dead; she felt them everywhere. *Helen. Helen.* But she couldn't see them, not the way she did before—her gray congregation. They were one now, like a fog rolling in, her mother and father and Elijah and Jonas, Dr. Carraway and all the rest. They were all there, she knew they were there, but she couldn't see them for who they were. She watched them go, a plume of smoke, sweeping into the air above her, above Rachel, and fading into the gauzy edge of a cloud.

Helen had hoped that once Rachel had seen who she was—just by looking at the face she had been born with—she would know why Helen had done the things she'd done. That they wouldn't even have to speak, to explain, to justify, defend. It would all be clear, once she was able to see her, and together they might be able to begin again.

But that isn't what happened.

Helen took another step toward her sister, and another. The rotten branches beneath her feet didn't even break: they crumbled. The ropey twine unraveled. But somehow it still held long enough for her to take another step toward her sister, and her sister another step toward her, until they were close enough to touch. Helen held out her hand for Rachel to take just as the last of the old rope finally snapped, as they knew it would, and the bridge fell, disappearing into the dark ravine.

But they didn't fall. For an instant they seemed to be floating, suspended somehow in the open air with nothing above them but sky and nothing below but a fathomless dark. And then, in a moment so brief it may not have actually happened, their faces—the masks they wore—transformed, and each saw the other as the other saw herself— not beautiful anymore, but not plain, either: but sisters. Just sisters. It was just the two of them now, and there was no magic or science or prayer, no great men and the memory of the great things they'd done; Roam and the rest of the world had disappeared. Because it wasn't about that. It was instead about the smallest things: a bird, a dog, a fever. Locoweed and a river, water and a rock. Most of all, though, it was about what happened to two girls on a rainy day, a day their parents had gone to Arcadia to see Dr. Beadles for the water they hoped would cure their Rachel. It began with a single lie.

One lie, and look at what had become of them! They almost smiled to think about it, that a moment so small, almost trivial, could change everything. But it did. It was like what happens to a leaf as it weaves itself down a stream, the way it can get caught on something, and how the other leaves and twigs following behind it, the bird feathers and snakeskin, the frog bones, the ants—nature's discarded parts—all flow up behind that first leaf and they get caught, too, and the stream eventually is dammed up, and stops. But water can't be stopped, it always finds a way around; it always makes another stream. So this is what they thought before they fell: what if, like this other stream, they could make another world? One in which everything unfolds just a little bit differently, one where that question—*What do I look like?*—was never answered, because it was never asked. Everything else would be the same there: one girl is beautiful, the other not; one can see, the other has been blind for years. Their parents have left them there alone. A moth rests against the window screen. The same rainy day has trapped the girls inside the house, and Helen is brushing her sister's hair.

*But then the rain stops, the clouds part and scatter, and the sun comes out, and the light bursts so brightly through the window that Helen has to shut her eyes. The sun slips beneath her silken eyelids anyway, as if it wants to show her something that, even with her eyes closed, she'll need the light to see. And in this heartbeat of a moment, sitting beside her sister, Helen sees it: Roam, all laid out before her, as if she's floating above it, flying above it. She sees the rain stop, and watches as the town comes to life. Doors open one by one. Like wary animals leaving their sheltered dens, people peer up at the sky: they can come out now. All morning long the rain has been falling, turning Roam into a soggy ghost town, but now that the sun is here the sidewalks quickly fill with life. Everybody has some business to attend to, some errand—or maybe, after being pent up for so long inside, they just need to take their dogs out for a walk.*

*The children who live in the old Yott place—there must be half a dozen of them now, at least—stream from their home and run fearlessly into the street, through big glassy puddles, shattering the skies reflected on each of* them. Then it's into the fields to play one of their games: today, hide-and-go-seek. Running past that giant oak at the edge of the field, its ambitious roots breaking through the sidewalk and the street itself, they all slap it, as if for luck. What a great climbing tree that would be—if they could only reach that first big branch.

And then there are the birds. When it rains they disappear, hiding somewhere in the dense forests at the edge of the field. But as soon as the storm is over, they burst free. All at once, the sky is full of them—hundreds. Red, green, yellow, blue. It's like a flying rainbow. It's the second most beautiful thing in the world.

Helen is one of those birds. That's what it feels like to her now, sitting beside her sister with her eyes closed. She can see everything: the people, the town, the mountains, the distant cities, a vast green continent slipping into limitless oceans. She can't fly high enough to know if they ever stop.

Then she opens her eyes. The air is a radiant riot of dust, a million anonymous worlds floating in the light. She's sitting on the bed with her sister, a beautiful day waiting outside the window. Suddenly everything feels new; suddenly, anything is possible. She takes her sister's hand. "Feel that?" she says. "That's the sun."

# ACKNOWLEDGMENTS

*I*mmeasurable thanks to all of those who helped me write, shape, and understand this book: Lillian Bayley, Nic Brown, Bruce Cohen, Leigh Huffine, Roger Kellison, Rachel Knowles, Barbara Marshall, Lauren Pearson, Amanda McPherson, Christine Pride, Katherine Sandoz, Alan Shapiro, all of my friends who support, love, and encourage me, and to everyone in the Creative Writing Program at the University of North Carolina. Joseph Regal and Markus Hoffman were especially vital as this book grew and changed, and also Sally Kim, my editor, whose careful eye and artful pen finally made Roam real. Thank you, Sally, and everyone at Touchstone.

And Laura Kellison Wallace, my wife. I cannot imagine doing this without you.

# ABOUT THE AUTHOR

DANIEL WALLACE is the author of five novels, including *Big Fish* and *Mr. Sebastian and the Negro Magician*. His novels have been translated into more than twenty-five languages. *Big Fish* was adapted for film in 2003 by John August and Tim Burton, and a musical inspired by the novel and film will open on Broadway in 2013. He lives in Chapel Hill, North Carolina, with his wife, Laura Kellison Wallace, where he's the director of the Creative Writing Program at UNC.